THE 1
OF ANTARCTICA

Did anything like the legendary Gorgon actually exist? Could it really turn men to stone with its mere gaze, or did it have powers even more horrible? Two American flyers found the answer in an ice-covered valley of Antarctica. They also found a lost city run by a woman of incredible beauty with a penchant for tyranny and lust.

Fasten your seatbelts as Richard S. Shaver and Chester S. Geier spin a grand tale of science fiction and fantasy in the great tradition of Edgar Rice Burroughs.

FOR A COMPLETE SECOND NOVEL, TURN TO PAGE 103

CAST OF CHARACTERS

RICK STACEY
Not only did he stumble onto a lost civilization in the wilds of Antarctica, but he soon found he was the only man alive who could save it from a monstrous creature from another world.

VERLA OF OLIN
She was a beautiful princess, and Stacey fell in love with her from the first moment he saw her—trapped inside a block of ice!

KORYL
The High Priestess of Upper Olin. She was perhaps the most beautiful, seductive woman in the world—with a heart of evil.

ZARDUC
The chief of Koryl's warriors. His unrequited love for the High Priestess kept him loyal—but for how long?

PHIL TOBIN
A mission into the wilds of Antarctica brought him face to face with an unspeakable horror from another dimension.

THE GORGON
Was it the legendary creature of Greek mythology, or was it something even more abominable?

PARN
On the surface he appeared to be just a common slave, but he knew the ins-and-outs of the Royal Palace better than anyone.

ICE CITY OF THE GORGON

by RICHARD S. SHAVER
and CHESTER S. GEIER

ARMCHAIR FICTION
PO Box 4369, Medford, Oregon 97501-0168

*For more information about Armchair Books and products, visit our
website at…*

www.armchairfiction.com

Or email us at…

armchairfiction@yahoo.com

CHAPTER ONE

A DARK patch appeared on the slope of a jagged ice ridge below. Rock—or the remains of a plane? Desperate hope surging through him, Stacey sent his own two-motored Lockheed Navy craft dipping down toward the tumbled and desolate Antarctic surface.

Fanged spires and pinnacles swelled upward threateningly. Between them lay snow, so deep and intensely white that it glittered blue. The ridges dropped down and away in bleak, sharp terraces, leveling into deep valleys or tortured ice fields. Here and there were deep canyons and chasms, veiled in blue shadow. Mountains towered in the near distance, their outlines harsh against the gray sky.

The whole made a fantastic etching in white and blue and gray. Somehow the other tints only served to emphasize the dominating whiteness. And yet, despite this white backdrop, a dusk hung over the scene, deep and filled with mystery. Against the dusk, clouds of snow, torn up and driven by the fierce, bitterly cold wind, writhed and twisted like pain-crazed wraiths.

The dark patch spread and took on detail, and then Stacey saw that it wasn't a plane. Just rock after all. Hopelessness, a sudden, aching weight inside him, he lifted the P2V Neptune back to its former altitude.

With the craft flying on an even keel, he glanced at Tobin, erect and tense in the adjoining seat. The other's freckled features were questioning.

"What happened, Rick?" he asked, raising his voice over the roar of the motors.

"Thought it was Hansen and Matthews. No dice, though." Stacey looked steadily into the dusk, watching the mountains ahead creep nearer. His hawkish, spare face was somber. He had amber eyes, made all the more striking by his sun-browned skin and coppery hair. Combined with unusually wide shoulders and a lithe, tall figure, his appearance was so distinctive that he seldom failed to become a center of immediate interest wherever he went—much to his annoyance and disgust.

Tobin nodded and the stiffness went out of him. He followed the direction of Stacey's eyes for several seconds, then spoke again.

"Think we'll find them?"

"If we keep looking long enough," Stacey said.

"We've been searching for almost a week already. After that amount of time, there can't be any hope—not in a place as wild and frigid as this." Tobin leaned closer, his intense gaze grimly earnest. "Each day we've been flying farther away from base. We can't keep it up, Rick. Right now we're searching territory that no one has ever seen before—territory that hasn't ever been photographed or mapped. If anything happens to us—"

Tobin didn't finish, but it wasn't necessary for him to do so. Stacey understood. If anything happened, it was the end. One of the three expedition planes had crashed several weeks before, and with Hansen and Matthews lost and perhaps dead, there would be no other craft available to conduct a search. The radio at base would summon help, of course, but help couldn't possibly arrive in time.

Stacey pressed his lips together tightly, striving to shake off his gloomy frame of mind. It was no use. He had to admit that the whole expedition had been dogged by bad luck from the very beginning. It seemed inevitable that some of it should eventually attach to Tobin and himself. They had been immune far too long.

Perhaps, Stacey thought, the whole mess was a result of man's attempt, as personified by the present expedition, to subdue the Antarctic and loot its ice-bound, age-old treasures. Uranium was the object in this case. A previous expedition had found traces of it, and with uranium now possessing high military importance, a second expedition had quickly been organized to determine just how vast the deposits were. Stacey and Tobin, together with Hansen and Matthews and the two flyers who had previously crashed, had been assigned to the expedition as an aerial photography and survey group.

IT HAD been hard work all the way. But the engineers at base had seemed confident. They had insisted, Stacey remembered, that mining operations could easily be carried out despite the handicaps of snow and ice, sub-zero cold and terrific winds, and a terrain that was rough and frozen. They had talked of new mining machinery, and Stacey had seen their plans for an underground mining operations base, heated, insulated from the cold, and containing facilities for every convenience.

But now he wondered if man's science and machines were enough. The Antarctic was a savage and dangerous region, as unknown and alien as another planet. And it seemed inhabited by hostile, invisible things that bitterly resented human intrusion and fought at every turn against it, fought with weapons of wind and snow, treacherous ice, and deadly cold. Fought, and all too frequently won. Stacey thought grimly of Hansen and Matthews and of the two before them.

He narrowed his tawny gaze at the mountains ahead, sensing the vast, absolute silence that existed beyond the roar of the Lockheed's twin motors. It was the silence of a place undisturbed for countless years by anything but the wind. And the wind had carved the ice ridges beneath the speeding plane into palaces, mosques, pagodas, ships—endless bizarre shapes. The terrain was a fantastic fairyland, illumined by fairy tints of white and blue and green and gray. It was beautiful in its weird, frigidly still fashion—but behind that beauty, Stacey knew, lurked a dozen forms of death, some swift and violent, some slow and insidiously lingering.

The mountains were creeping nearer. If for some reason Hansen and Matthews had been unable to clear the peaks, Stacey thought, that was where he would find them—lying very quiet and frozen amid the ruins of their Lockheed somewhere along the base of the range. His guess seemed a good one. These were mountains of a height and sheer, rugged mass such as were to be found in only a few other parts of the world. Colossi, they were, spreading their enormous, blocky shoulders in silent menace against the gray and sullen sky. The wind was whipping long plumes of snow from the jagged peaks, plumes that were like congealed breaths issuing from beings huge and warm and balefully sentient.

Presently the massive summits were towering close. Stacey lifted the Lockheed, fighting the steady down pressure of the terrific wind outside. He wanted to clear the peaks with plenty to spare, otherwise a sudden blast of wind might smash them against one of those masses of steel-hard rock and knife-sharp ice.

Slowly the plane went over, swaying and jerking in the wind's rush, over and beyond and then down—one wing dipping dangerously. But the range had been passed, and now the steep slopes fell away sharply into a series of broad valleys far below.

Stacey guided the Lockheed down, following the slopes toward more level ground. He was jolted out of his preoccupation with flying at the hard pressure of Tobin's gloved hand on his arm. Tobin was pointing tensely.

"Down there, Rick…see it?"

After a moment of squinting intently, Stacey saw it. About mid-way on one of the slopes to the right, something projected from the snow that seemed too dark and regular in shape to be ice. A wing, Stacey realized in another instant. He felt the old eagerness return, but subdued now, mingled with a feeling of dread and cold.

He swung the Lockheed around and toward the upthrust wing. Details appeared swiftly with decreasing distance. He saw the body of the wrecked plane, then—broken and crumpled. The other wing and the tail assembly were scattered dozens of yards away, barely visible in the deep drifts.

ONLY the cold and the dread were left in Stacey now. He had been close in his guess regarding the fate of Hansen and Matthews. They had cleared the peaks, though. And it seemed that something had happened almost immediately afterward. Perhaps strong wind currents had driven the plane out of control. But the two had crashed there, on the slope.

Tobin had binoculars at his eyes and was studying the wreck intently. "No sign of life," he announced at last.

"Any tracks in the snow?" Stacey called back.

Tobin shook his head slowly. "They're still inside, Rick. This was something they wouldn't walk away from."

Stacey took a deep, unsteady breath. "Pictures, Phil."

Tobin unbuckled his safety straps and left his seat, moving carefully toward the large camera mounted over a hatch near the middle of the plane. He began snapping pictures as Stacey swung the Lockheed around again and came back over the wreck.

It was the least they could do, Stacey thought bitterly. There was no place to land, unless it was in one of the valleys far below. But that would have meant a long climb upward—too dangerous to risk. At that, however, Stacey felt willing to try it if he knew the two men were alive. But the wreck had been violent and complete, and nothing had disturbed the snow around it after the fragments had settled. There was no doubt but that Hansen and Matthews were dead.

Stacey swung the plane around once more, and then Tobin returned to his seat. Finally, lifting the Lockheed's nose, Stacey began climbing for altitude in preparation for returning over the peaks. The search was finished, he knew. He glanced for the last time at the wing protruding like a gravestone from the snow and lifted one gloved hand in a salute.

Ahead and up the peaks towered hard and sharp, long streamers of snow stretching away from them in the fierce wind. The plane climbed steadily, its motors thrumming.

Stacey thought eagerly of base. It would be good to be back to where there was life and warmth and the security that came of solid contact with the ground. He would appreciate these things more than ever now. He knew he would never forget the picture of the wing high on a lonely mountain slope. He—

The right motor missed a beat.

Stacey's hands froze on the controls. Ice seemed to form along the back of his neck, creeping up into his mind. He glanced at Tobin and saw in his eyes the same alarm that must have been mirrored in his own.

The motor had picked up once more. Now it missed again. Then it coughed—and died.

Stacey darted a look at the instruments. They showed plenty of gas and oil remaining for the return to base. There was only one other explanation for the dead motor.

"Ice in the fuel lines," he told Tobin. "Something must have gone wrong with the water screen on the refuel hose back at base."

"What can we do?" Tobin asked anxiously.

"We'll have to land somewhere. The fuel lines have to be cleared. We wouldn't get over these mountains on one motor."

Tobin glanced downward as Stacey began fighting the list and drag of the dead motor. "There might be level ground in one of the valleys down there, Rick. Think you can make it?"

STACEY nodded briefly, his features set in grim lines. The Lockheed was slipping toward the right at an angle, and only his skilled manipulations of the controls kept the craft from going into a spin. He let the nose continue to drop, lifting the right wing at just the proper moment. Aided by the remaining motor, the plane went into a long glide downward. Past the mountain slopes, it soared, approaching the nearest of the broad valleys below, which began to open up like the interior of some enormous flower.

And then the left motor began missing. Seconds later, it, too, went dead.

In the abrupt silence, Stacey could feel his heart pumping loudly. He fought to stretch the plane's downward glide toward the valley, knowing with a frantic clarity that his and Tobin's only hope now rested on reaching level gorground.

An eternity seemed to inch past. Wind keened past the plane, and the ice terraces and snow slopes dropped past with blurred swiftness. Then the mouth of the valley swallowed the Lockheed, and only short hundreds of yards ahead the slope at last leveled off.

Stacey battled to keep the plane's nose up the remaining distance. If they hit the tumbled drifts at the foot of the slope, serious damage to the Lockheed was certain to result. Another plane wing would point its grim message at the sky. But this time, Stacey thought, it would mark the frozen graves of Lieutenant Rickard Stacey and Lieutenant (j.g.) Philip Tobin.

With only a few feet to spare, the plane cleared the drifts, and then its runners were gliding over the smooth expanse of snow beyond. A short time later the braking flaps brought the Lockheed safely to a stop.

Stacey relaxed in his seat with a long sigh of relief. "Well, here we are!" he announced finally.

Tobin grunted. "A couple of hundred miles from nowhere in particular. Anyway, we're still in one piece. And clearing the fuel lines shouldn't be too much of a job."

Unbuckling his safety straps, Stacey leaned toward the windshield, peering into the greater confines of the valley ahead. The valley was roughly triangular in shape and several miles in extent, with the plane situated at what seemed the apex. Mountains loomed bleakly on every side, and the mysterious Antarctic dusk seemed thicker here. There was a deep, unearthly silence, broken only by the low moaning of the wind.

Scattered over the valley floor were a great number of curious ice formations, cone-like in shape, tapering toward the top. Stacey had noticed them in a preoccupied way while landing, but now something about the formations struck him as strange. They seemed too numerous and too identical in outline to be natural.

"Hand me the glasses," he told Tobin.

With the binoculars focussed on the formations, Stacey made two discoveries, one within moments of the other. Startled, incredulous, he whirled back to Tobin.

"Good Lord, Phil...it looks like—" He stammered momentarily, took a deep breath, then continued. "It looks like there are...*people*...inside those overgrown icicles, or whatever those things are!"

"People…" Tobin gasped. "Are ya nuts, boss?"

"People," Stacey repeated. "And beyond the icicles are the tops of what look like buildings. Here, take a look."

Long seconds later, Tobin took the binoculars from his eyes. He had an almost dazed look on his face.

"You…you're right. Those ice pillars have people inside of them. They must be frozen…dead. And there…there's a city—or what's left of a city—in the distance beyond."

Tobin handed the binoculars back to Stacy and the two looked at each other in stunned silence for several seconds, the wind whipping between them.

"We've stumbled onto something big," Stacey muttered. "And we're going to have to find out just what it is."

CHAPTER TWO

THEIR preparations were few and quickly completed. Both wore thick, warmly lined leather flying suits, and over these, for additional protection against the cold, they pulled hooded fur parkas, which they took from their supply of emergency equipment. There were canvas packs with shoulder slings, containing food and cooking utensils, together with such items as a compass, signal flares, a Colt .45 automatic, and ammunition. They slipped the weapons, which were already loaded, into convenient pockets beneath their fur parkas. Then, carrying snowshoes and long staffs tipped with steel grapnels, they left the plane.

Donning the snowshoes, they set out across the valley floor toward the nearest of the strange pillar-like ice formations. They had been trained in the use of snowshoes, as well as other Antarctic equipment, and they made swift progress.

Stacey was tense with anticipation. People, here—in the Antarctic! It seemed beyond the realms of imagination to be true. But he had seen the figures within the ice pillars—and their forms were undeniably human. Tobin had seen them, too.

"Could they somehow be alive?" Stacey asked himself under his breath.

He glanced toward the towers of what appeared to be a crumbling city far in the distance. Towers which, to the unaided eye, looked like continuations of the pillars scattered over the valley. He decided the answer to his question was no—the bodies in the ice pillars couldn't possibly be alive. With a city relatively close at hand, Stacey decided it was most likely that the pillars were icy graves of some sort.

The idea seemed confirmed when he and Tobin at last stood before one of the pillars. They looked in awe at the monolithic shaft for several moments. Then, wiping the frost from the surface, they gazed in on the lonesome body inside. Within it was a woman, exotically lovely, her slender form unclothed and very still. Her eyes were closed as though in sleep, but it did not seem to be a peaceful one, for an expression of despair was frozen on her small, delicate face.

Stacey then discovered something that was even more disturbing. When he peered in closely he could see that the woman's hands were bound by chains to a smaller pillar inside the outer one. Death, it appeared, hadn't come naturally to this woman. Stacey felt uneasy by this.

To his amazement he also found that the pillar did not consist of ice, as he had earlier surmised. It was transparent, with a yellowish tint, and it appeared to be made of some kind of plastic or hard wax.

And it seemed to be hollow.

Tobin's round face was awed and perplexed. He turned to Stacey and spoke in a hushed voice.

"This doesn't make any sense, boss. That woman in there...she's chained...*chained.* Do you see it?"

Stacey nodded, "Something happened to her that couldn't have been very nice."

"I wonder if she's even dead," Tobin went on. "Doesn't seem likely that she is...I mean if she has to be kept chained down like that..."

"That might have been necessary—before she died," Stacey said slowly. He glanced around and felt the strangeness of the scene and the utter silence that hung over it creep into him with a chill that was not due entirely to the bitter cold. He made a sudden gesture to Tobin and strode toward another pillar a short distance away.

WITHIN the pillar was a man, tall and splendidly proportioned. His features, though essentially masculine, had the same exotic quality as that of the woman. It was a quality for which Stacey could find no resemblance in any race he knew. The man's figure, like that of the woman, was unclothed, but his eyes were open. They were distended in a stare of abject horror and fear, as though he had died with his gaze fastened upon something utterly loathsome. And his hands, too, were chained.

"Wish I knew how long they've been like that," Tobin wondered aloud as he and Stacey turned away.

"Not very long," Stacey replied.

"What?" Tobin responded incredulously.

"Think about it, Phil. If these structures had been out here any length of time—years perhaps—they most certainly would be covered over with snow and ice."

Tobin was silent for some seconds, gazing at the towers of the mysterious city in the dim distance. Finally he spoke. "This is getting creepy, Rick. If you're right...that means people are still living here. Right here—in the heart of the Antarctic."

It was an unnerving statement. There was more silence between them as the frigid wind rushed through and seemed to laugh at them.

"Not very pleasant people I'm afraid," Stacey muttered, his face grim. "I have an idea that we'd better watch our step."

They were in the midst of the pillars now, stopping before each, gazing silently at the figures within. The people seemed to consist of men and women in equal numbers, and not all were young or unclothed. But they shared in common a dread and fright that had left its indelible stamp upon their faces.

And then Stacey came to a pillar before which he halted with startled abruptness, awe and admiration sweeping the chilling uneasiness from his mind. Chained inside the pillar, frozen and statuesque as were all the others, was a young woman—but a woman unlike any Stacey had seen in the previous pillars. There was somehow a difference in everything about her, intangible, yet unmistakable, as though she were of a higher degree than the eerily immobile figures all around. The conviction seemed borne out by the fact that her pillar was set apart from the others and raised upon a dais of ice.

"A princess," Stacey whispered. "You could only have been a princess. Or a queen…"

The woman was young and slim, but exquisitely rounded, her bare form gleaming with a pearl-like luster in the dusk. Dark hair fell in shining, heavy waves well below her waist. Her delicate features were perfectly molded—and they were composed, as though some fine, proud spirit within her had resisted showing any trace of fear. Her eyes were closed, the dark lashes long and soft on the swelling contours of her cheeks.

She was beautiful in a way Stacey could not recall ever having seen in his life, yet it was something more than this that captivated him. It was as though his ideal of womanhood had finally materialized—and it was more wondrous than anything he had ever imagined.

He had a sudden, deep sense of tragedy. Unconsciously, and without even the knowledge that this woman had ever existed, he knew that he had yearned for her all of his life. And now he had found her—but too late. Something had ended the brightness and the sweetness of her, leaving a cold and still expression, transfixed within a pillar of some unknown substance that had been deposited about her in some unimaginable way.

Stacey knew he would never be the same again for having seen this woman. And rebellion rose within him at the thought that her loss should be irrevocable. With a feeling born of desperation, he speculated once more on the possibility that the bodies within the pillars might still be alive—somehow. He wondered if people existed in the city beyond.

A latent determination gathered within him. If people were actually still there—alive somehow—they might know how to awaken and release this woman. Perhaps they could—

Stacey's thoughts were interrupted by an explosive gasp. He whirled to find Tobin pointing in unbelieving horror at an object that was streaking toward them. In the next instant Rick Stacey went rigid with shock, his mind revolting in stark incredulity at what he saw...

It was a head—floating in mid-air.

Approaching over the snow, out of the worst nightmare imaginable, came a huge, horrific head, floating through the wind without any visible means of propulsion or support, yet moving with uncanny speed...

COMPLETELY bodiless, the head was—and huge, all of five feet in height. The features were unmistakably feminine, horrifically beautiful in a way that was strange and alien—a beauty that was evil, even sadistic. The great red lips were stretched in a rapacious leer, exposing large, sharp teeth. Baleful fires flickered within the red-tinted, slit-pupiled eyes. Covering the head, instead of hair, were living ropes of flesh, writhing snake-like about the vast face, each strand scaled and dappled like the skin of a python, shining, at once beautiful and terrible. It was sheer horror.

The weird monstrosity suddenly brought to Stacey a recollection of pictures he had seen of the Gorgon of ancient Greek mythology, whose glance was capable of turning men into stone. And somehow the objectivity of the thought enabled him to wrench his mind free of the paralyzing dread that the approaching apparition had struck into him. He darted a hand into the opening of his parka, fumbling for his Colt .45.

"Go for your gun, Phil!" he hissed at his stunned companion. "Get ready to start shooting!"

As though sensing his intention, the head abruptly slowed. The scarlet, flaming eyes narrowed—and Stacey felt something like an icy hand grasp fiercely within his mind, seeking, probing, then holding him motionless with an overpowering mental force.

A complete paralysis came over him. Only his thoughts seemed able to move, whirling in panic and despair.

Within him was a suspicion that verged on horrible certainty. Was it possible that the Gorgon was no creature of myth after all—that this abomination in front of him was one of its descendants? Or—incredibly—was it possible that this was the original Gorgon itself, having somehow survived throughout the centuries in this forgotten valley deep in the heart of Antarctica?

He didn't know. He was aware only that the nightmarish monster had rendered him a helpless victim for whatever evil plans it had in mind.

Once more the head began moving toward them, moving with stealthy care this time, as though having realized that the two men were strangers. The red-tinted eyes were still narrowed, intent and wary, the scarlet lips curved in a soundless snarl. Closer, closer, the head drifted. It finally floated to a stop a few yards away—and the nearness of it sent waves of revulsion through Stacey, so intense that they bordered on pain.

Now the reddish, slit-pupiled eyes slowly widened, became fixed and unblinking, glittering with hypnotic steadiness. Stacey felt an icy hand stir within his mind, moving with sinister purpose. Dimly he realized what was happening. The monster's chill, powerful thoughts were probing and searching his memory centers—draining him of knowledge.

A long time seemed to pass. Stacey felt as though he was floating, disembodied in a murky void, while cold fingers plucked and prodded at his awareness. Then, slowly, he became conscious of his surroundings once more. He saw the head close before him, and even as he strove shudderingly and futilely to move away, one of the living ropes of flesh covering the head darted at him with the speed of a striking serpent. He felt a sharp pain in his thigh.

Flames seemed to spread through him from the point of contact, like ripples spreading over the surface of water. The flames touched his mind—and it seemed a great light blazed briefly within him, bringing a new clarity and vividness of being, a sharpening and heightening of perceptions that seemed to open up a whole new sense of awareness. He grew conscious of things he had not previously noticed, of outlines and details, of shades and tones strange to him. He knew that his mind was involved, for his brain seemed to have become painfully tender and sensitive, as though each nerve had been stripped of insulation—laid bare to the cold, probing mental fingers of the nightmarish creature under whose power he had fallen.

HIS new senses told him that what had happened to him was also happening to Tobin. And he surmised that the same fate had overtaken the splendid race of people now imprisoned within the pillars.

A mocking chuckle sounded in Stacey's mind. And then came a mental voice, soft and insidiously sweet, with an undertone that was chillingly alien.

"You are correct in your assumptions. I *am* the Gorgon. What you see about you is my...handiwork. As for other details that yet puzzle you, soon you will learn—very soon."

The chuckle came again. It faded slowly, submerging beneath a current of dark purpose. He sent out a tentative finger of thought in an attempt to learn what that purpose was, but he obtained nothing save a curious impression of strain, as though the head—or Gorgon as the unearthly being called itself—was concentrating intently upon the performance of some difficult task. Though tense and apprehensive, Stacey reacted with shock to the fact that the head's name should be identical to that of the mythical creature he had been thinking of just short moments before. He wondered in a dim way what the actual relationship was.

Then everything was crowded from his mind by the

awareness of what was now taking place. The huge head, grotesque and repulsive, yet oddly beautiful, had moved in close to Tobin, poising itself before him. From the tips of the snake-like strands—coiling like hair about the terrifying, yet woman-like face—a whitish mist began to flow, settling and thickening about Tobin's rigid form.

Stacey recognized the manifestation as similar to that by which a spider spins a web, or a moth a cocoon, but on a vastly greater scale. And not unlike a huge spider, the Gorgon began weaving and bobbing about Tobin, shaping the soft and plastic substance with its tentacular growths, which seemed as deft and swift as fingers.

Behind Tobin a small pillar took shape. Chains appeared, securing his wrists to the pillar. Then, completely enclosing Tobin and the small pillar, a large one quickly formed. When the Gorgon at last ceased its rapid movements, Tobin was encased like a fly in amber, immobile, statuesque—an exact replica of the weirdly imprisoned people scattered over the valley floor.

With the uncanny depth of perception that had come to him, Stacey sensed Tobin's thoughts. The other was sick with despair, and the effect upon Stacey was all the more intense for the knowledge that, within moments, he would share a similar fate. It couldn't happen, he told himself. It mustn't happen. But even as the desperate thoughts flashed through his mind, he knew there was nothing he could do. He was paralyzed, helpless, unable to move so much as an eyelid. It appeared certain that he and Tobin were doomed.

The Gorgon turned toward Stacey, the great slit-pupiled, reddish eyes lit with a deep exultation at the horror of his knowledge of what was about to happen to him. The cold mental fingers explored his mind again, feeling out each nuance of his dread—sucking at his emotions as a spider might suck at his juices, with a relish and a tasting and an inner satisfaction that accompanies a hearty meal.

"You have seen the Gorgon's handiwork, my human friend,"

the mocking thought formed in his brain. "Now you understand—now you know what awaits you."

There was a soft chuckle. The monster slowly moved closer to Stacey, its reddish orbs enrapt, gloating. From the tips of the snake-like appendages about its face, the whitish mist once more began to issue, settling and thickening around him. The stuff felt warm, yet no more substantial than smoke. But as the creature began weaving and bobbing about him, swiftly shaping his prison, the mist rapidly began to grow dense and solid. Within a short time it was as firm as a coating of plastic or ice.

THE Gorgon was finished. It hovered before Stacey, gazing into his unblinking eyes with a vast delight, preening its dark thoughts before the mirror of his mind.

"You and your companion are now in the Gorgon's power. And the Gorgon is pleased, for you are both young and strong. For such as you, the Gorgon has a need."

"A need?" Stacey's thoughts echoed automatically. "What do you mean by that?"

"The Gorgon is building a structure, a bridge of sorts. What you see here"—and the monster's thoughts gestured like a hand at the pillars dotting the valley—"are links in that bridge. When the last link is in place, *all* of the Gorgon will enter your world."

"All?" Stacey echoed again, his interest rising above the sick dejection that filled him.

"What you see of me here is not my complete self—so to speak. The rest of what might be called "my body" exists in another world. To be more specific—another dimension. You must be wondering about the nature of my true appearance. I will show you."

Slowly a picture formed in Stacey's mind. As it took on shape and detail, he was filled with incredulity and bewilderment, made all the more intense by a growing sense of horror.

For the Gorgon was strange and alien almost beyond comprehension. The creature consisted of a number of separate bodies or members, each a distinct entity and able to function independently of the whole. The parts were made altogether one by a psychic and physiological connection so complex and deep-reaching that Stacey was able to grasp only the vaguest implications of it. His mind could not embrace the complete extent of this weird being. He was unable to fully comprehend the creature's size, its intricacy of detail and function, and its sheer, superhuman abilities.

But he certainly knew he'd been rendered helpless and made prisoner by the uncanny powers of this "portion" of the Gorgon that existed here on Earth. And he surmised logically that those powers would be increased incalculably if the creature was able to assume its complete aspect. At the moment it appeared that nothing could prevail against it. If the Gorgon finished building its "human bridge," and if all of its being came into the world of men, it would surely result in a catastrophe for human civilization.

"There is nothing to prevent me from coming through," the monster's jeering thought broke in. "My work is almost done. Soon your world will become part of my domain, and I will do with it…as I please. And I have many interesting plans—of that you can be sure."

And Stacey saw what that would be. The jeering thoughts sketched a picture in his mind whose details were made all the more horrible by a fierce eagerness, a ravening hunger, and sadistic cruelty. The Gorgon considered human beings as little better than cattle. And as cattle they would be—fed upon.

The world would become a vast ranch, a wild and barbaric place in which people would be bred and herded. There were also fleeting suggestions of tortures and other evil practices, which made Stacey sick with loathing and dread.

His raw emotions seemed to excite the monster. Its cold fingers of thought began stabbing at the tender, over-sensitive perceptions that his new awareness had given him. Great waves of pain beat through him repeatedly, crowding his agonized mind perilously close to the brink of madness. He knew that somehow his suffering gave the Gorgon's head enormous pleasure and stimulation, as though his torment was a source of satisfaction more potent than liquor or drugs.

Stacey did not lose consciousness. In his new state of being, that seemed impossible to do. Yet his reactions to pain reached a saturation point that for the time being rendered him useless for the Gorgon's purposes. Still palpably excited, the creature darted over to Tobin's pillar, and Stacey's dimmed and pain-hazed perceptions told him that his companion was now enduring a similar experience.

The Gorgon's sadistic excitement reached a state bordering on frenzy. Abandoning Tobin at last, it went to another pillar, inside of which was the lovely woman who had so strongly attracted Stacey earlier. The creature's thoughts jabbed and slashed at the mind of the woman, but Stacey sensed dissatisfaction from the Gorgon, as though the woman was shielding herself against the pain. Furious, but reluctant to postpone its sport the length of time necessary to beat down the woman's barriers, the head rushed away toward the other pillars further beyond. It paused before each, whipping up fear and feeding upon it, until a cloud of suffering seemed to hang over the entire valley.

Sick and filled with infinite despair, Stacey thought of the Gorgon loose and rampant upon the world—thought of it tormenting the entire human race as it was now tormenting the helpless prisoners within their pillars of this icy valley.

CHAPTER THREE

STACEY'S awareness of the Gorgon's presence gradually faded. It seemed that the monster had finally wearied of its sadistic activities and left the valley.

A calm descended that had in it something almost of peace. Then a voice spoke in Stacey's mind. With the strange, all-embracing awareness that had come to him, he recognized the mental tones as those of Tobin.

"Rick?" Tobin was saying. "Rick? Can you hear me?"

"Yes…yes I can hear you."

"Rick—that thing…what it was thinking…what it plans to do…" Tobin's thought were incoherent with a deep horror that was not for himself.

"I know what you mean," Stacey said slowly. "It would be the worst thing that could possibly happen to the world."

Tobin was silent a moment. He seemed to be getting himself in control. Finally he said:

"We can't let that thing get loose, Rick. We've got to stop it before it's too late. The rest of the world has to be warned."

"I've been thinking about that," Stacey returned grimly. "I haven't been able to think about anything else. But I don't know how we're going to get out of these icicles we're in."

"We've got to find a way…we've just got to!"

Stacey said nothing. He kept his gloomy thoughts masked.

"Rick?" Tobin asked after a moment.

"Still here."

"How are we able to talk to each other like this?"

"I think the head did something to us…to our minds. Remember the way she stung us with those snakes on her head? Somehow the sting made us telepathic."

A warm thought brushed Stacey's mind softly. "You are correct, stranger."

Stacey felt a queer thrill. He knew the soundless words came from the lovely woman in the pillar nearby, who had so deeply fascinated him. He had been aware for some time that she was not dead, as he had at first guessed, but held in some kind of suspended animation—as were Tobin and himself. But only now his full attention settled upon her.

"Thank you," he said. "I was just guessing, but it's nice to have you support me."

The warm thought seemed to smile this time. "I am pleased to accept your thanks. You see, stranger, there are great powers slumbering in the human mind. The telepathic ability is one of them. The Gorgon is able to awaken this ability by means of her sting, which paralyzes those portions of the brain whose functions ordinarily block it. But enough of the Gorgon. We shall have more than enough time in which to speak of her later. Who are you? From where do you come? There are vague pictures in your mind which greatly interest me. I am Verla of Olin."

Stacey introduced himself, not omitting to include Tobin. Then, with the flashing, swift mental speech that was so much more rapid than spoken words, he described the United States, its people and civilization. He sketched a picture of the other nations of the world in the attempt to give the woman the perspective necessary to appreciate the finer points of his own homeland. Finally he told her of the expedition to the Antarctic, and of their search for the missing flyers, which had resulted in their discovery of the valley and their capture by the Gorgon.

The warm thoughts of the woman were touched with awe. "It is wonderful, Rick Stacey, the picture of the outside world that you have given me. It…why…it seems more like a beautiful story than a reality! But I don't doubt that what you have told me is real. There is truth in your thoughts—and kindness. More, Rick Stacey, there is a wisdom in your mind such as few men in Olin possess, including our scholars of the ancient knowledge."

STACEY gave a mental shrug to conceal emotions in which pleasure and embarrassment were mingled. He asked, "Is Olin the name for your land?"

"It is now more precisely the name for the city alone, for only there does life still exist. But once it was the name for the city and the surrounding valleys. That was in the long ago, when, as legends say, Olin was a warm land, a land of grass and trees and flowers."

She paused a moment, sadness tingeing her thoughts, and Stacey recalled a scientist back at base having mentioned that Antarctica was once a tropical paradise. Then the woman continued her explanations. "There are not many people left in the city, only a few thousand at the most. Existence has grown more difficult through the centuries, and only the fittest had survived. The ancient machines that warmed the city and produced food and clothes and the other necessities of life have broken down one by one. These machines were vast and complex. The descendants of the men who had built them had not known how to keep them in repair."

Stacey was interested in the machines. "Do you know how they function?" he asked. "How do they produce food and clothes? The people of my land do not have such machines."

Verla was unable to answer in detail. But what she did communicate to Stacey startled him. The ancients of Olin had possessed atomic power! And it was through atomic transmutation that the wondrous machines that remained produced clothing and food. Taking as raw material stone, metal, wood, and earth—even such unsubstantial stuff as air itself—the machines turned out edible things, bolts of cloth, bars and sheets of metal, not to overlook a steady output of light and heat. The atomic motors would function as long as the metal ingeniously fashioned about them endured. But the grinding pressure of centuries had slowly weakened the metal bodies of the machines, and their atomic hearts had stopped one by one.

"You seem surprised by the power that the ancients of Olin were able to harness in their machines," Verla told Stacey. "Don't the men of your land have such power?"

"In a very crude form," Stacey said. "They have just learned to release it in the form of weapons called bombs, though now they are experimenting with atomic fires called piles, which they hope to harness to machinery to produce light and heat. Transmutation has already been accomplished on a small scale. To the people of my land, these things are remarkable, for ours is still a young civilization. But since you have had these things for a very long time, it seems that is not so with your people."

"We are an old race," Verla said. "Olin was great long

before the coming of the ice."

The great age of the city, her soft mental voice went on after a moment, was shown by the vast depth of ice which now covered it. Only tall towers were still visible. This portion of the city above the ice was known as Upper Olin. The portion below was called Lower Olin.

And Lower Olin, she explained, was enormous in extent, for the city had been very large. Far beneath the ice were innumerable tunnels and corridors, connecting the great buried buildings. But as might have been expected, only a very tiny portion of Lower Olin was inhabited. The people there were very different in character from those who lived in Upper Olin. They were a good and industrious people. Conscious of their ancient glories, they were struggling to attain once more what the indolence of their predecessors had lost.

"The people of Lower Olin," Verla's thoughts finished proudly, "are my people."

And for the first time the full significance of the title Verla of Olin dawned upon Stacey. She was a princess, the hereditary ruler of Olin. He recalled having sensed her royal countenance at first sight of her within the pillar. Now he knew he hadn't been wrong in calling her a princess, though the term then had been more from admiration than anything else.

"But what of those in Upper Olin?" he asked. "Aren't they your people also?"

INSTANT scorn filled the woman's response. "They are not my people, Rick. If they were, I wouldn't be here. Nor would these others—including you and your friend. The people of Upper Olin are rebels against the ancient line—outlaws and heartless murderers. Worse, they are the creatures and willing tools of the Gorgon!"

"Are you telling me that monster has human allies?" Stacey asked in astonishment.

"Yes—and the most clever and dangerous of these is Koryl, the High Priestess. For in Upper Olin, you see, the Gorgon is worshipped as a goddess. Thus far have fallen the descendants of the ancient great of Olin. Koryl is beautiful—I admit this willingly. Her beauty has driven men into ecstasy. Yet few will deny that she is also scheming and cruel. And just as cruel, though without her cleverness, is Zarduc, the chief of her warriors. Koryl serves the Gorgon, but Zarduc serves Koryl."

"I think I can understand Zarduc's side of the situation," Stacey said musingly. "But I don't see why Koryl should help the Gorgon—or for that matter why the Gorgon should help Koryl."

"It is because Koryl alone understands the secret and mysterious process by which the gateway between the Gorgon's world and ours is kept open. So you see, Koryl serves the Gorgon, yet the Gorgon serves Koryl. It is an unholy alliance. That, perhaps, is why the Gorgon does not tamper mentally with Koryl, fearing that the ability to fully open the gateway will be lost. And that is evidently why the Gorgon has imprisoned us within these pillars, planning to use our combined minds or life energies in some fashion that will overcome Koryl's advantage."

"I wonder if Koryl knows that."

Verla's answering thought was faintly startled. "Perhaps not, though she is clever—and ambitious. Koryl is using the Gorgon's help to achieve great personal power. Many of the warriors of upper Olin despise the High Priestess. There have even been several minor rebellions. However, with the Gorgon as her ally, these minor insurrections have met with disaster. Some of the bodies within these pillars are actually rebellious warriors. Already Koryl is in possession of all Upper Olin. And almost daily Zarduc and the Gorgon make deeper raids into Lower Olin. It was on one such raid that I was captured. That was not long ago—a few weeks, according to your measurement of time."

"And Koryl allowed the Gorgon to place you here?" Stacey said.

"Yes. Koryl has hated me most of all my life. I think she

would have killed me, except that subjecting me to perpetual torment as a prisoner of the Gorgon offered her greater satisfaction."

"But if you were captured, how is it that your people in Lower Olin still remain?"

"I ventured too far from the hidden places while leading a small band in quest of ancient machines that could be used by us as weapons against Koryl," Verla explained. "As I have told you, Lower Olin is vast in extent. My people are difficult to locate. But frequently small groups leave to seek machines or supplies. It is then that they risk capture by the Gorgon or Zarduc."

"They show courage," Stacey said in quick admiration. "And it would seem they're the only hope we have for regaining our freedom. Do you think they might make an attempt to rescue us, Verla?"

"There is an excellent chance they might. That is why I have not despaired too much at being imprisoned. Jendon, one of the wisest of the scholars in Lower Olin, has an idea for overcoming the Gorgon's superhuman powers. He was working feverishly on it when I saw him last."

"The Gorgon…" Stacey's thought was filled with anger and disgust. "Everything seems to center around the Gorgon. Has the creature always been in Olin?"

"Not always." Verla explained, the silent words flashing in complete images and ideas across the screen of her mind.

In the distant past, a scientist of Olin had accidentally discovered how to open up the gateway between Earth and the other-dimension world of the Gorgon. But it was an incomplete gateway, such that only the Gorgon's head could traverse through it. Because of the strong psychic and physiological link between the head and other bodily parts, the Gorgon's sphere of activity was kept confined to Olin, as the city and its enclosing valley were nearest the gateway. Thus the monster could not become an immediate threat to the rest of the world until it managed to bring the remainder of its incomprehensibly alien body through.

THE scientist who first opened the gateway, was an ancestor of Koryl. Like Koryl, he too hungered for personal power and used a Gorgon's uncanny abilities to achieve his aims, the most immediate of which was the overthrow of the rulers of Olin. He succeeded in this end, though shortly afterward another scientist fathomed the secret of the gateway and closed it. Separated from its other bodily parts, the psychic and physiological link severed, the head of that Gorgon almost immediately died. And—deprived of his monstrous ally— Koryl's ancestor soon met a like fate.

"The story has become a legend," Verla told Stacey. "Perhaps the people of your land know of it, for at that time the cold was settling over Olin and many were leaving for warmer lands. They would have spread the story, so that it became a legend beyond Olin also."

"Evidently they did," Stacey agreed. "I have read of such a legend, though it seems to have been considerably changed by time and much repeating." He outlined briefly the ancient Grecian myth of Perseus and the Gorgon, Medusa.

Verla resumed her explanation. The scientist who had overcome the Gorgon in the distant past was one of Verla's direct ancestors. This was the principle reason for Koryl's intense hatred of her. Made immensely popular by his feat, the scientist became a ruler of Olin. He did much to keep alive Olin's declining greatness, a task made increasingly difficult for his descendants by the cold and the ice, which began to grow ever more serious.

Olin went into a swift decline. It was not until the past few hundred years that its inhabitants began to shake off the fetters of superstition and barbarism, and in doing so begin the long climb upward. In Verla's time, great progress had already been made in regaining the knowledge of the ancient machines and records. There had been a promise of even greater things to come.

"And then," Verla said bitterly, "Koryl discovered long-hidden instructions for opening the gateway, which had been left by her ancestor scientist. She allowed another Gorgon to enter this world, allying herself with the monster as her traitorous forebear had done in the past.

"War immediately followed. For myself and the subjects loyal to me it was a losing war. We were forced to flee Upper Olin and take refuge in the lowest levels of the city, where we have been at bay ever since."

"Now Koryl considers herself the High Priestess of all Olin, and life in her part of the city, I have heard, is an unending celebration of her victory. There is feasting, drinking, and the wildest kind of revelry. Almost each day there are dances and contests of some sort. Slaves are pitted against each other in bloody sports, forced to kill each other under the threat of horrible torture. And there are ceremonies centering about the worship of the Gorgon, in which slaves or captives are offered as sacrifices to the monster."

"What a mess." Stacey's entire being was appalled and sickened. "And the same thing is going to happen to the lands beyond Olin unless we can somehow prevent it. If all of the Gorgon gets through the gateway, the creature may be too powerful for even the advanced science of my own people to stop."

"If it comes through," Verla returned bleakly, "there will not be one Gorgon—others will follow. It's only because the Gorgon is as yet unable to enter in its entirety that more of its kind haven't appeared. I do not understand the exact reason, but it is as though the Gorgon were blocking the gateway."

"More!" Stacey gasped. "As if one wasn't enough!" His thoughts collapsed hopelessly, and he remained sunk in a gloomy mental silence.

AFTER a time Verla's thoughts touched him like a gentle and comforting hand. He found himself communicating with her again, telling her, in response to her questions, of the kind of clothing and ornaments in fashion among the women of his land, and explaining the customs that existed between the sexes there. It was not until later that he realized how cleverly she had made him forget his despondence.

He had a sense of growing intimacy that was very pleasant. In the direct contact of mind to mind, there was little one could hide from the other. Any attempt at concealment was instantly detectable. Thus, despite the short time he had been acquainted with her, Stacey came to know more of Verla of Olin than he would normally have learned in years with another woman. And what he learned was in every way sweet and fine, completely in keeping with what his eyes had told him of her exceptional loveliness. He was certain now that this woman was his ideal, yet with a shyness he had not hitherto known he possessed, he sought to keep his feelings hidden.

He had felt a smattering of guilt regarding his sudden feelings for her, until he discovered that Verla was hiding something, too. And in the end their very efforts gave them both away.

Verla's secret, Stacey found, was—too his delight—much like his own.

Hand in mental hand, they wandered the enchanting pathways that existed for them alone. Until Verla's thoughts flared in sudden alarm.

"Rick—someone approaches."

And as though her dread was a ripple widening in a pool of water, a mental echo of trepidation rose from the pillar-folk.

"It is the Gorgon! And with her—Koryl!"

Instinctively, Stacey knew what that meant. And Verla evidently knew also.

"Koryl has learned of you, Rick. She comes to see what manner of men you and your friend Phil Tobin are. Rick...I'm afraid for you."

Trying futilely to comfort the woman, Stacey waited. And then, into his limited view soared a strange bubble-shaped craft, within which sat a group of people in brightly-colored garments.

In front of the machine floated the Gorgon.

CHAPTER FOUR

BEFORE the pillars containing Stacey and Tobin the monster hovered to a stop. A moment later the bubble craft stopped, too, settling lightly to the snow. A door opened in the transparent side, and one by one its passengers emerged.

A man and a woman preceded the others. There was that about their appearance and bearing that almost at once enabled Stacey to identify them as Koryl and Zarduc. An instant later a whisper of thought from Verla confirmed his guess.

After the pair came several men and women. They were of varying ages and almost without exception were fine physical specimens. They were light in coloring, as were all the people of Olin that Stacey had seen so far. He would have classed them as unusually attractive were it not for the effects of dissipation clearly visible in their faces. The boisterous, wild life of Upper Olin was leaving its mark.

All wore short skirts of some metallic material, glittering and multi-colored, with ornate and richly jeweled harnesses covering the upper half of their bodies. On their feet were jewel-embossed buskins that laced to the knee. Both men and women wore elaborate head coverings, the women tall, fantastically arabesqued tiaras, the men lavishly decorated helmets, surmounted by colored plumes or high, scroll-like crests.

At first Stacey wondered why they did not suffer from the cold. Then he saw that all were covered with a thin, transparent over-garment that somehow provided effective insulation.

Stacey could not read their thoughts, something that seemed to be possible only to those within the pillars. But it was obvious that most of the group were enjoying a lark. They were laughing and talking excitedly, jostling each other in their eagerness to peer at Stacey and Tobin.

After his initial, comprehensive scrutiny of the others, Stacey devoted his attention to Koryl and Zarduc—particularly to Koryl, for despite what he knew of her character, the High Priestess fascinated him.

Verla had told him that Koryl was beautiful, that men had killed themselves over her. But with a picture of evil in his mind, the description had meant little. Now he saw that Koryl's beauty was incredible—even outrageous.

Her body, revealed by her brief costume, was perfection itself, like a poem in flesh modeled by some godlike master sculptor. She was as slim as a golden flame burning in an utter absence of wind, yet somehow lushly rounded and curved. Her skin was white and utterly flawless, with a faint rose tint. From under the tall, crown-shaped tiara atop her small head fell a mass of curling blonde hair, as long and heavy as a short cloak and the color of molten gold. Her face was slightly triangular, the chin dimpled and the lips full and sensuous, the color of a strong man's blood freshly spilled upon snow. There was passion in those lips, Stacey thought—and cruelty.

He found himself looking into her eyes, and with it came the sensation of sinking into endless depths. Those eyes were a clear aquamarine green, large and tilted, and fringed heavily with golden brown lashes. He wrenched himself from their fathomless, sea-like embrace with great effort, turning his awareness—as though in search of escape—upon Zarduc.

THE man was tall and superbly muscled, with aquiline features that were too harsh and self-centered in cast to be entirely handsome. From beneath his ornate helmet dark red hair curled almost to his shoulders. His skin was almost as fair as that of the women about him, though numerous scars— evidently relics of past battles—covered his splendid warrior's body. His eyes were a pale and icy blue, narrowed now in a slight frown as he gazed at Stacey. A latent scowl twisted his too-full lips.

Stacey sensed a feeling of hostility from Zarduc. He was at a loss to understand the reason, for he was unable either by sound or expression to do anything that could arouse the chieftain's dislike. A moment later, directing his awareness once more at Koryl, the answer became plain.

Other emotions had replaced the purely objective interest that had first shown on her face. Her green eyes were lidded and slumberous as they traveled over Stacey's features, noting his sun-bronzed skin, touching the firm line of his lips and the spread of his shoulders, evident even beneath his fur parka. Her slow, appraising glance returned to his coppery hair and lingered on his amber eyes. The sensuous curve of her lips deepened in a faint smile.

Zarduc turned to her and spoke abruptly, motioning toward the bubble-shaped craft. Koryl shook herself slightly, as though awakening from a dream. A mask seemed to slide over her features. She spoke briefly to Zarduc—obviously in refusal, for the man's scowl deepened.

He began to quarrel now, his gestures swifter and even expressing a degree of anger. But with an imperiously silencing wave of one slim white hand, Koryl turned away.

Zarduc flushed and tightened his lips. He was plainly agitated, but it seemed that he didn't dare protest any further against whatever Koryl had in mind.

It was apparent to Stacey the warrior chief somehow feared Koryl—feared her almost to the same extent that he was ensnared by her breathtaking beauty. Stacey knew the Gorgon was involved, and he wondered how the situation might be altered if Koryl was ever without the monster's protection.

The exchange between the two had not gone unnoticed by the others of the group. They seemed keenly aware of the power and status of both Koryl and Zarduc, an awareness that was reflected by their sycophantic reaction to the moods of the two powerful personages. The group had suddenly grown uneasily silent, avoiding Zarduc's disconcerted glances.

Koryl was facing the Gorgon, who hovered several feet to one side of the group. The High Priestess' exquisite lips did not move, but Stacey knew she was in communication with the monster. And as though a faint echo of her mental voice reached him from the monster's mind, he understood what Koryl was saying.

"Great one from beyond the gateway, I desire you to release these two men. It was a mistake to imprison them thus. They are strangers from a far land and it is certainly possible they may possess information that would be of great importance to us. I would speak with them…" Koryl's lips arched into a half-smile, "…especially with the one of the yellow eyes and the face of a hunting hawk."

"But they are strangers from the outside world. They may be quite dangerous, my High Priestess," the Gorgon's cold thought returned. "They possess strange weapons and knowledge, and might even cause you serious harm should they be allowed free in Olin."

"I will take suitable precautions, great one. And with you to aid me, I'm feel confident that nothing could go wrong."

"You forget that there are many things that I must attend to. Should there be a dangerous turn of events, I might not be present to give you aid and assistance when you need it the most."

Koryl waved off the Gorgon's concerns. "I am willing to take the risk."

"This is madness," the Gorgon replied with a sudden sharpness of tone, anger stirring in its dark, alien mind. "I am emphatically against your wishes, my High Priestess."

Koryl straightened rigidly, her green eyes flaming. "You exceed yourself, great one! Remember who controls the gateway. You will indeed become only a head should you extend further my displeasure. Release these two—at once!"

SOMETHING exceeding rage flashed in the Gorgon's strange, cold mind. The flash awoke an instant, involuntary shudder of fright in Stacey and he felt a surge of deep-buried, primeval dread. It was a rage so vast that it ceased to be emotion. And it went as suddenly as it had come, hidden behind a screen of evil cunning.

Stacey realized that Koryl would someday pay dearly for her arrogance. At present she had the Gorgon's aid and protection, but these were things secured by her control of the gateway. They would most certainly vanish if she ever lost that control.

There were ugly crosscurrents here that disturbed Stacey. The Gorgon, forced to do Koryl's bidding, secretly building a mysterious bridge of pillar-encased human beings. Zarduc, bewitched by Koryl's incredible loveliness, yet hating and fearing her. And Koryl, domineering and cruel, inflamed by ambition, trampling ruthlessly over the feelings of those in her power.

It was an unstable human atomic pile, Stacey thought, swiftly reaching critical mass. If it ever reached a point of detonation, there would be horrendous ramifications a thousand times over.

He also didn't like the idea of being released into Koryl's custody, even though it offered a chance of escape. He knew that he might all too easily fall under her captivating spell. And if he were able to resist her, he knew as well that resistance would most likely endanger him. Aside from this, he shunned the idea of being separated from Verla. The mental union they had consummated had become exceedingly pleasant—more complete in many respects than any physical union could have been.

But he had not choice in the matter—that was clear. The Gorgon at last responded reluctantly to Koryl's demand.

Hideous, alien, yet somehow beautiful, the great head floated closer to Stacey's pillar. Once again he detected in its cold thoughts an impression of strain, but a different sort of strain than he had previously sensed. Some other strange process was taking place. Something, Stacey knew, that would release him from the pillar.

From the Gorgon's mind issued an incomprehensible flow of force that became an increasing sound in Stacey's mind—high and keen and nerve-wracking. It rose still higher, causing a certain degree of pain within Stacey's brain. The sound seemed to strike into the very substance of the pillar, causing it to vibrate in the same manner that a thin glass goblet vibrates to the sustained, high note of a violin. And as a goblet may be thus shattered, so the material of the pillar began to fall in a fine powder about Stacey. The wind seized the powder as it loosened and bore it away in thin, grayish vapors.

Within moments, the pillar was gone. Stacey was still held in paralysis, but free now of his prison.

The head turned to Tobin's pillar, and the process was repeated. Then one of the monster's tentacular growths began moving along Tobin's leg as though searching for something. The tentacle found what it was looking for and made a plucking motion too swift for the eye to follow. Whatever had been removed from Tobin's leg, however, remained invisible.

Returning to Stacey, the Gorgon sent an exploring tentacle along his leg also. He remembered the sting he had felt before the paralysis had gripped him. He wondered now if the monster were searching for the source of the sting, to remove from the wound something like the stinger of a bee or a wasp. Even as he wondered, the tentacle paused—and plucked. The object, whatever it had been, was gone. Seconds later, Stacey felt the paralysis draining from him.

HIS telepathic powers were leaving him, too. He realized this as the uncanny clarity and keenness of his mind began to fade. Almost too late he remembered Verla. Summoning his dwindling mental powers for one last effort, he called out to her.

"Goodbye, Verla. I promise not to forget you...do you understand?"

"Rick! Yes—and farewell...dear one."

The treasured mental tones vanished. The old drab and blunted world existed around him once again. He moved his arms slowly, thinking with regret of his lost god-hood.

Then he turned his head—and became aware of Koryl. Her beauty seized at him, held him enrapt and fascinated. She seemed even more exquisite at close range than his view of her from the pillar had hinted. He looked into her eyes and found himself sinking as before into their watery depths. Dimly he was aware that they were glittering with excitement, that a faint smile of eagerness lifted the corners of her full, red lips.

The long, gold-brown lashes slowly lowered. Stacey recovered from his momentary rapture with a sensation of rising through ocean depths. He heard Koryl speak in a rich contralto, voicing a question. He shook his head to show that he did not understand—the actual spoken language of Olin conveyed nothing to him. He felt dizzy still, and he was grateful for the revivifying touch of the frigid wind on his face.

Koryl nodded her sleek head quickly and flashed a dazzling smile. She had evidently anticipated Stacey's lack of comprehension and it seemed she knew what to do regarding it. Turning once more to the Gorgon, she resumed her silent mental communication with the creature.

Stacey found the monster gazing at him remotely, a sullen light smoldering deep within its great reddish orbs. Its thoughts formed coldly in his mind.

"The High Priestess requests that you and your companion be taught the language of Olin. It shall be done, stranger from a far land. But think not that you have escaped the Gorgon's power."

A tentacle flicked out, touching Stacey's head. He recoiled instinctively, but the cold, snake-like thing quickly followed the movement, retaining contact. Recovering himself, Stacey remained quiet.

Another tentacle touched Tobin also, and still another came to rest against Koryl's white forehead. A contact with Koryl had been made, Stacey realized, in which the Gorgon was to play the role of a catalyst or power source.

In another moment a weird sensation of numbness spread through Stacey's mind, as though a force of some kind had gripped his brain. The force began to move about within him, impressing upon certain of his memory centers a duplicate of the speech patterns supplied by the mind of Koryl. For long minutes the incredible process went on. New synapse paths were blazed, new neuron linkages formed.

And then, before the confusion in Stacey's mind had time to

subside, it was over. He felt the frigid wind on his face again. The haze before his eyes began to lift, and the colors that swam formlessly before him resolved themselves into the shapes of men and women. He saw Koryl close before him, her exquisite features anxious. Her contralto voice sounded softly in his ears.

"You have not been injured?"

"I...I'm all right." And then Stacey gasped. "Why...why I can understand you now..."

"Of course, stranger. And your friend as well."

"But...how did it happen? As far as I know, such a thing is impossible."

Koryl shrugged her white, sleekly rounded shoulders. "Few things are impossible to the Gorgon. She possesses great knowledge and powers."

"So I see." Stacey rubbed the back of his hand slowly across his forehead and glanced at Tobin. The other returned his look blankly, blue eyes dazed.

STILL struggling to accustom himself to what had happened, Stacey's gaze chanced across the pillar within which was Verla's slim, exotically lovely figure. He stared at her with a faint surprise, fully aware for the first time of the barrier that now existed between them. The intimacy they had shared now seemed merely a dream.

"You find her attractive?" Koryl asked softly, following the direction of Stacey's eyes.

He recovered himself quickly. He wanted to avoid exposing Verla to harm by arousing Koryl's jealousy. He said:

"All the women here seem attractive."

Koryl's lips lifted in a slow smile. Beneath lowered lids her green eyes were intent and hard, "Some more so than others, perhaps?"

Deliberately he let his eyes travel over her. He nodded. "That's true. I was trying to be a gentleman and give all the ladies credit."

"A wise gentleman remembers that some ladies deserve a

greater amount of credit," Koryl said.

Zarduc growled, "Must we spend the entire day in this place, Koryl? You may find the conversation interesting, but it makes me wish for strong drink—or to wring a throat or two."

Koryl's rich laughter chimed on the cold air. Her watery gaze was mocking. "Do you have any particular throats in mind, bloody one?"

"Aye, that I have." The chieftain's baleful glance settled on Stacey.

Koryl laughed again. With a sudden, lithe movement she came close to Stacey and linked her arm in his. She gestured with her free hand at the bubble-like craft. "There are better places in which to carry on our conversation. We shall return to the city." She glanced up at Stacey as the pressure of her arm urged him into motion. "You and your companion are my guests, of course. And you shall remain such...as long as you both conduct yourselves in a manner befitting guests. But I'm sure you will appreciate my hospitality after your sojourn in the pillars of the Gorgon."

Stacey returned her gaze grimly. "I understand what you mean," he said.

They reached the transparent bubble craft. Stacey noted curiously that the machine was about a dozen feet in diameter and seemed constructed of some material like glass or clear plastic. A short ladder led up to a deck near the middle of the craft. Here a continuous bench followed the curve of the wall. In the middle of the transparent floor was a slender pedestal or column, on top of which were a number of levers, obviously controls. Stacey could see that the column went through the floor, merging into the propulsion mechanism below. This seemed very simple in detail. Stacey had a strong urge to examine it at close hand.

Stacey followed Koryl—up the ladder and into the circular cabin. She gestured him to a seat on the bench beside her, and with a faint grin—knowing he could hardly do otherwise—he complied.

Tobin entered next, his blue eyes round with interest as he, too, examined the craft. His bewilderment seemed to have left him.

"Are you okay, boss?"

"Doing fine, Phil...just fine. You look a little dazed."

"Yeah...I guess so."

Then came Zarduc, followed by the others. Taking their cue from Koryl, the group returned to high spirits again, laughing and jostling as they took their seats.

Zarduc took his place before the controls, and presently the craft lifted into the air, the Gorgon following a short distance behind.

CHAPTER FIVE

STACEY watched Zarduc for a moment, noting at the same time the bubble craft's swift ascent. There was only a faint humming sound from the propulsion mechanism. The lack of noise or vibration, combined with the transparent walls, gave Stacey the odd sensation of floating in the air.

The pillars spread over the valley floor were dwindling in size and detail. Stacey sought for the one in which Verla was encased. With an aching sense of loss, he realized that he could no longer find it. Grimly he told himself that he would return. He intended to make every effort to free the woman.

The craft ceased rising and shifted effortlessly into horizontal flight. Stacey found himself admiring Zarduc's deft handling of the controls. Barbarian though he might be in other ways, the man had the abilities of a natural pilot.

Koryl said, "You seem greatly interested in the operation of the air ship. Don't the people of your land possess such machines?"

Stacey nodded. "Yes, though they are much different in appearance and operation." He didn't think it necessary to add that the aircraft of his race were in some respects inferior to the bubble ship.

Koryl added shrewdly, "Then that must be the method by which you arrived in Olin."

Stacey nodded again.

"What became of your machine?"

"It has been seriously damaged," Stacey lied. It would be best, he thought, for Koryl to consider him completely in her power. That way his and Tobin's chances of escape would be increased. If they ever did get out of Olin, the plane would be waiting for them—intact. The ice in the fuel lines could be removed without too much difficulty.

He embroidered on the falsehood, explaining that the plane's engines had stopped because of the cold and that it had crashed while he and Tobin attempted to land. Koryl followed his story with excitedly widened green eyes.

"It is fortunate that you escaped harm," she murmured at last. Then she frowned prettily. "Do you realize that you have not yet told me your name?"

Stacey hastened to make up for the omission, as was clearly expected of him. He introduced Tobin and himself, giving their naval airforce rank.

"A warrior!" Koryl exclaimed in delight. She whirled to Zarduc. "Do you hear, my bloody one? These men are warriors in their own land."

The brooding scowl with which the other had been piloting the bubble ship grew darker. "They may not be very great warriors in this land, however," he grunted.

"That remains to be seen." Koryl returned her attention to Stacey. "Being a warrior, I'm assuming you've you fought in many battles?"

"There have been quite a few." Stacey replied.

He had entered the Pacific War while it was still getting under way, and had seen more than his share of the fighting. He told Koryl of this, exaggerating details here and there to satisfy her evident eagerness for the bloodily dramatic.

Then, prompted by her questions, he went on to tell her of the lands and people of the outer world, repeating substantially what he had previously told Verla. As he talked, he watched the progress of the bubble ship toward the spires that marked the location of the ice-covered city of Olin.

THE spires had grown steadily in size. Seen from the valley, they had appeared small and featureless, but now it was evident that they were huge—fully as large as the skyscrapers of a modern American city. The spires lacked the simplicity of modern American architecture, however. They were elaborately terraced and ornamented, covered with numerous carvings and bas-reliefs. Lavish use of metal, marble, and rainbow-hued tile added to the appearance of ornateness and grandeur. The visible portion of the city had a fantastic quality, as though it was imaginative rather than real. It was a fairy city, limned weirdly against the bleak background of ice and snow.

Stacey could find no suggestion of streets or avenues, though he knew in the past there must have been splendid thoroughfares among the great buildings, and parks and gardens as well. But now there was only a blanket of snow and ice. Stacey saw few signs of life. Once or twice a bubble ship glinted briefly in the far distance as it moved among the spires. Otherwise an oppressive air of desertion hung over the city.

Over what seemed the approximate center of Olin, Zarduc finally sent the bubble craft dropping down to a landing. Their destination, Stacey saw, was a building larger and more lavishly decorated than the rest. About this dominating central spire, which was surmounted by a huge metal statue, a number of smaller spires were grouped. The walls of all were elaborately carved and inlaid. Very broad, arched windows, vaguely Gothic in outline, appeared at regular intervals.

The central spire dropped away in a series of widening terraces. Upon the topmost of these, Zarduc settled the bubble ship to a landing.

Koryl caught Stacey's glance and gestured. "This is the ancient palace of the rulers of Olin. It is here that I, the High Priestess of the Gorgon, hold power."

Stacey nodded as though the information were news to him. He noticed Tobin's faintly puzzled look and shook his head slightly. For some reason, Koryl seemed unaware of the telepathic communication possible to those within the pillars, and Stacey preferred that she remain ignorant of the fact. Escape for Tobin and he would be easier if Koryl did not suspect that they had been prejudiced against her by their contact with Verla.

Beckoning to Stacey, Koryl rose and lithely descended from the ship. A number of armed men, obviously guards, had appeared on the terrace from a broad doorway in the building. Their weapons, Stacey noted curiously, consisted of a device like a flare-muzzled rifle, a sword, and a dagger. He decided that not many of the ancient weapons were left if such less efficient arms as a sword were also used.

Koryl swept into the building escorted by the guards, who seemed cringingly servile in her presence. Walking a few steps behind her with Tobin, Stacey found himself in a broad hall, which was luxuriously decorated in the exotically ornate style he had already noted as typical of Olin.

Koryl had advanced only a short distance down the hall, when a group of women appeared and clustered about her. They began to remove her transparent covering, while others fell to arranging her cape of golden hair and dabbing her face with perfumed lotions. Their ministrations were accompanied by many curious glances at Stacey and Tobin.

As Stacey watched, slightly bewildered by the activity, another group appeared, this time consisting of a number of men. Zarduc and the others were now attended to. When Zarduc's covering was removed, he was obsequiously handed a sword and dagger and a pistol-shaped device with a flaring muzzle like that of the rifles held by the guards. With the Gorgon present, Stacey decided, Zarduc had previously no need for weapons. Thought of the monster made him glance about, but it was no longer in evidence.

KORYL finally waved her attendants aside. "I shall leave

you to see that our guests are made comfortable for the present," she told Zarduc. "Conduct them to the proper chambers and see that they are provided with every convenience."

Zarduc nodded somewhat sourly. "Is that all, my High Priestess? Do you not also wish me to bathe and feed them? These, it seems, are what you consider the more important duties of the chief of your warriors."

"With the Gorgon to aid you, my great chief, you do not have too much to do," Koryl answered firmly. She turned to Stacey, her features softening. "Farewell for now, Rick...Stacey. I shall see you again...soon."

Stacey nodded. He was disturbed at himself for feeling a slight sense of eagerness by the faint suggestion of promise in her voice. Emotions clashing, he watched as she strode away in the midst of her attendants, a vision of bewitching loveliness.

She was utterly heartless, he knew, and vain and arrogant as well. In her ruthless quest for power, she had allied herself with an evil and virtually omnipotent monster from some unknown extra-dimensional realm, murdering and enslaving her own people. Yet even these things somehow seemed mitigated by her overpowering, extravagant beauty. She could easily make a fool out of a man, he thought. And he wondered if he was going to be that man. Avoiding it was going to be difficult. For others had already fallen under her spell and Zarduc was clearly one of these. The muscled chieftain might protest against her frequently humiliating commands, but in the end he obeyed them—as he was doing now.

As if aware of Stacey's musing, Zarduc turned to him with a fierce scowl. One of his big, scarred hands rested on the curving butt of the flare-muzzled pistol at his belt. He grunted:

"If this matter were left to my choice, stranger, I would chop you into pieces and make you swallow every single one of them."

"I have as much choice in this matter as you do," Stacey returned with a shrug. "There's no reason for hard feelings between us."

Zarduc's scowl faded slightly. "You speak like a man of sense—but I fear you may not have any sense left once Koryl sets to work on you."

Turning to the guards, the chieftain barked swift commands. An escort formed about Stacey and Tobin, and they were led down the corridor. Zarduc, marching with military precision in the lead, set a brisk pace.

At the end of the corridor they descended to a lower floor of the building by means of an elevator-like platform in a circular shaft, which seemed to move through some process of gravity nullification, since no cables were in evidence. Zarduc led the way down another corridor, stopping presently before an arched doorway. He gestured Stacey and Tobin into the room beyond.

"You both will remain here for the present," he said. "And by remain, I'll have you understand that I mean exactly that. There will be guards posted outside the door to see that you do not set yourselves to 'wandering' about the palace."

"I was under the impression we were guests," Stacey said.

Zarduc lifted his big shoulders. "Only where the High Priestess is concerned. The presence of you and your friend here in Olin is of her choosing—not mine. I shall deal with you in my own way if necessary." His pale blue eyes fastened grimly on Stacey. "You will be wise to remember that, stranger. Koryl may be taken with you for the moment, but you will do well not to make too much of it. I have certain prior…'claims'…you might say. I am also second in command in this city, which means I am not without powerful rights of my own. I can make things most unpleasant for you, should you…shall we say…go too far in your efforts to become close to the High Priestess."

"And Koryl will make unpleasant things happen to me if I don't go far enough," Stacey pointed out matter-of-factly.

One corner of Zarduc's full lips rose in a thin, wolfish smile. "That is indeed a precarious situation for you to be in, stranger.

"Look," Stacey said. "You don't want us here. As far as that goes, my friend and I don't want to be here. So why not help us to…end our visit here? It seems that would solve the problem for all of us. Am I right?"

"It would accomplish nothing, stranger. You have admitted that your airship is wrecked. And without it, the Gorgon would recapture you before you could get very far."

STACEY briefly considered telling Zarduc that his plane was essentially undamaged, but he didn't know what effect the information might have. The plane was his and Tobin's ace in the hole, and he balked at running even the slightest risk of losing it. He shrugged and remained silent.

Zarduc prepared to leave. "I will send servants to look after your needs. In the meantime, bear in mind that guards will be stationed beyond the door. And bear in mind as well the warning I've given you."

Then the chieftain turned and strode from the room, the door closing with an air of finality behind him. Stacey and Tobin were alone, gazing at each other in hopeless silence.

"Well there's someone who wants to be your best friend," Tobin commented under his breath.

"I can tell were going to be pals for a long, long time," Stacey answered back. He then gazed about their quarters. "Look at this place will you?"

Stacey's eyes examined the room. It was large and luxuriously furnished. And it was pleasantly warm, as the entire building seemed to be. For the first time Stacey became fully aware of the warmth. He began slowly to strip off his fur parka and the leather flying suit beneath.

Tobin shortly followed suit, dropping listlessly onto a low, very broad couch, which was strewn thickly with pillows. "I thought being chained to those pillars was bad enough, Rick, but this place could turn out to be worse—a lot worse."

Stacey nodded wryly. "If Koryl doesn't get the attention she wants from us—especially from me I suspect—she'll most likely hand us back over to the Gorgon. And if I become a little *too* friendly with her, my 'pal,' Zarduc, will have a wonderful time sliding one of his knives into my back."

"There's the plane, Rick. They don't know it's still in good shape. I watched Zarduc operating the ship that brought us here and it looks easy enough to operate. If we could somehow get a hold of one, we could reach the plane before the Gorgon or anyone else knows what's going on."

"It might work—but I don't know if I want to try it just yet."

"Why not? You know the fix you're in."

"There's Verla—the woman in the pillar next to us. I'd like to help her. She was something special…very special. And I'd like to help her people, too." He shook his head and laughed a little under his breath. "I know it sounds a bit crazy, Phil, but there's something about her that compels me to want to stay— at least for the time being. If we could get in touch with some of her followers from down below, the ones in Lower Olin, we might be able to work out some kind of a plan. We'd probably need their help anyway if we really want to get out of this place. It'll all depend on how long I can stall off Koryl and Zarduc." He looked wryly at Tobin. "And that…should be quite a tap dance."

Tobin started to protest, but then nodded slowly. "I understand how you feel, Rick. There aren't many women around like this Verla. I mean she's not exactly the kind a' gal you'd find on a street corner in downtown New York. If she was even faintly interested in me, I'm sure I'd tear the whole city apart for her." He put his hand on Stacey's shoulder. "All right, Rick, you're the boss. We'll stick it out." Tobin's round features became slightly mirthful. "Maybe there's another broad like Verla somewhere down in Lower Olin. Who knows…?"

Another silence fell. Stacey went to investigate a doorway in one of the splendidly carved and inlaid walls of the chamber. He found himself gazing into a tile-walled room that was obviously a bath, for in the center was a broad waist-high cylinder of carved marble that could only have been a tub. He was examining this at close hand when Tobin appeared in the doorway.

"Visitors, Rick."

Returning to the chamber, Stacey saw that two youths had entered. They were simply dressed and without ornaments of any kind. He decided they must be the servants Zarduc mentioned he would send.

"Make yourselves comfortable, boys," Stacey said with a grin, gesturing to a couch. "In my land we're in the habit of helping ourselves—unless we can afford not to."

"But...but it isn't proper—" one of the two blurted out, his young face bewildered. "It is our duty to serve you."

"If you refuse our service, we will be punished for having displeased you," the other added.

"You must be joking. Punished?" Stacey considered a moment, scratching his chin. "Well...I'll tell you what, the two of you can show me and my friend how to use some of the things around here that are strange to us. That way nobody'll be able to say you didn't do your job. How's that? But jobs like washing my back? Sorry...I'll take care of myself."

The two reluctantly accepted the compromise. Their names, Stacey learned, were Parn and Trek. Parn was the taller and more mature of the pair, obviously the leader. Both, however, were finely proportioned, their features clean-cut and intelligent.

Guided by the instructions of the two, Stacey and Tobin bathed, one after another. The tub was filled and emptied by manipulating a series of metal flowers ornamenting the inner rim. Drying was accomplished by a device set in the wall that seemed to draw moisture into itself. Finished with the bath, Stacey and Tobin were shown how to apply a lotion-like liquid that completely dissolved the whisker stubble on their faces.

"That's one thing I'd like to take back with me," Tobin said in admiration. "A guy could make a fortune with that stuff in the States."

STACEY nodded in bemused fashion, his thoughts centering around a different matter as he finished dressing. He turned finally to Parn.

"You said something about being punished if your service was refused. What did you mean by that? Losing your wages, getting scolded—or being thrown to the Gorgon?"

"A fate almost as bad as being thrown to the Gorgon," Parn replied.

"Where I come from a servant would simply quit. Is it possible that you can't quit—that you and Trek are being forced to do this kind of work?"

"We're slaves," Trek said abruptly, a long-pent bitterness surging into his face.

Stacey said softly, "Then I gather that you two aren't in sympathy with Koryl and her followers in Upper Olin."

Quivering visibly, Trek glanced at Parn. But the other remained silent, his features wooden. Trek bit his lip and remained silent, too.

Stacey hadn't overlooked the possibility that the two might be spies. But spies, he concluded, would have been eager to supply him with information in the hope of drawing out damaging statements or admissions. The behavior of Parn and Trek amply indicated that they were no henchmen of Koryl or Zarduc.

Blind confidence grabbed Stacey. He knew he might be taking a terrible chance by saying too much to these two strangers, but he opted to risk it. He spoke swiftly, leaning in close to them.

"I've been *inside* one of the pillars, a captive, and I've communicated with Verla, the Princess from Lower Olin."

"Rick, don't say too much," Tobin interrupted.

"It's okay, Phil."

"But—"

"Phil…please…"

Tobin paused, an anxious look on his face. "All right, boss. Hope you know what you're doing."

Stacey turned back to the two servants and continued on. "That's how I know so much about Olin. Verla and the people of Lower Olin have my full sympathy. And though I'm a comparative stranger, I'd like to help them. The first thing I'd like to do is free Verla from the pillars. But I'm going to need help. Verla told me of a man named Jendon. He's also from Lower Olin and he's the only one I know of who can give the kind of help I need. Somehow my friend and I must get out of the palace and reach this man. Together we should be able to free Verla…somehow. That would mean new hope for Verla's people."

"But you are a guest of Koryl" Trek said sharply.

"A guest in name only. The guards outside the door aren't exactly friendly."

Trek's lips quivered again, but Parn quickly laid a hand on his shoulder. Parn's face was still wooden, and Stacey knew that it would be impossible at the present moment to overcome the youth's suspicions. Yet he didn't entirely despair. The seed had been planted. Stacey felt mildly optimistic that it would eventually bear fruit.

The door suddenly opened. Zarduc stalked into the room, a black scowl on his face.

CHAPTER SIX

A COLD wave of alarm washed over Stacey. Had Zarduc somehow heard what he had said to Parn and Trek? If so, Stacey knew—at the very least—that precautions would be taken to prevent him from ever getting into contact with the people of Lower Olin.

But in another moment it became clear that Zarduc's scowl was due to a different reason. And that reason, Stacey deduced, was most likely Koryl. Zarduc had probably become embroiled in another quarrel with her—a quarrel from which he had again emerged second best.

Stacey smiled a grim, inward smile. Zarduc's emotions were slowly rising to a dangerous level. Judging from the reputedly violent, bloodthirsty nature of the man, serious things were going to start happening sooner or later.

Zarduc paid no attention to Parn and Trek other than to order them from the room with a sharp gesture. Then he concentrated the full force of his scowl on Stacey.

"All bathed and perfumed, eh, my pretty one?"

Stacey grinned faintly. "And you've been rolling in the muck as usual, eh, my lovely one?"

While Tobin coughed in a humorous fashion, Zarduc grew rigid, his lips pinching together into a pale line.

"Warrior's blood, stranger, you go too far with your insults."

"No farther than you go with yours," Stacey said.

Zarduc's hand wavered over the hilt of the dagger on his belt. A long, straining interval passed. Slowly the furious chieftain grew calm.

"I'm unable to take forthright measures here and now, stranger—but I'll have my revenge before long."

"Revenge? Revenge for what?"

"Bear that in mind." Zarduc's icy blue gaze impaled Stacey for a few moments longer. Then he nodded his helmeted head in the direction of the door. "Now you will come with me. Koryl has ordered a banquet held in your 'honor.' I'm sure you wouldn't want to keep her waiting."

Shrugging, Stacey followed with Tobin as the chieftain stalked from the room. Beneath his outward unconcern, Stacey's thoughts were grim. He knew Zarduc bitterly resented the two Americans' presence in Upper Olin. And it seemed logical that the man had hit upon, or was at least planning some scheme for removing them. Stacey didn't know what that scheme was, but he felt certain that it would be unpleasant—and fatal.

He bleakly promised himself that he would put up a whale of a fight. And—he touched the automatic in a hip pocket of his gray khaki trousers—he had the means with which to do it. Tobin was also still in possession of his gun. Amazingly, they hadn't been searched for weapons when they were freed from their pillars. Perhaps Koryl and Zarduc had been too confident of the Gorgon's protection to bother. Or perhaps, judging from the conspicuous size of the weapons in Upper Olin, it had been assumed from the fact that no armament was in direct evidence upon Stacey and Tobin, that they had simply not possessed any.

With guards surrounding them and Zarduc in the lead, Stacey and Tobin were taken through the ornate corridors, to another of the circular shafts with its elevator-like platform. They descended to a still lower floor of the building. A walk through further corridors brought them finally to a vast and splendidly decorated dining hall, which echoed to the boisterous talk and laughter of a large gathering of men and women.

The noise swiftly faded as Zarduc appeared with Stacey and Tobin. Excited whispers and curious stares greeted the two men from the outer world.

ZARDUC grew straighter and more military in bearing, as though becoming more than ever conscious of his importance. He led the way toward the apex of a very long, low table that was built in the form of an angle. Instead of chairs, there were thick cushions on both sides of the two branches of the table, and the gathering sat or reclined on these. Stacey was briefly reminded of the banquets of ancient Rome, which had taken place in a much similar fashion.

Glancing toward the open end of the angle formed by the table, Stacey saw a group of over a dozen plainly clad women who were busying themselves before three huge metal and tile cabinets. These seemed to be machines of some sort, for they were covered with a multitude of wheels and levers and differently colored lights. A moment later Stacey realized that these were the food producing machines that Verla had mentioned.

As he neared the apex of the table, Stacey noticed for the first time that Koryl was already present. Directly before the apex, she reclined on a deeply upholstered, low couch, the only one in the room. She had exchanged the harness and skirt which she had worn previously for an iridescent, jeweled robe which flowed in revealing, gauzy folds over the rich curves of her figure. She wore a tiara even larger and more splendid than the first Stacey had seen, and from under this her mantle of hair fell in a golden flood about her white shoulders. She was, he decided, slightly terrific. Hollywood would have been wild about her.

Red lips parted in a dazzling smile, Koryl gestured Stacey to a seat on the cushions at her right, indicating that Tobin was to place himself beside Stacey. In cold silence, his glance at her sullen, Zarduc dropped to the cushions at Koryl's left. The chieftain proceeded to stare, obviously brooding, at the table before him.

Koryl leaned toward Stacey, her watery eyes bright and confiding. "My people are very much interested in you."

"I'm quite flattered," Stacey said. "But I'd say they're wasting their time. I'm not so very important where I came from."

"But you are important here," Koryl returned. She leaned closer, the jeweled robe slipping dangerously along the sleek curves of her shoulders. "In fact, Rick Stacey, you could become very important here in time."

It was with difficulty that Stacey kept his eyes from straying to the dwindling boundaries of the robe. He shrugged and said, "I'm not too interested in becoming important. From my experience, important people usually have a lot of troubles."

"That's not necessarily true in Upper Olin," Koryl said with a laugh, though it was evident that Stacey's answer had not pleased her. With a quick, almost fretful motion, she pulled the robe back up over her shoulders.

The servant girls before the three huge food machines had now finished their preparations. Bearing steaming bowls and platters, they advanced in a carefully formed wedge toward the apex of the table. Koryl first was served, then Stacey, Tobin, and Zarduc. Finally attention was given to the others nearest the apex, and in turn to those further away. The importance of the guests present at the two branches of the table obviously fell in proportion to their distance from Koryl.

THE food, Stacey found, was spicy and exotic in flavor, though palatable. It consisted of variously colored jellies and pastes, with several other dishes that had the appearance, texture, and taste of meat. However artificial the whole might have seemed, Stacey knew that it was undoubtedly highly nutritious.

In addition to the main foods there was a variety of breads and sweet pastries, with numerous beakers and flasks of colored liquids, which were evidently liquors and wines. Koryl selected one of the containers and personally filled Stacey's goblet. She smiled at him, her pique of a moment before apparently forgotten.

He sipped at the contents of his goblet—and gasped in surprise. The stuff was potent. The little he swallowed surged in waves of heady warmth to his brain. He would have to be careful. Too much of the liquid and he'd go out like a light.

Later, however, he found that this was not true. A large quantity could be imbibed without too much obvious effect. While intoxication resulted, there was no loss of consciousness. Nor were there any ill effects afterward.

Stacey's attention was diverted from the food by a flurry of activity in the space beyond the open end formed by the angle of the table. A group of men had appeared, laboriously moving the huge food machines to one side of the hall. After them came a gathering of men and women dressed in bright costumes, the men carrying strange devices, which proved shortly to be musical instruments. A number of large metal bowls supported by tripods were distributed about in a star-like pattern.

Tendrils of smoke coiled upwards from these, filling the hall with a fragrant blue haze.

The musicians took their places at one side of the hall, and presently the sound of their instruments rose and blended in a growing flood of melody. Higher the music rose, and higher, taking on a swift and pagan tempo that caught at the pulses irresistibly. Stacey had never heard music like it before. It seemed to carry elements of jazz, yet held an insistent undertone of qualities that were wild and primitive. He found the music stirring him in a way that he definitely was unaccustomed to. He wasn't sure if he liked this feeling

The costumed girls had been poised among the tripods, statuesque, arms outspread. Now they swept together in a dance that increased in pace to the rhythm of the melody flooding in throbbing waves throughout the hall. They whirled faster and ever faster, weaving in and out among the tripods, merging and separating, twisting and leaping.

Stacey watched until he became aware of a faint dizziness that seemed in some way to be accompanied by a sense of excitement and stimulation. He decided that this was the effect of the faint blue smoke curling from the bowls. He had been careful not to drink the contents of his goblet too quickly and too often.

This, he noticed, was something that his pal Tobin had failed to do. The other was surrounded by a group of pretty and scantily clad women, who were plying him with questions and filling his goblet as rapidly as he emptied it. It was evident that Tobin was having the time of his life. His features were flushed, and he laughed often as he teased his listeners.

But for that matter, Stacey observed that most of the other guests were already in an even worse condition. With shouts and laughs that rose above the wild, pulse-quickening music, they were indulging in uninhibited horseplay and lovemaking. Quarrels were many and frequent. At one point, two men rose unsteadily to their feet and threw themselves at each other in a fierce if clumsy fight with long daggers. The duel ended abruptly as one of them fell to the floor with a nasty gash in his side. He was carried from the hall amid scattered handclaps for the victor. Except for this, the fight had attracted little attention.

THE banquet was turning into a debauch much too rapidly for Stacey's peace of mind. There were undercurrents of unruly savagery beneath the veneer of culture that overlay the life of Upper Olin. The potent drinks combined with the strangely stimulating blue smoke and the pagan music were tearing that veneer away. The savagery was coming to the surface, reaching a level where anything might happen.

While observing events about him, Stacey managed to keep responding to questions and conversational sallies directed at him by Koryl. Now he turned his full attention to her.

"Do you think your party is getting a bit...out of hand?"

She gave an unconcerned shrug. "I can always summon some of the guards to restore order...or even the Gorgon, if necessary. But affairs of this sort are desirable in a way. They release inner pressures that would otherwise seek more dangerous outlets." She studied Stacey with a mocking smile. "I gather that you don't approve of what you're seeing."

"Can't say I do," he said. "I suppose I'm just an old-fashioned boy from the States. Does this sort of thing go on all the time?"

"As often as anyone can find an excuse for it. There is not much else to do in Upper Olin."

"I can think of a lot of things to do."

"Really? Do enlighten me."

"Well, there's the advancement of knowledge, the improving of living conditions."

Koryl shrugged again. "Those things are for men too old to enjoy pleasure. Or for dreamers."

"Wouldn't you agree that the worth of a civilization is often measured by the work of its dreamers?" Stacey queried.

"Perhaps—though we of Upper Olin live to enjoy living. We find enough of 'worth' in that. I can see, Rick Stacey, that you are something of a dreamer yourself."

"I suppose I am."

"Of what do you dream?"

"The things dreamers usually dream about."

"Women among them? Beautiful women?"

Stacey grinned slightly. "Depending on the time and place,

yes." He thought suddenly and with a pang of Verla.

"No doubt you have many women in your own land," Koryl went on.

"I've known many in my time," Stacey replied. "But a man in my profession doesn't get to know them well. It's a here to-day, gone tomorrow sort of life."

Koryl chuckled at this. "Then—you have no mate, no children?"

"Suppose I told you I had a dozen mates and an army of children?"

Koryl's mocking smile flashed again. "I wouldn't be too surprised, I suppose. But even if there was truth in that, it wouldn't be of any importance…not here…not now."

"Zarduc might not think so," Stacey said, glancing over at the warrior chief. He had noticed that the chieftain was slyly eavesdropping on his conversation with Koryl.

Becoming aware that his stratagem had been discovered, Zarduc flushed angrily. Koryl's next words fanned the anger into a blaze of inner rage.

"What Zarduc thinks does not concern me."

"There was a time when it did," the chieftain shot back. "That was before the coming of this cursed stranger. I am not blind, my High Priestess, to the fact that you have taken a fancy to him."

"And why not, my bloody one? Our newfound friend, Rick Stacey, is…quite nice. I find talking with him to be a challenge, a constant contest of wits that is most enjoyable. That is more than I can say for your relentless state of bad humor and poor manners."

"But he has no right to any claims on you."

"Nor do you have a right to any claims, my bloody one."

"How dare you," Zarduc muttered softly under his breath.

"Please remember my dear Zarduc—lest you incur my wrath—that I have given you certain favors because of your po-sition, and even your loyalty, but you must not assume too much from this. I am the High Priestess of the Gorgon and the ruler of Upper Olin. What I give, I have every power to rescind."

ZARDUC abruptly leaned forward, his pale blue eyes glittering and intense. "You have forgotten something, my High Priestess. You've forgotten the warriors' code."

She stiffened, concern flashing into her face. "You don't dare invoke the code, Zarduc. I forbid it..."

With a grin of triumph the chieftain shook his head slowly. "You know you can't forbid it, Koryl. No ruler has ever defied the code, not when two warriors were involved. And never when one of them was a chieftain. You can ill-afford to make an exception now."

"You think not? You think not, Zarduc?" Koryl began gathering herself as though to rise, her green eyes blazing. "The rulers of the past did not have the Gorgon to aid them. *I* do. If you defy me, I shall have the Gorgon add you to her collection of victims in the pillars."

"Think, Koryl," Zarduc returned quietly. "By defying the code, you will set the whole warrior class against you. Many of them already despise you. Think of the small rebellions you've had in recent times—and the warriors are many, the Gorgon only one. And the Gorgon cannot be everywhere at once. She has great power, but lacks the advantage of numbers. And what of your plans of conquest? Without warriors to aid the Gorgon in her attacks against the lower regions of the city, many dangers could soon threaten your rule in Upper Olin. Perhaps from the people of Lower Olin...perhaps from the warriors themselves."

Koryl relaxed slowly, her lower lip caught between her teeth. By slow degrees, an expression of defeat spread over her face. Finally she turned to Stacey.

"Rick Stacey, Zarduc has invoked the ancient warriors' code by which he may engage you in a duel to defend his honor—a duel to the death. I am forced by tradition to allow this duel, since you are both warriors. And since you *are* a warrior, Rick Stacey, you cannot refuse to take part. Else he wins by default, and you will be banished from Olin."

"That suits me just fine," Stacey said. "Tobin and I will leave right now if you say so."

Koryl shook her head slowly. "In this case, I cannot allow you to go free. There is too much danger in what you may tell the outer world. You and your companion will be returned to the pillars of the Gorgon."

"Hold on just a minute," Stacey said. "I don't see how I got mixed up in this to begin with. What in the world did I do to make Zarduc want to defend his honor? I haven't done a damn thing."

"You took my place in Koryl's favors," Zarduc interjected. "According to the warriors' code, I can compel you to engage in this duel. This will show Koryl which of us is the better warrior, and thus...the better man."

Koryl said tonelessly, "Do you accept, Rick Stacey?"

"I don't suppose I'd gain much by refusing."

"Boss, you can't do this," Tobin broke in.

"I don't really have much choice, Phil."

Within Stacey a dull anger surged. He saw it all now. This was what Zarduc had been planning since his arrival at the palace. The man had been devilishly clever, issuing his challenge at a well-attended gathering with many notable citizens present, leaving no loophole in his scheme through which Stacey or Koryl could evade his designs.

As though aware of Stacey's thoughts, the chieftain grinned mockingly, "As the injured party, I have the choice of weapons, stranger. Also the choice of place and time. The weapons, then, daggers. The place, *here*—the time, *now!*"

CHAPTER SEVEN

ZARDUC rose quickly to his feet. Vaulting the table, he strode several paces toward the open end, his arms raised for silence. The music stopped, the dancing girls became motionless, the talk and laughter faded.

"I announce a duel," Zarduc said in ringing tones that seemed to fill the hall. "It will take place at once. The participants are myself and the stranger who has come to us from the outer world."

A tumult of excitement broke loose. The hall echoed with cheers and bursts of hand clapping.

Zarduc began removing his outer clothing. Finally he stood ready, wearing only a short metallic skirt and laced buskins and gripping a dagger whose blade glittered evilly in the light.

Stacey had the strange sensation that he was living a dream. The way events had suddenly built up to a serious crisis had been so abrupt that somehow it didn't seem real.

He felt Koryl grip his arm. Her low, tense voice sounded in his ears.

"Go, Rick Stacey. Fight. Fight and win—for me!"

He rose to his feet. Someone thrust a dagger into his hand. Still with that dream-like feeling, he stepped over the table and walked slowly toward Zarduc.

Across a space of a dozen feet they at last faced each other, circling slowly. There was no time to think of preparations or strategy. Zarduc suddenly darted forward, his blade stabbing at Stacey's chest.

The swift movement jolted Stacey into full alertness. Into his mind flashed memories of a judo course he had taken. He would need every bit of it now. He was anything but an expert in knife fighting, as Zarduc very obviously was.

Stacey darted aside, his leg outstretched. In the next instant he felt Zarduc's weight jar against the limb, but he was not quick enough to seize the other's knife wrist as it flashed by.

Tripped, Zarduc plunged to the floor. Stacey, too, was out of balance, falling to one knee. Before he could recover and take advantage of Zarduc's momentarily prone position, the chieftain leaped once more to his feet.

Fury twisted across the man's face. But a new caution was there as well. He began circling carefully, moving easily and lightly on his feet, his eyes narrowed and intent.

Zarduc shifted, feinting, then closing in as Stacey gave back. Stacey's mind was cold and tense. Retreat. That was the thing. This was no time for heroics. Retreat—then turn the force of the enemy's own onslaught against him.

Again and again Zarduc feinted. And then, crouching low, he rushed, having maneuvered Stacey into a position where the tripping strategy could not be repeated.

Stacey stepped forward. His forearm crashed against Zarduc's knife wrist, knocking it harmlessly to one side. Then, feet braced, he took the full force of Zarduc's rush against his hip, turning with it, his elbow smashing between the other's shoulders.

ZARDUC started to go down. But with a cat-like swiftness and an amazing presence of mind, he caught Stacey around the leg. And then, as he hit the floor, he gave a powerful tug that brought Stacey half atop him. Instantly Zarduc twisted, whirling himself over Stacey, one muscular hand fastening on Stacey's throat. The other hand—gripping the dagger—rose high, poised, and swept down.

Desperately Stacey countered with his wrist. He was almost too late. He felt a searing pain as Zarduc's blade glanced along his forearm, slicing across the surface flesh. An immediate attack with his own blade was impossible, for that hand was pinned beneath him.

Stacey writhed with frantic violence, vividly and painfully aware of the iron fingers clutching at his throat. The breath he needed so badly was being cut off. His efforts did not succeed in dislodging Zarduc from atop him, but he managed to pull his knife hand free. Clumsily he swept the point at Zarduc's face.

The warrior chief twisted his head aside with barely an inch to spare. He was forced to release Stacey's throat to protect himself from the menace of the swooping blade. He caught Stacey's forearm, shifting his grip an instant later to the wrist, forcing it to one side. His own knife wrist was already held in the laboring clutch of Stacey's other hand.

Furiously they strained, one striving to bring his knifepoint into deadly contact with the other. It was a contest of sheer strength. Weakened by having had his breath choked off, Stacey did not dare let it continue. He had to do something—and fast.

He allowed his resistance momentarily to weaken. Zarduc eagerly pressed his advantage, driving his full weight behind his knife hand. Stacey had planned for that. He heaved around under the force of the thrust, twisting Zarduc to one side… back…and over.

The trick might have allowed him to thrust his dagger down against Zarduc's loosened grip, but the warrior chief had gained an understanding of Stacey's fighting tactics. He kept moving, now using Stacey's own inertia against him. Pulling Stacey in his wake, Zarduc sought to pin him down once more. The momentum, however, was too great to overcome. Stacey added to it by pulling in turn. They rolled over and over along the floor until the bulk of the low table brought them up short. Each struggled savagely for the advantage, twisting and heaving.

The hall was a scene of wild disorder. Most of the guests were on their feet, shouting and cheering. As many of the cheers were for Stacey as for Zarduc.

Koryl alone had retained her seat. She sat tensely at the edge of the low couch, her green eyes shining with excitement.

Tobin was among those who took little or no interest in the struggle, mainly because of the many drinks he had virtually inhaled. He was mumbling incoherently as he lay among the cushions, his head pillowed on the lap of a pretty dark-haired girl.

Stacey and Zarduc had rolled away from the table. But now, as they thrashed and twisted over the floor, Stacey abruptly found himself jammed against it. Before his mind had time to grasp Zarduc's intention, he felt the back of his knife hand shoved savagely against the table's sharp edge. Numbness shot through his arm, and an instant later he realized that the dagger had flown from his involuntarily splayed fingers.

He was unarmed. And he knew he would remain so.

Zarduc would give him no opportunity to recover the weapon. This, Stacey remembered, was a fight to the death.

SOMETHING exploded in his mind. With a burst of strength, fired by reserves of energy that he hadn't known he possessed, he heaved violently with his legs, throwing Zarduc over him and half across the table. Then he writhed aside, twisted to hands and knees, and pushed himself erect.

Even as he turned to face his combatant once more, Zarduc lunged at Stacey, the dagger held high. Stacey almost grinned. It was a perfect set-up.

He ducked under the stroke, catching Zarduc's knife wrist as it descended. Then the full force of Zarduc's rushing body came down on his shoulders. He was ready for it. He twisted and Zarduc flew through the air, going completely over the table and hitting the floor on the other side amid the screams of startled guests in the vicinity.

Smiling faintly, a hard, cold, and wholly merciless smile, Stacey went after his man. He leaped the table, bent, caught the dazed warrior chieftain by the hair, and hauled him half upright. Stacey's other hand, balled into a rock-like fist, smashed into Zarduc's chest. Zarduc straightened with a gasp of pain, and then another fist thudded against his jaw, driving him back.

Stacey followed step by step, raining in one punishing blow after another. Under the onslaught Zarduc's last feeble defenses crumbled. The dagger had dropped from his hand. He tottered weakly, eyes half closed, legs buckling.

The gathering in the hall had gone mad. As one, they were now cheering Stacey on, shrieking for blood. He knew he could easily have satisfied them. Zarduc's fallen dagger was within easy reach. But he could not find it within himself to take the man's life.

Instead he brought up his right fist in a short, chopping blow that took Zarduc flush on the jaw. The chieftain dropped limply and lay still.

It was only then that Stacey awoke to the din of cheering all about him.

Koryl hurried forth. "You were wonderful," she cried above the noise. "I haven't seen such skilled fighting in a very long time." She gazed, wide-eyed, at Stacey for several seconds, then her gold-brown lashes lowered and a slow smile curved the corners of her red lips. "You have fought for my favors, Rick Stacey. And you have won. I am now yours...gladly and willingly."

Stacey returned her glance. She was intoxicatingly beautiful, the very essence of desirable womanhood. But he also remembered she was evil and cruel as well. And again he found himself thinking of Verla. Even now, superimposed on Koryl's face, he saw a picture of the imprisoned woman's hauntingly beautiful features. That lovely face would always be in his mind.

Koryl's face came back into focus a moment later. To cover up his hesitation, he rubbed a hand wearily over his forehead.

"You have offered me a great honor," he told her. "But right now I'm hardly in a condition to take advantage of it. What I need the most right now is a chance to rest."

"And what of Zarduc?" she said, pointing to the fallen warrior. "He still lives."

"No killing tonight, Koryl."

The crowd reacted to this with jeers, a goblet was even thrown into the center of the floor, but Koryl spun around and waved her hands in a gesture for silence. The crowd was instantly hushed. She then looked at Stacey, a mischievous smile spreading across her face.

"For Zarduc the humiliation you have served upon him will be far worse than death." Koryl chuckled a little at her own words. "So be it." She then clapped her hands. "I shall have servants take you to your chambers at once." She gestured a hand toward the drunken body of Stacey's companion. "And your friend, too." As she turned to walk away, she glanced back over her shoulder. "Rest well, my dear Stacey."

Back in the room, Tobin sprawled upon one of the couches and fell quickly into a deep slumber. As he stood looking over his snoring companion, full realization came to Stacey of what his fight with Zarduc had meant. It had made him more deeply entangled with Koryl than he'd ever planned. To keep her at a distance now would prove to be most difficult. And if she awoke too quickly to the fact that he had no sincere interest in her, the results might well be disastrous and at the very least would impair his plans for escape.

HE THOUGHT desperately of Parn and Trek. They were his only hope at present of getting into contact with the people of Lower Olin—especially with Verla's friend, Jendon. And it seemed a frail hope at best, but it was the only hope he had. He could think of nothing else that would enable him to flee Upper Olin and free Verla without the Gorgon's interference. Another uncertainty was Jendon himself. Verla had said he was striving to devise a way of overcoming the Gorgon's superhuman abilities—had he made any progress in that regard?

The question remained unanswered in the days that passed. Stacey, however, was given little time to think of it. Each day was filled with a constant round of activities. He went sight-seeing about Upper Olin with Koryl, Tobin, and a group of others, sometimes afoot, clad in the transparent protective suits, but more often in the bubble ships. On these latter occasions desperate thoughts of seizing control had come to Stacey. He still had his automatic, as did Tobin. But the Gorgon was always in close attendance. He remembered all too well his first attempt to use his gun on the monster, which had resulted in his becoming a captive in the pillar.

A variety of sports and games filled in the other hours. Both men and women took part in most of these. Some were as innocuous as activities like cards or table tennis, others were as strenuous as rugged sports like football or basketball, requiring great strength and endurance. There were contests with weapons in which only slaves took part, fighting to the death—sometimes both died. Stacey knew that the men selected were forced to participate under the threat of things worse than death, perhaps even prolonged torture. He could only watch in helpless and utter disgust as the degenerate, pleasure-mad life of Upper Olin reached a sickening crescendo.

Duels between Koryl's nobles otherwise filled in the program. Some of these duels featured—much to Stacey's surprise—participants that were women. These were frequently grim and bloody affairs, and the more grim and bloody, the greater was the delight of the spectators.

Once Stacey attended a ceremony of worship involving the Gorgon. This took place in a vast chamber on one of the floors of the palace just below the ice level, which had been fitted up as a temple. Lighted by only a few widely spaced atom torches, the chamber was filled with weird shadows. In one of the walls, covering a circular space roughly seven feet across, was something that—at first glance—looked like a window. But it was quite opaque, a pale blue in color, the surface shimmering and pulsing and covered with countless tiny pinpoints of light.

As he gazed at the phenomenon, Stacey had the strange but insistent impression that he was looking into a vast distance, world beyond world, to a point where the universe ended and others even more remote and mysterious began. Simultaneously he had a dizzy, confused feeling, as though he was plummeting through endless depths. It was only when he closed his eyes that this feeling left him. At that moment Stacey realized that he had not looked through a window, but through an opening that led into the unknown, an extra-dimensional realm from which the Gorgon had come. That was his first glimpse of the gateway...

BEFORE and immediately below the shimmering, pale blue circle in the wall was a waist-high block of carved marble, which was unmistakably an altar. Koryl took her place before this, arms raised high, voicing a quick chant. She wore an elaborate headdress from which fell long folds of a filmy, pale blue material, obviously a symbolic representation of the gateway. Beneath the semi-transparent draperies her perfectly curved and otherwise unadorned figure showed in misty silhouette.

Koryl's chant echoed through the chamber, rising to a climax. Watching, Stacey saw a shadow appear on the shimmering surface of the gateway. The shadow deepened, and then, slowly, as though emerging from some viscous substance, the Gorgon appeared. The monster floated entirely through the opening and hung poised over the altar.

Koryl's voice rose to a cry of triumph, then abruptly stilled. She turned, one hand raised in a signal.

Two men in ceremonial robes appeared, carrying between them the bound and writhing body of a young girl. Sobbing hysterically, the girl was placed upon the altar. She tried to roll off, but before she reached the edge, the Gorgon turned its flaming red eyes upon her, and she became utterly motionless.

The assemblage within the temple began straining forward eagerly, their faces lit with ghoulish anticipation. The reason became clear to Stacey a moment later. For as the Gorgon gazed down at its victim, it began to emit powerful waves of mental radiation—waves that told of a terrible hunger and a cruel gloating. The monster began to—*feed*—sucking the life essence from the body of the girl.

And as it fed, the waves of mental radiation grew even stronger, flooding into the minds of the worshipers. Stacey experienced a feeling of dark ecstasy, so intense that it was almost unbearable, momentarily sweeping all reason from his brain. Deep within him he was revolted and sickened, but somehow could not resist the vast pleasure and delight that poured into him like an electric current.

For long moments it went on, and then the waves diminished in force, leaving behind a deep sense of pleasure and wellbeing. The Gorgon was finished. It moved slowly, sated, and disappeared into the gateway.

Sanity returned to Stacey. He peered curiously at the body of the girl on the altar. Rage and pity filled him as he saw that it had become strangely shrunken, as though it had been drained, emptied. He knew the girl was dead.

THAT evening he paced the floor of his and Tobin's chamber angrily.

"What a rotten, perverted existence they lead here," he told Tobin. "I can't stand any more of this."

"There's not much we can do about it right now, boss."

"I'm telling you I'm at the end of my rope. If something doesn't happen soon, I'm going to wind up doing something rash—and most likely it'll be right in front of our she-devil friend, Koryl. That'll change her mind about me—fast."

Tobin shook his sandy head forebodingly. "I'd been hoping that Parn and Trek might trust us enough by now to help us. Who knows, they might even be able to show us a way out. But I haven't seen them around lately." Tobin shrugged his shoulders indifferently and smiled. "Maybe Koryl or Zarduc got suspicious and fed 'em to their Gorgon pal."

"We're finished if anything has happened to them," Stacey said grimly. "I've put off Koryl's advances long enough and I'm pretty certain she's running out of patience with my 'politeness.' I think she may be getting ready for some kind of a showdown. But whatever happens, I'm not going back to the pillars—and I intend on raising plenty of hell before I'm through."

Tobin started to speak, but at that moment a faint, grinding noise sent Stacey and him whirling around in surprise.

"What the hell was that?" Stacey wondered aloud.

They had been alone in the room, preparing for slumber. The unusual noise made them freeze momentarily. They stood, silently listening. Then a carved panel opened in a nearby wall.

Through the opening stepped Parn.

The youth gestured for silence. "Come with me," he said. "Hurry…Jendon is waiting you."

CHAPTER EIGHT

FOR a moment Stacey stood rooted, an incredulous surge of excitement and joy rushing through him. Then he moved forward and grasped Parn's shoulders.

"Jendon…he knows? You got through to him? Where is he?"

"Some distance from here. I told him about what you told me—about your wanting to help the Princess, and our people. He knows we're taking a big risk in trusting you." Parn looked Stacey up and down. "I'll kill you myself if you've lied to us."

"I haven't lied to you," Stacey replied with a straight face.

Tobin chimed in, "Rick here is about as straight and narrow as they come, pal."

"Then come with me—both of you. Jendon has everything in readiness. But you must hurry. We're in danger every second we remain here."

Nodding, Stacey turned swiftly to Tobin. "Come on, Phil. We've got to get our stuff together."

Short minutes later, Stacey and Tobin followed Parn through the opening. They were in a narrow, musty-smelling passageway between walls, Stacey saw in the light of the glow-tube Parn carried. The passageway led for a short distance before it turned abruptly to the left. The branching passageway now before them was longer. It terminated finally in a small, square room, where—in the floor—there was a circular shaft. An elevator platform hung within the shaft, and when Stacey and Tobin stood beside him on the platform, Parn sent it dropping smoothly downward.

Smooth rock walls flashed by at great speed. The descent seemed interminable. Then at last the platform slowed and finally stopped.

It was cold at this level. Parn was prepared for it, wearing a transparent covering.

"Do we have much further to go?" Stacey asked, the slightest hint of impatience in his voice.

Parn nodded as they walked along. "Jendon could not approach too close to the palace. There was too much danger of being discovered."

"How did you get word to him?"

"Through a messenger who operates in the hidden tunnels,

like these we're in now. I'm one of the agents of Mernos. I send needed information to Lower Olin. In short...I'm a spy."

Tobin smiled. "Good for you, kid."

"Who is Mernos?" Stacey asked.

"He's the Regent of Lower Olin, ruling in the place of Verla. A wise and kind man. But I had great difficulty in assuring him that you and your companion could be trusted. What won him over was the fact that you had already gained Verla's trust."

The trio advanced into a large underground room. Parn walked to the far wall. He pressed a concealed switch and a hidden panel slid open. They crossed a huge chamber that was dark and cold and unfurnished, their way lighted only by the dim beams of Parn's glow-tube. The route led through a series of corridors and then through a long tunnel under the ice. At last they came to a flight of steps that cut into the ice and led upward. Quite unexpectedly, Stacey and Tobin found themselves outside. A biting wind blew against their faces as they gazed back at the ornate tower of the palace, now a considerable distance away.

Stacey stiffened in dismay as he saw a bubble ship come soaring toward them several feet above the ice. He began reaching frantically to the pocket in which his automatic lay hidden.

"It's Jendon," Parn explained. "He's been waiting for us."

The bubble ship landed, brief introductions were exchanged, and the trio hastily crowded into it. Jendon proved to be a tall, white-haired older fellow, though vigorous in appearance. He greeted Stacey and Tobin warmly, then returned his attention to the controls. Under his manipulations, the bubble ship raced low over the ground until the towers of Olin began to fade into the distance. The pillars of the Gorgon soon appeared in the valley ahead. Jendon then turned the controls over to Parn.

"The task before us is to free Verla," he told Stacey. "And we must do this as quickly as possible, lest the Gorgon appear."

"But I thought you were working on something to overcome the Gorgon," Stacey said.

"Yeah," Tobin added. "This Gorgon's not exactly someone I'd like to get reacquainted with."

Stacey spoke again. "From what I understand of the situation, it isn't possible to rescue anyone from the pillars unless there's a way of preventing the Gorgon's interference."

JENDON smiled. "I have found that way, stranger. But since the creature cannot be killed by any means that we currently possess, there is the risk that it will summon help. Freeing Verla from the pillar may take more time than we'll have at our disposal."

Jendon turned to where a number of strange articles lay on the floor of the bubble ship. He picked up a device roughly two feet across that looked like a shield. The outer side was a smooth, bright metal, polished to a mirror-like surface. The inner side was concave and held in its center a box-like affair of metal, from which numerous wires radiated to a circular helix attached to the inner rim of the device.

"It's with this that I hope to keep the Gorgon from taking us captive," Jendon explained. "The idea for it came from ancient records describing an apparatus with which an ancestor of Princess Verla defeated the first Gorgon to appear in Olin."

Stacey examined the device curiously. "What will it do?"

"According to the ancient records, it will turn the Gorgon's own mental forces against her—like a mental mirror—reflecting them back at her and increasing their intensity in such a way that will make them unbearably painful. This is the only method at our disposal for coping with the Gorgon's terrible powers."

Stacey's thoughts revisited the classic Greek myth again. If a Gorgon had actually existed in ancient times, the Greeks had surely distorted the actual facts in numerous ways. Certainly men weren't turned to stone upon its gaze. However, the portion of the legend dealing with the mirror-surfaced shield used by Perseus to overcome the Gorgon seemed curiously close to the truth. Briefly it struck him how incredible it was that creatures and weapons of legend should come alive in the modern age. He shrugged these thoughts off, however, and returned to thinking of the harsh dangers that lay immediately before them. He leaned toward Jendon.

"Are you certain this device will work?"

The old scientist smiled faintly and shrugged. "That remains to be seen. I haven't had time to experiment with it extensively." He gave Stacey a reassuring glance. "I'm hopeful, though. I followed the ancient records carefully. If they are correct—and I believe they are—then the device should function as we hope."

"What about Verla? How do you intend to free her?"

"The method is simple. I shall first use a series of strong vibrations to dissolve the substance of the pillar, much as the Gorgon does herself. These vibrations are produced by an apparatus not unlike the weapons used in Olin. You've undoubtedly seen them."

Stacey nodded quickly. He had learned that the flare-muzzled pistols and rifles, so ever present in Upper Olin, operated by releasing vibrations that could stun—even kill.

Jendon went on, "Once the pillar has been dissolved, Verla may be released from her paralysis by removing the stinger from her body that was placed there by the Gorgon. The mere process of removing the stinger, however, will alert the Gorgon to what we're doing. This was the unfortunate experience of several rescue expeditions in the past. There is some sort of mental bond between the Gorgon and these tiny stingers that it places in the bodies of its victims. Perhaps it is this contact with the Gorgon's mind that keeps them in paralysis. It's a matter I don't fully understand, as yet."

Stacey nodded thoughtfully, recalling his telepathic communication with Verla. Evidently this had somehow been made possible by the presence of the stingers and their link with the enormous mental forces of the Gorgon.

HE SAW that the bubble ship was now moving among the pillars. The one that encased Verla should be at the other end of the valley, near the spot where he and Tobin had first landed in the plane. He pointed out directions to Parn. The youth nodded and accelerated the ship to a rapid pace.

When they reached the approximate location of Verla's pillar, Parn slowed the speed of the craft. The bubble ship settled slowly onto the icy floor of the valley. There was a crunching sound as it bit into the snow. Stacey helped Jendon gather up the equipment, then led the way as the foursome exited the ship.

"We must hurry," Jendon said. "Do you know exactly where Verla's pillar is?"

Stacey gestured. "Right in here, somewhere. It's on an ice dais. That should make it easy to find."

He led the way again, searching quickly. A few moments later he raised his arm and pointed.

"There it is."

Stacey took a step, then stiffened into shocked rigidity, a horrible dismay sweeping through his mind.

The dais was empty—Verla and the pillar were gone.

For a long moment Stacey stood motionless, sagging, mentally and physically numbed. From behind he heard Tobin's cry of surprise, followed a moment later by the startled voices of Jendon and Parn as they became aware of what was wrong.

A sudden, desperate thought of hope roused Stacey into motion again. Perhaps he was mistaken about the location. Verla's pillar might be on another ice dais not far away.

Frantically, hoping against hope, he began to search again.

"Where ya going, boss?" Tobin shouted through the cold.

"We've got to keep looking. This may not be the same dais."

Tobin and the others rejoined the search. But it was soon evident there was nothing to find. Stacey was forced at last to accept the chilling fact that Verla had vanished.

"Koryl's behind this—damn her," he muttered thickly. "She must have guessed. She must have realized my 'politeness' was because of my feelings for Verla."

"But how in the world would Koryl have even known you had feelings for her," Tobin asked. "You didn't tell her did you?"

"No...no I didn't. But think back, Phil. That day the Gorgon released us—she saw me staring into Verla's pillar. She sensed my attraction. She even asked if I found her attractive. Perhaps even the Gorgon told her."

"What do you intend to do now?" Jendon asked.

"I'm going back to Upper Olin," Stacey replied, a resolute look on his face. "I don't know how I'm going to do it, but somehow I'm going to force Koryl to tell me what she's done with Verla."

Jendon shook his white locks. "That wouldn't be wise, my friend. Koryl undoubtedly knows by now that you've escaped. And when she learns that your motive for doing so was to free Verla, she will become most angry—angry enough to have your head I'm afraid. Koryl is not the kind that would ever allow herself to be considered second to another woman, especially by a man to whom she has shown inter—"

Jendon broke off sharply as Parn grasped his shoulder and pointed.

"The Gorgon!" Parn cried. "The Gorgon comes!"

CHAPTER NINE

IN THE next instant Stacey saw the monster. It was soaring over the pillars in the distance, approaching in their direction with angry speed. He glanced quickly at the bubble ship. They had made a potentially fatal mistake in moving so far away from it.

"Stand behind me—" Jendon commanded sharply. "Place yourselves behind the shield. Hurry—it's our only hope!"

While Stacey and the others gathered in single file at his back, Jendon lifted the shield-like device defensively before him, touching a switch in the box that was fastened to the inner side. A faint radiance rose from the helix circling the rim.

Stacey fumbled for his automatic, a hard knot of tension within him. He didn't know if he would get a chance to use the weapon, but he intended to try. He knew everything depended on Jendon's device. Would it work? If it didn't, they would be helpless—completely at the Gorgon's mercy.

The creature was close now, descending toward them. Stacey could see the vengeful expression upon its repulsively alien yet somehow beautiful face. Whatever it had in mind could only be extremely unpleasant. He fought to steady his automatic, an unbearable tension gripping his gun hand.

Then the Gorgon became aware of Jendon's shield-like device.

It came to an abrupt stop, its slit-pupiled eyes narrowing speculatively. For what seemed a long time the monster considered the mirror-bright surface that was turned in its direction. Then, its lips curling in a soundless snarl of contempt and defiance, it began moving forward.

To Stacey it seemed the end was near. Within a short span of seconds he and the others would be in range of the monster's terrible mental forces.

Tobin gripped Stacey's arm. "You've been a real pal, boss."

"You, too, Phil."

The Gorgon was almost on top of them. And then, scant yards away, it stopped with a bewildering suddenness. It almost seemed to bounce backward—as though an invisible wall had shot up before the creature, barring its progress.

A startled expression replaced the contempt that had been on its appendage-covered face. The Gorgon seemed shocked by a sensation it had never experienced before in all of its wicked existence. And that sensation, it swiftly became obvious, was *pain*.

Jendon's device was apparently working.

Its face twisted in a grimace of agony, the Gorgon abruptly retreated. At a safe distance it considered the foursome again. Then, without warning, the Gorgon flashed into motion again, sweeping around in an arc, attempting to attack the group from the side where it would not be directly repelled by Jendon's device.

Despite his age, Jendon's reactions were still swift. As the Gorgon bolted to the side, he moved with remarkable swiftness, swinging the shield around and bringing it to bear on the creature's on-side rush. Once again the Gorgon jolted to a stop, its face twisted in agony.

PRESSING forward with the shield, Jendon now attacked. At his first movement the Gorgon jerked back convulsively, both rage and shock registered on its face. It had probably never been attacked before by any living creature. Jendon moved forward more swiftly, following up his advantage. Again the Gorgon retreated, reluctant, raging, but unable to withstand the torturous reflections of the shield. Finally it whirled and began racing back toward the towers of Olin.

Stacey gripped Jendon's shoulders in triumph. "Holy smoke—it worked!" he cried.

"Did you see that thing run?" Tobin shouted into his ear.

Parn collapsed into a sitting position on the icy surface, tears of relief gathering in his eyes.

"It worked," Stacey repeated. He started to laugh. "Looks like we won't have to worry about our Gorgon friend for awhile—"

Tobin was whooping and shouting as he did a victory dance in the snow.

Jendon smiled wearily, but quickly sobered. "The Gorgon retreats, but it goes to summon help. We can't remain here much longer—unless we wish to do battle with Zarduc and his warriors."

They hurried back to where they had left the bubble ship. Parn took over the controls once more, and within moments they were soaring toward the city. At Jendon's directions Parn maneuvered the vessel so as to approach Olin from one of its more isolated sides, this being a precaution against discovery by those inside the city.

Stacey was torn by conflicting impulses. Despite the victory over the Gorgon, the shock of Verla's loss was still keen. He had a wild urge to confront Koryl and demand to know what she had done with her. But at the same time he knew this would most likely prove to be suicidal. Reluctantly, he decided the wisest course would be to return with Jendon to Lower Olin, where a more effective plan could be devised for freeing Verla. He told Jendon of his decision, and the old scientist voiced instant approval.

"It is the best thing to do. You needn't fear that Koryl will harm Verla anytime soon. Having Verla in her possession gives Koryl a certain power over you—and us. And she relishes it."

Stacey nodded slowly. "That's what I'm afraid of."

They reached the outskirts of the city. Parn kept the ship moving low over the ground, taking advantage of the cover provided by the buildings intervening between them and the palace.

Watching the terraces of the distant structure, Stacey saw a number of bubble ships take off and begin speeding toward the valley. He glanced at Jendon, who had also observed the departure of the pursuing ships.

"We must hurry," the old man said. "They'll return and search the city immediately upon finding that we've left the valley."

Parn increased the speed of the ship until the ice-buried buildings flashed past in blurred succession. Jendon watched intently. Presently he touched Parn's shoulder and spoke a few words, pointing. Parn nodded and slowed the bubble ship's speed.

Stacey saw that they were in what appeared to be a completely abandoned section of the city. The tops of the buildings that protruded from the snow here were almost all in ruins. As he watched, the ship descended toward a gaping hole in the roof of one of the structures. Darkness swallowed them until Parn touched a switch that sent a wide beam of light sweeping ahead of the ship.

Through a series of vast, empty rooms the vessel floated, descending finally through a broad shaft. At the bottom was a long tunnel in the ice. Parn followed this for a time, turning at last into a number of others. Stacey was soon bewildered by the complexity of the network. He wondered how much longer the trip would continue. Then suddenly the bubble ship turned into a tunnel that was brilliantly lighted.

AT THE end of this lighted tunnel a number of men stood guard beside a mounted weapon that looked vaguely like an artillery piece. Jendon identified himself, and the ship was allowed to continue through.

Other lighted tunnels appeared, much larger in size and gradually giving way to a series of low caverns whose roofs were supported by immensely thick columns of ice. Stacey realized that they were in what was in effect an underground city. Here were the actual streets and lower portions of the buildings of Olin. Numerous people were about, and here and there a bubble ship moved among the columns.

Parn brought their own bubble ship to a stop before a great stone stairway that led up to a pair of huge metal doors, above which the roof of the cavern began.

Jendon turned to Stacey and Tobin. "This is the end of our journey for the present. The building before you is the headquarters of Mernos, who—as you perhaps know—is the Regent of Lower Olin, ruling in the place of Princess Verla. We will speak with him at once."

As they left the ship, a party of guards hurried toward them down the stairway, weapons held at the ready. Jendon again identified himself, and this time an escort was formed to accompany them into the building.

They were ushered into a large room, which was furnished with an effect of dignified luxury. Mernos was not present, but the captain of the guards left word that the Regent would be summoned immediately.

Stacey dropped onto a couch, closing his eyes with a sigh of weariness. His thoughts ran over the sequence of events of the past several days—the search for the missing flyers and the almost nightmarish sequence of events that had followed, culminating in his presence here. He wondered what the future held for him and he thought hopelessly of Verla.

The sound of people entering the room brought him erect. Striding forward was a tall, middle-aged man with grizzled hair and a care-worn, patrician face. The robe he wore and the decorations on it indicated that he was a person of stature— obviously Mernos himself. The Regent was smiling warmly. Behind him followed a slender, auburn-haired woman, her features pert and vivacious.

Jendon hastened to perform introductions. The newcomer was the Regent, Mernos, as Stacey had surmised. The woman proved to be his daughter, Loren. Stacey noticed that Tobin took an immediate interest in the woman, and despite her shyness, she seemed equally interested.

"Word of you and your companion has reached me," Mernos told Stacey. "I'm delighted to meet you and to know that you stand on our side of this struggle. Your aid will be greatly appreciated in what lies ahead for us. But there are immediate matters that appear incomplete. Where is Princess Verla? Did you succeed in freeing her?"

"I'm afraid not," Stacey replied. "When we reached the spot where she had been held, we found that the pillar containing her body had been taken—undoubtedly the handiwork of Koryl."

Mernos shook his grizzled head in quiet despair.

"The liberation of Princess Verla would have meant new hope for Lower Olin. The people have fallen into a state of depression in recent weeks. It's been spreading almost like a disease. If this overall feeling of despair continues to fester, I'm afraid our resistance, as a people, to Koryl and her minions will begin to crumble."

"The situation isn't entirely hopeless," Stacey returned. "Thanks to Jendon, you now have a means of defense against the Gorgon."

Stacey gave an account of their skirmish with the otherworldly monster. Mernos seemed most pleased.

"This is wonderful news," the Regent commented. "We've lived in fear of that creature for so many years. I never thought we'd have an effective means of combating it. We owe you much, Jendon."

Jendon gave a quick, polite bow of acknowledgement. "Thank you, your highness."

"I can't help thinking that this will give us a much better chance of rescuing your princess," Stacey added. "Stop and consider the situation, without the overwhelming mental powers of the Gorgon to stand behind her warriors, Koryl is now exposed to a direct attack by the people of Lower Olin." Stacey smiled. "Gives you something to think about, doesn't it?"

"You got that right, pal," Tobin added.

"There may be something in what they say, your highness," Jendon said thoughtfully. "The device would have to be heavily protected by our forces, but it's conceivable it could work for us in a combat situation. I might be able to increase its range so that the Gorgon could be kept at bay from a greater distance. That would allow us to more easily protect the device and at the same give our men more of a free range should they engage Koryl's warriors in direct combat."

"Can you make more of these devices?" the Regent asked eagerly.

"Oh...I'm sure I could," Jendon replied, "if you give me the time and equipment. The question is...do we *have* the time? Koryl will undoubtedly plan an attack soon—unless we can attack her first."

"An attack..." Mernos' eyes gleamed. "Can you imagine the expression on Koryl's face? We of Lower Olin have never even conceived that such a thing could ever be possible. The Gorgon's power was always the difference. It stacked the odds in Koryl's favor. But now...perhaps..." A look of determination came over the Regent's features. "Far too long have we run from the Gorgon and Koryl."

LATER that day Stacey, Tobin, Jendon, and the Regent

launched into a discussion of plans. They were joined by a number of other high-ranking officials of Lower Olin. Everything, the Regent pointed out, depended on Jendon's device. The entire success of any offensive against Koryl depended on equipping the attacking forces with as many of the shields as possible. Thus, the manufacture of the shields would be given the highest priority. All available materials and manpower were to be made available for the task.

"You'll be working against time," the Regent told Jendon, "but your earlier point is well taken." Mernos then spoke to the rest of the group. "We must all remember that Koryl will not be idle while we're preparing for this. We know she's in regular communication with the Gorgon, so it's safe to assume that she knows about Jendon's device and its dire effects. Her warriors may be preparing an offensive against us as we speak. We must do everything possible to strike against her before she can strike against us. The future of our people and the life of our princess hang in the balance."

Jendon nodded gravely. "I don't think the shields will prove too difficult to manufacture. We should be able to produce a good quantity of them within a short number of days."

"Do everything you can to speed up the process," Mernos said, gripping Jendon's arm in a physical expression of support.

"We'll certainly do our best, your highness."

"That's good," said Stacey. He turned to Mernos. "The next consideration is men and weapons. How many warriors are there in Lower Olin? What condition are they in and how well equipped are they?"

The Regent said heavily, "We do not have many warriors at this present time—certainly not as many as Zarduc has under his command in Upper Olin. There have been serious losses in past encounters with Zarduc and the Gorgon. But what we lack in numbers, I think we can make up for in other ways."

"How's that," asked Tobin.

"The remaining warriors of Lower Olin," Mernos went on to explain, "are the product of grim survival, the unfit having been weeded out in past battles. They compose a body of fighters who are, almost without exception, strong, quick, and shrewd. In addition, they've been in constant training for the day Koryl would make an all-out attempt to conquer Lower Olin.

"Sounds like the ancient Spartans," Stacey observed.

Mernos looked quizzically at Stacey. "Who were the ancient Spartans?"

"They were toughest bunch of brawlers the ancient world ever knew," Tobin interjected. "Sounds like your boys are up to the task, though."

"I believe they are," Mernos replied, a subdued gleam of confidence in his eyes. "Regarding equipment, our warriors possess a large number of ancient flying war machines. There have always been a greater number of these machines stockpiled in the lower levels of the city than in Koryl's districts. The military scholars of Lower Olin—scholar being synonymous with scientist—developed and manufactured these machines in the lower levels of the city. So this is one big advantage that we have—and our warriors have been carefully trained in their operation."

Stacey's eyes were glittering with excitement. As Mernos finished speaking, he rose and began to pace the floor.

"I don't want to sound over-optimistic," Stacey said, "but the situation sounds far better than I dared hope for. One thing that's really working against us, though, is that so many of the people here in Lower Olin are filled with thoughts of despair—especially when it comes to the whole aspect of the Gorgon. But now you have a viable defense against it. We'll be able to meet Koryl and Zarduc on nearly equal terms." Stacey whirled back to Mernos. "I have some advanced training in military tactics. I can probably help you plan your assault."

Mernos nodded toward Stacey. "We would be grateful for your aid."

"Your chieftains...I'd like to talk with them. And I'd like for you to supply me with maps of the city. We'll begin making plans for an attack against Koryl immediately."

The meeting continued far into the morning. When at last it broke up, details for an invasion of Upper Olin had been carefully worked out. To the chieftains was left the task of assigning units under their command to certain specific duties.

Only then did Stacey realize how tired he was. He readily accepted Mernos' suggestion that he turn in for a rest. He and Tobin were ushered to a guestroom, and within minutes of their arrival, Rick Stacey and Phil Tobin were sound asleep.

As soon as Stacey awoke, he went to see how Jendon was progressing on the manufacture of the shield-like weapons. A number of the devices were already under construction in the old scientist's laboratory. With no other matters that required immediate attention, Stacey and Tobin willingly offered their services.

Toward evening Stacey decided to pay Mernos a visit and learn how the other preparations were coming along. Tobin grasped eagerly at the opportunity to see Loren again. He had spoken of her almost continually since their meeting.

"Nice dame...huh, boss?"

"I wouldn't call her a 'dame' to her face, Phil," Stacey replied, smiling.

Mernos looked strangely distressed when Stacey and Tobin strode into his office. He looked up with grim eyes and said slowly, "We've received a message—and it concerns you, Rick. Word from Koryl was just brought to us by courier. Koryl demands that you return to Upper Olin at once—or Verla will be executed."

CHAPTER TEN

STACEY sighed. "I expected that. But I'd been hoping for a little more time. As it is—" He ran his hand through his already disheveled hair. "—we'll have to make serious changes in our plans. Without the time we need, an entirely new plan will have to be implemented if we want to save the Princess' life. I do have an idea, though." Stacey stopped for a moment, rubbing his chin thoughtfully.

"Our chieftains were most impressed with your initial plan of attack." Mernos broke in. "I don't think you'll have any trouble getting their approval for any changes you have."

"It'll be delicate, and there *is* a much higher risk of failure. But I don't think we have any other options at this point—if we want to save the Princess, that is." He straightened up purposefully. "I'd like to have another meeting with the chieftains, if possible—right away. I'll need to explain the new changes I have in mind. In the meantime, I'd like word sent to Parn that he needs to get ready to take me back to Upper Olin."

The emergency conference took place a short time later. Stacey detailed the change in plan made necessary by Koryl's ultimatum to Mernos and the chieftains.

"Put simply, Parn will help me gain entrance into the royal palace. It's my intention to confront Koryl—forcibly if necessary—and force her to reveal the whereabouts of Princess Verla."

"Are you mad?" one of the chieftains blurted out. "That's suicide." Several of the others seem to scoff at the idea.

"My dear Stacey," Mernos added, "while we admire your courage, such a plan would surely have a disastrous ending for you—and the Princess."

"Parn helped Tobin and me escape from Upper Olin because of his knowledge of a system of secret passageways within the Palace itself. I know for a fact that there is one such passageway that leads directly into one of Koryl's private chambers. I saw her enter through it myself just days ago."

"How did you come to be in one of her private chambers?" Mernos asked.

Stacey took a deep breath, a slight look of embarrassment on his face. "By royal command—and it was only with the greatest of efforts on my part that I was able to escape from her...charms. My 'politeness' no doubt agitated the High Priestess to a great degree. At any rate, I don't believe she knew I had seen her enter. The room is a private lounge off a hallway near her main living quarters."

"I know the room—and the passageway into it," said Parn. "It used to be a favorite meeting place for Koryl and Zarduc. As far as I know, the passageways are known only to a handful of people—the High Priestess and one or two others. I don't think even Zarduc knows of their existence. I discovered them quite by accident. I've explored them many times—usually late at night—and I know them well."

Stacey continued, "Once we reach the room we might have to improvise a bit. We may have to get rough with a guard or two. But they surely won't be expecting anything like this and we'll certainly have the element of surprise in our favor. With a little bit of luck we might be able to gain entrance into Koryl's living quarters. Once inside, Parn and I will force her to reveal the Princess' location." Stacey looked grimly at Mernos. "And I won't be afraid to get a bit rough if I have to."

"The High Priestess usually has two guards in the main corridor leading to her private living quarters," Parn added.

"Like I said," Stacey replied, "it may get a bit rough." He looked back at Mernos. "Once we find out were the Princess is being held, we'll try to find her and release her. Hopefully we'll be able to use the secret passageways again. We'll either have to subdue Koryl completely, or take her with us—at gunpoint if necessary." Stacey patted the pocket containing his automatic. "When we find the Princess, Parn will bring her back to Lower Olin through the passageways. I'll remain behind."

"For what purpose," Mernos asked.

"To try to find and destroy the gateway of the Gorgon. It's in a temple below the main levels of the palace. I was there once with Koryl. If I can find it, I'm sure I can wreck it— perhaps beyond repair. However, it's entirely possible that the Gorgon will be present, so I'll be needing one of Jendon's shielding devices. I'll have to carry it with me. From what I've learned, if I can close this gateway—with the Gorgon on this side—the creature will die."

The meeting went on for another hour. Plans were also laid

for the forces of Lower Olin, armed with as many shielding devices as possible, to enter the palace through the hidden passageways a short time after Stacey's and Parn's gaining entrance. They would capture and hold all-important positions, while reinforcements arrived by air with war machines to forestall any organized counter-attack by Zarduc and his warriors. The whole thing depended on close coordination and timing, and Stacey grimly emphasized this point to his listeners.

With the details of attack fully mapped out, Stacey and Parn were ready to leave. Tobin approached him, an earnest expression on his face.

"I'm coming with you, Rick."

Stacey smiled and put his arm around Tobin's shoulder, leaning in close to him. "Not this time, pal."

"But, boss—"

"You're the best co-pilot anybody ever had, Phil, but Parn's going to be sitting next to me on this one. Besides, this is really a two-man job. You come in with the others." Stacey winked at him. "You'll probably end up rescuing me from our Gorgon pal."

Tobin reluctantly gave in. With hurried farewells, Stacey started away. Parn was waiting for him. Pausing only long enough to take along one of Jendon's shield devices, Stacey and Parn climbed into a bubble ship and set out for Upper Olin.

Reaching the surface, Parn guided the ship slowly and carefully toward the palace, moving only a few feet above the ice. Behind the bulk of a partly ruined tower, he finally set the craft down carefully in the snow. Then he led the way outside, stepping swiftly toward a large slab of marble that lay against a jumble of masonry at the tower's side. He lifted the slab aside, and steps leading down into the ice tunnel appeared.

Stacey and Parn moved quickly and confidently now, retracing the route to the interior of the palace that they had traveled the previous evening. Parn knew of no secret paths leading to Koryl's private living quarters—these, if they had existed, would have been discovered in his earlier treks through the passageways.

As they walked through the cold tunnel, Stacey thought of a new twist for their plans.

"You say there are only two guards stationed near Koryl's living chambers?" Stacey asked Parn.

"I've never seen more than two at one time," he answered.

"If we can somehow lure them into to the private lounge, we might be able to overwhelm them and take their uniforms. That would certainly make it easier to gain direct entrance into Koryl's chambers."

"It might work. Perhaps I could bait them."

"Perhaps."

THE opening of a panel brought them at last to the unoccupied private lounge on the floor of the palace where Koryl was located. Stacey was surprised at how easily things had gone so far. Parn went to the door in the room, opened it, and peered cautiously into the hall. He turned back to Stacey, nodding.

"I can see the guards. They're stationed right in front of Koryl's door." He took a deep breath, cold sweat beading up on his forehead. "Get ready, Rick. I'm going to lure them in here after me. They don't take too kindly to slaves wondering freely about the palace. Once they're inside I can help, but it's going to be mostly up to you."

Stacey gripped the other's arm briefly. "Bring on your guards. You can depend on me."

Parn slipped out into the hall, and Stacey took up a position to one side of the door, gripping his automatic by the barrel. He waited as long seconds dragged past, his blood pumped heavily in his veins.

He stiffened tensely as quick footsteps sounded in the hall. Parn darted into the room, taking up his position at the side of the door opposite Stacey. Moments later two uniformed figures burst into the room, swords gripped in their hands. The guards were looking around quizzically as Stacey and Parn leaped at their backside.

It was over in a few seconds. Stacey hammered the back of one of the guard's heads with the butt of his automatic. The man collapsed to the floor in a heap. Blood dribbled from behind his ear. Parn pulled the other to the floor. He and Stacey pounded hard blows into his face. Stacey then pulled the guard's head up and smashed it into the hard surface of the floor. His struggles ceased immediately. It was over. Neither guard had even had the chance to cry out. Stacey and Parn then stripped their unconscious foes of their uniforms and bound them securely with braided ropes that formed part of the window hangings in the room. They stuffed part of their own discarded garments thickly into the guards' mouths, then drug them into a nearby closet.

Donning the uniforms that they had stripped from their victims, Stacey and Parn strode out into the hall.

Stacey held the shield behind him under his cloak. It was a bit awkward, but it didn't appear too obvious. He and Parn walked briskly, giving the appearance of men on an important duty. Fortunately, they didn't encounter any other persons in the corridor. It had all seemed so easy. Stacey and his companion reached the door leading into Koryl's quarters moments later. The hearts of both men were pounding rapidly.

"Will there be anyone else in there with her—perhaps more guards?" Stacey whispered to Parn.

"I think it will be unlikely," he whispered back. "Perhaps a servant girl or two. There are many rooms beyond this door, but her private bedroom is at the end of an inner hallway."

"We'll deal with the servant girls if we have to."

Parn opened the door and they entered—they were inside Koryl's living quarters! He led Stacey down the hallway toward Koryl's sleeping chamber, skirting quickly past the outer rooms where servant girls might be present. The hallway turned and narrowed. They abruptly faced a beautiful, ornate door. Parn grasped the handle, listened a moment, then hurled the door open.

Koryl was pacing the floor of a barbaric, yet luxurious bedroom. At their entrance she whirled furiously.

"What is the meaning of this? Why—" Recognizing Stacey and Parn, she broke off, drawing a quick breath in preparation for a scream.

Stacey reached her in a bound, one arm circling her waist, a hand fastening about her throat. He said with deadly softness, "Quiet, Koryl. Shouting an alarm will mean your death."

She looked into his grim face and relaxed slowly, biting her lip. "Again you have made a fool of me, Rick Stacey. I had never thought it possible of a man. How did you get here…dressed in these uniforms?"

"Never mind, Koryl. The only thing we're going to talk about is Verla. Where are you keeping the Princess?"

"Rick—look at me," she said quietly, her expression becoming soft. Do you not find me beautiful?"

"I do."

"Then why is it that you prefer a mere child like Verla to a woman like me?"

Stacey nodded gravely. "You *are* beautiful, Koryl. You're perhaps the most beautiful woman I've ever seen—but you're evil, too—remarkably evil. And you wield your beauty like a whip. I never imagined anything so beautiful could be so completely vile. The Princess, though, the Princess is sweet and good. She's got real blood in her veins. I'm afraid all you've got is ice."

"Look at me, Rick." Koryl stared hard into Stacey's eyes. It was an almost hypnotic stare. "You know that Verla can't offer you what I can give."

"You're only saying this to save your neck."

"Rick, we must hurry," Parn jumped in.

Koryl continued. "I offer you power and a life of wealth and luxury. And I offer you a love that few men could ever know. You have not yet known my arms. Nor is it too late. You'll have my heart—and my body. For a man such as you I'm willing to forgive anything."

"It's no good, Koryl," Stacey returned doggedly. "All I'm interested in is the location of the Princess." Stacey's grip tightened around her, his eyes hardened, and he spoke with a steel-toned voice. "Now where is she?"

In Stacey's grasp Koryl's magnificent body suddenly grew taut with rage. "You refuse me? You refuse Koryl...the High Priestess of Olin? So be it."

Koryl then spat in Stacey's face.

"You devil, you," he whispered harshly into her ear.

"As for Verla—your beautiful, virginal princess—you will *never* know where her 'highness' is hidden. She'll be dust before you find her. Kill me if you wish—but I will not reveal her location."

STACEY'S face was pinched and cold. He thought of closing his hands on her throat and choking the life out of her. Then he shook his head slowly. "No...I won't kill you, Koryl. That would be the easy way out for you, wouldn't it? What I will do is leave you a calling card from the people of Lower Olin—and you'll carry it with you the rest of your life." He gave a slight smirk. "Ever heard of plastic surgery?"

A blank expression of ignorance came over Koryl's face.

"Perhaps your advances in the field of medicine aren't that far along yet." Stacey gazed down at Parn's knife, hanging in its sheath on the side of his belt. "I'm going to perform it on you—my dear High Priestess—right now. Your face is so incredibly beautiful, almost god-like. Men have marveled at it all of your life. But after I've performed my 'surgery,' no man will ever look at you the same way again."

Stacey's fingers tightened on Koryl's throat, shutting off her breath. He whirled to Parn.

"Your knife...give it to me!"

In another swift motion, Stacey had Koryl pressed helplessly to the floor. Parn's dagger point against the soft whiteness of her cheek. He spoke in a low, oddly remote voice.

"We'll take that lovely hair of yours first, Koryl. Then your face. The scars will be deep—most noticeable I'm afraid. You'll find it rather unpleasant looking at them. And certainly no man will ever *want* to look at them."

She spoke with an effort, her watery eyes suddenly wide with an emotional appeal. "You…you wouldn't allow such a horrible thing to happen, Rick. You may hate me, but it isn't in you to be so merciless…"

"Wanna bet?"

With his forearm pressing against her throat, he caught a handful of her golden hair, slipped the edge of the dagger under it, and drew the blade back sharply. The locks of hair came free in his hand.

Koryl gasped.

"Your hair first, Koryl. Like this." He held the strands up for her to see. "Little by little, until it's all gone. Then…your face." Stacey's face quivered and grew red with intensity. Even Parn looked taken aback.

"Stop!" Koryl whispered loudly. She closed her eyes as an expression of submission came over her face. "I'll…I'll tell you what you want to know." She hesitated for a moment, looking at Stacey with both anger and fear in her eyes. Finally she spoke, "Verla's being kept prisoner in a room not far from here. I will…lead you to her."

Stacey made no move. He studied Koryl a moment, then smiled a slow, thin smile. He seized another handful of hair—and again the dagger flashed.

He laid the second locks of hair gently beside the first.

A shudder swept Koryl. Something in her face seemed to shatter like fragile glass. She closed her eyes again.

"The temple…Verla's in the temple."

Stacey rose from the floor, pulling up the High Priestess along with him.

Then he threw an uppercut into her jaw.

Koryl collapsed onto the floor again—completely unconscious.

"Hurry," he commanded Parn, "while she's still out." Like

the guards before her, Stacey and Parn used makeshift bonds to bound and gag Koryl. She lay motionless on the floor, her eyes still closed.

Snatching up his shield and cloak, Stacey started from the room. "The temple, Parn. Hurry!"

Another brisk walk through the halls, another pretense of important duty. An elevator platform took them down to the lower floor of the building where the temple was situated. There appeared to be no guards on duty.

Flush with impatience, Stacey ran through the dim, silent halls until the great metal door of the temple appeared. Only then did caution come into his mind. Stealthily now he and Parn moved forward. Stacey slowly swung the door inward.

The shadow-filled expanse of the temple chamber yawned before him, vast, pervaded by a deep and menacing quiet. In the far wall behind the altar, the inter-dimensional gateway shimmered, bathing the altar below it in waves of pale radiance that was not quite natural light. At the foot of the altar was the slender, wraith-like form of Verla. And in the shadows to one side something lurked…

From those shadows the Gorgon rushed.

A terrible surge of fear rushed through Stacey. He swung up the shield, feeling frantically for the activating switch.

"Parn! Get behind me!"

The Gorgon's chill, paralyzing thoughts almost took grasp of his mind. But in the next instant the faint radiance leaped out from the helix in the rim of the shield, and the Gorgon recoiled as though it had been touched by fire.

The monster then exploded into furious action. Leaping, darting, whirling, it sought with enormous energy and determination to find a weak point in the invisible barrier of the shield. Again and again it flinched back from the torturing emanations, but some bleak and desperate will to survive drove it repeatedly to the attack.

STACEY never knew where he summoned the superhuman

strength and agility necessary to keep the monster at bay. Parn—still behind him—bounced along with his every move. At one point the young man literally screamed in terror. But Stacey matched the Gorgon's every turn and leap, slowly yet inexorably driving it back—further and further.

Thoughts flashed through Stacey's mind. Why had the Gorgon chosen to remain in the temple? Was it to keep guard over Verla? Or was it there to protect the gateway and the mysterious machinery that controlled it? The Gorgon could not operate the machinery itself—this much Stacey knew. He also knew that if the gateway closed it would sever the precious psychic link between the head and its other components that lurked in waiting on the other side. The gateway was partially open, but only the head of the Gorgon could traverse through it. And Koryl was the only one who knew the secret of operating the machinery to its fullest capacity. Thus, the Gorgon remained in her power.

"Stay behind me, Parn," Stacey shouted at one point. He feared the young man was near exhaustion.

The Gorgon continued its onslaught. Evidently it had known somehow—perhaps through its extraordinary mental powers—that Stacey and Parn would appear.

Renewed strength flowed through Stacey's frame. He fought grimly, with a quiet and relentless savagery. He didn't know how much time passed. It might have been minutes, it might have been hours.

Slowly, slowly, the Gorgon began to weaken from its relentless contact with the agonizing radiations of the shield. The hysterical fury and determination began to fade from its alien face. Weariness came, then despair, and finally...defeat. With a final leap that must have drained the monster's final dregs of strength, it hurled itself backward and up, vanishing through the gateway with a burst of light.

"Parn!" Stacey cried urgently. "The shield. Hold it here in front of the gateway—like this. Keep watch for your very life."

While the other stood guard with the shield, Stacey hurried

toward the altar, pausing only long enough to touch Verla's hair briefly. She was securely tied with smooth, gleaming strands of some material that was evidently produced by the Gorgon. She was awake and smiling tearfully, though she seemed too weak to utter a sound.

Stacey fell to examining the altar, a great sense of urgency within him. The front of the marble block showed nothing to indicate what he sought, nor the sides. But at the rear he found worn places along a joint in one of the stones. He inserted the tips of his fingers, pulled, and the slab came free in his grasp.

Contained in a cavity within the altar was a mass of tubes and intricate wire coils, moving, twinkling, humming with a faintly sweet melody. Lips curled in a wolfish grin, Stacey thrust a leg into the cavity.

And kicked as hard as he could.

The twinkling died in a bright flash. Stacey kept kicking at the delicate core of the inner machinery. The humming rose to a painful crescendo—then faded. Stacey looked up.

The gateway was gone.

Only then did he return to Verla, cutting loose her bonds. Slowly and gently he gathered her into his arms. It was the first time he had touched her in a physical sense. Time, for a few moments, ceased to have any meaning. Parn and the temple seemed to disappear around him. There was only Verla and the beating of his heart in a vast stillness.

There was all of that—and then there was Parn's shout of alarm. With the sensation of being rudely wakened from a dream, Stacey turned. He saw a woman come bursting into the chamber, hair fluttering behind her in a golden cloud.

Koryl!

And from the doorway at her rear boiled a troop of warriors, swords and vibration pistols glinting in their hands.

"Take them alive!" she screamed.

For a moment Stacey went numb with surprise. He watched as Koryl's men rushed toward them. Then he reached for his automatic. However, he had barely pulled the gun free when the wave of warriors slammed into him, hurling him back and downward. Fists beat at him. Hands groped and clutched. Repeated surges of pain flashed through him as blows were struck. His consciousness clouded for a few moments. He was eventually hauled to his feet, a helpless captive.

He was fully aware of the all-embracing extent of the catastrophe.

CHAPTER ELEVEN

ONE FACE in particular took shape out of the turbulent ring of faces that surrounded him. Koryl's face. She was smiling with a certain sadistic eagerness.

"So, my friend from the outside world. Now it will be your turn to experience…what did you call it…plastic surgery? But this will only be a small, small portion of what is yet to come. You shall come to know every possible degree of torment before I'm finally done with you."

She laughed, the rich contralto tones reverberating off the walls of the darkened chamber. "But before I start with you, I'll give my attention to the lovely Verla." She gestured at the weakened figure of the Princess, then looked back to Stacey. "Look at her—so exquisite, yet so helpless. Where are your heroics now?" She stepped up, face to face with Stacey. "You would have scarred my face for life—disfigured me horribly. How will you feel when your dear princess has the face of a troll?" She flashed a slight but wicked smile. "This revenge…will be *sweet*. Your beloved will suffer in kind."

"Wait…" Stacey gasped in desperation. "Wait, Koryl. Do anything you want with me—anything at all. But I beg you to leave the Princess out of this."

"Ah…so the torment begins." She laughed softly again. "Save your breath. You'll be needing it soon."

"Koryl…" Stacey said, a surprisingly relaxed look coming over his face. "Don't you realize what's happened down here?" He shook his head in a scolding manner, like a mother who's about to admonish an ill-behaved child. "You're not being very observant. Look about you, Koryl…look over at the temple wall." Stacey's eyes glanced to the solid wall where the inter-dimensional door had once been. "The gateway, Koryl. The gateway is gone—and so is the Gorgon."

The High Priestess gasped. "Gone?"

She whirled about and stared at the wall above the altar. Incredulous, she then ran to the altar itself, bending over to peer into the rear cavity. Another gasp came from her lips. Very slowly she straightened up, a grim look on her face.

There were sudden murmurs among the warriors. Stacey and Parn heard one of them mutter…

"The power of the High Priestess is broken."

Koryl's eyes darted across the faces of her men, some looked around at each other, others appeared deep in contemplation. An intangible something formed within the room, a distinct change of attitude…a distinct feeling of *differentness.*

Koryl, sensing this, said abruptly, "To the loyal men who remain with me, I promise power and glory. And to those who serve me most faithfully…my love."

Stacey realized that the situation at hand might spell an abrupt end for Koryl's power. The chamber was suddenly filled with taut nerves. The High Priestess had long dominated these warriors, as she had dominated everyone else within her kingdom—and there was great resentment because of it. Up until this moment, she had been able to keep Upper Olin under her full control because of the power provided by her unholy partnership with the Gorgon. But now the Gorgon was gone—vanished permanently into the nether world from whence it came. Koryl now looked at the warriors with a mounting sense of trepidation.

The warriors continued to glance at one another, as though trying to discern from each other's expressions exactly what the other was thinking.

Who would be loyal to whom?

Some of them began to form into small groups, continuing

to mutter amongst themselves. Koryl tried to assemble them in front of her again, but she was largely ignored. Stacey and Parn saw hands begin tightening about sword hilts and pistol butts. Anxiety was building up quickly. The overall tension was suddenly broken when another group of warriors suddenly burst into the chamber.

In the lead was Zarduc.

"What goes on here?" he demanded. His pale blue eyes glanced quickly from Stacey to Koryl. Then he looked above and behind Koryl, at the wall where the gateway had once been. One of his men nudged him from behind.

"The gateway, my lord!"

"By heavens!" Zarduc exclaimed. He looked about the temple, feverishly searching for the monstrous form of the Gorgon.

It was not to be seen.

His gaze then narrowed to the High Priestess. Slowly he began to smile.

"The Gorgon has departed from our world, Koryl?"

"Yes," she said. "Gone." Her voice was flat.

"I see," Zarduc replied. "Well…it appears you have lost a most important ally." Zarduc raised his eyebrows to the High Priestess as though inviting a response.

"It makes no difference," she shot back matter-of-factly. "Why should it? I am the High Priestess of Upper Olin and you are my loyal chief of warriors."

"Most interesting," Zarduc responded, largely ignoring Koryl's comments. His smile broadened as he paced back and forth in front of her. "Is it possible for the door to be reopened?"

Koryl looked to the floor. She knew it was pointless to lie.

"No," she responded quietly, almost in a whisper. "The door cannot be reopened."

Zarduc sauntered in elaborate fashion toward Koryl and stopped directly before her. He gave her a quick, sarcastic bow. Then he stood spread-legged before her, his thumbs actually hooked in his belt.

"So it all comes to this...my beautiful one. Your biggest power piece, the Gorgon, is gone—gone forever with no chance of return." He moved up to within an inch or two of Koryl's face. "I think you know what the ramifications of all this will mean."

"It means nothing, Zarduc..."

THE chieftain shook his red mane gravely. "It means your tyranny and highhandedness has come to and end, for me, the warriors of Olin, and a great many others." A painful expression came over his face. "I was loyal, Koryl—and I gave you my heart. I gave you my *heart.*" Zarduc turned and walked back a few steps. "I could have tolerated your cruelty and even your over-indulging life-style—I even participated in it...willingly." He shook his head in a resigned manner. "But you used my affections to make me a fool...and a disgrace. You taught me many things, Koryl, and now I know there is more to a woman than a seductive face and a beautiful body. These things you still have—but they are no longer of any meaning to me."

"You're wrong, Zarduc." Koryl said softly. "They can still mean everything to you. Don't think that it's too late." She swayed forward entreatingly, a disarming picture of repentant loveliness. "I, too, have learned a lesson, Zarduc. But you must allow me to prove it to you. Even a High Priestess can make errors in judgement."

"No," Zarduc said flatly.

Koryl was close to him now. "Come to me my darling." In a blurred flash of motion, she struck. The small dagger leaped from the girdle at her waist—and buried itself into Zarduc's broad chest.

"To me!" she cried, stepping back lithely. "To me! Power and glory to my defenders."

The sides were formed now. Swords flashed, pistol barrels glinted.

The temple exploded into pandemonium.

Shouting amid the clash of arms, warrior threw himself against warrior in a wild battle for supremacy. Grotesque shadows gyrated and flickered on the walls of the temple as the chamber exploded into an orgy of blood. Many warriors fell— fatally wounded by their own comrades.

Zarduc had not fallen, though. He stood rigidly for several moments, staring in disbelief at the knife lodged into his chest. With grim, terrible effort he withdrew the weapon and dropped it to the floor. Blood literally spewed from the opening in his chest. He then drew the vibration pistol from his belt. Koryl's eyes widened in terror as the weapon raised in her direction. Madly she tried to flee.

Deliberately, almost casually, Zarduc fired.

The invisible beam caught Koryl full in the back. She stopped abruptly, stiffening into a statuesque pose of horror and fright. Her beautiful body then collapsed to the floor. The furiously weaving legs of fighting warriors soon hid her quivering body from view.

Zarduc stood erect for a few moments longer. Then, as two wrestling figures crashed into him, he finally dropped, his blood draining onto the temple floor.

An arm about Verla, Stacey watched the wave of battle reach its peak and begin to subside. Many of the warriors lay dead or wounded. Some had fled. Only a few struggled on, and their weariness was clearly evident. Stacey then gestured to Parn, gathered up Verla in his arms, and moved toward the entrance of the temple. One warrior tried wearily to stop them. Stacey simply raised a foot and kicked the man to the floor. The remaining warriors paid no attention to them.

With Verla held close against him, Stacey hurried around the sides of the chamber, moving toward the door. He stopped abruptly in despair, though, as another group of men suddenly appeared.

"Rick!" Tobin exclaimed.

Stacey then recognized Tobin and the chieftains of Lower

Olin. His body sagged in relief. He kissed the Princess on the forehead.

It was over.

* * *

VERLA put down her goblet and glanced across the table at Stacey. "I had been hoping that you'd be able to remain here with us in Olin, Rick. But from what you've told me, it seems I have no chance of persuading you to stay."

"I'm sorry, your highness."

A certain sadness crept into Verla's eyes. "You're an honorable man, Rick Stacey."

He nodded gratefully, and for a moment the banquet hall faded about him. It had been a glorious feast, yet vastly more restrained than those that had taken place under the rule of Koryl. He thought of the several idyllic days that had passed since the liberation of the city, and pain came with the realization that those days were coming to an end. With Koryl and Zarduc both dead and the Gorgon's menace removed forever, the warriors of Lower Olin had quickly triumphed. The city was united once more, and Verla reigned in the upper half as her ancestors once had.

"Phil Tobin and I are still in the service of our own country," Stacey said. "And although our duty makes it necessary for us to return to the outside world, I'm sure that same duty will someday bring us back to you." He glanced at Tobin. "Wouldn't you agree, Phil?"

Tobin, who was unashamedly holding hands with Loren, nodded slowly. "I suppose you're right, boss. And I'm also betting we'll be back sooner than you think. I can't imagine it any other way. They'll send us out with an expedition as soon as we make our report. After all..." He raised his glass. "...who better to lead an expedition back to Olin that the boys who discovered it."

"Here, here!" cried Verla.

"That brings up a serious question, though" Stacey said contemplatively. "I'm not certain that Verla and her people would care to have the outer world know about the existence of Olin."

"But why not?" Verla asked. "We have nothing to hide from the outside world."

"That's partly the trouble," Stacey answered. "The people of the outer world are not all filled with sweetness. There are some who are very much like Koryl and Zarduc."

Verla shrugged her gleaming shoulders. "If allowing such types into Olin brings you back any faster, Rick, I shall bear with them. But you must tell them for me that they will have to be on their best behavior."

Stacey nodded politely at this.

The Princess smiled then said coyly, "I shall make it clearly understood that *I* rule in Olin."

Mernos and Jendon grinned at this.

Mernos said, "There is much you have learn about Verla, Rick. Lesson number one is that she has a very definite will of her own."

Both Rick and the Princess laughed at this.

"Contact with the outer world would be profitable in many ways," Jendon put in. "It would do much to help complete Olin's rebirth. And I am curious about outer world science. There must be many fascinating and useful things to learn." His eyes glittered.

"So be it," Stacey proclaimed. "The world shall know of Olin. And...*your highness*...I promise you my friend Phil and I will be back again someday...someday soon."

"I'll be waiting," Verla said. "For you, Rick, there will always be a place in Olin—beside my throne."

THE END

THE BATTLE OF THE GODS...

Welcome to Asgard, the land of the ancient gods: Odin, Thor, Loki, and all the other immortals. However, If the fates were correct, a terrible disaster would soon befall Odin and his mighty sons. Then there was a visitor from the outside world—a mortal man from the 20th Century. His name was Leif Svensen and in his hands appeared to rest the future of Asgard. Could it possibly be that a mere mortal could change the destiny of the gods?

Here is a wild tale of fantasy and adventure, spun by one of the best known authors of the golden age of science fantasy…Lester Del Rey.

CAST OF CHARACTERS

LEIF SVENSEN
Just an average guy who never thought of himself as the "hero" type—until he found himself in the mythical kingdom of Asgard!

FULLA
As a goddess in Asgard she lived the life of an immortal, but her heart belonged to a mortal man of Earth.

LEE SVENSEN
He spent most of his life laughing at danger—and it got him a one-way ticket to Asgard and an audience with the gods.

LOKI
The sly god that not even Odin could trust, yet his shrewdness might help save Asgard from defeat.

THOR
Put a hammer in his hand and stand back! This mighty Norse god could fend off dozens of invading giants.

ODIN
The King of the gods. His mythical kingdom faced an impending doom that only a mortal from Earth had a chance of stopping.

WHEN THE WORLD TOTTERED

By
LESTER DEL REY

ARMCHAIR FICTION
PO Box 4369, Medford, Oregon   97501-0168

*For more information about Armchair Books and products, visit our
website at…*

www.armchairfiction.com

Or email us at…

armchairfiction@yahoo.com

CHAPTER ONE

LEIF SVENSEN threw the last split log against the saw, feeding it automatically by the whine of the blade. Then he straightened his lean body, knocked the blond hair back from his eyes, and kicked off the motor. The mechanical growl faded down to nothing, letting the drone of the wind and the pinging of icy crystals on the metal roof come through. He scowled at it and began beating his hands together to warm them.

"Fine way to end September," he said, but there was no surprise in his voice. It was a purely routine remark, and his visitor took it as such, though his own scowl deepened.

"Yeah. Radio says there's a blizzard running from Dakota clear down to Kentucky. Guess we're just getting the edge. Helluva year—no summer, killing frost in early August, now this. I hear some people claim it's the end of the world."

He lifted inquiring eyes that mirrored doubt and reluctance to express his own ideas without encouragement, waiting for Leif's response. Then he shrugged. "Made up your mind about your dog?"

"It's still made up, if that's what you mean," Leif answered flatly. "He's been chained the last two weeks. And I'm not going to kill him because of a bunch of lies. Is that what you came about, Summers?"

Summers hesitated, trying to play safe and straddle the fence, as usual. "Just figured I'd better warn you they're holding a meeting on it. Al Storm had two pigs killed last night, big tracks around like a wolf—or your dog. Storm's mighty put out—figures the dog's gotta go, and seems to want to take you with him. With food getting scarce and all... Well, I just thought I'd tell you. Maybe you better attend the meeting."

Leif nodded. Summers was right, at that. With the loss of crops and the crisis in food over the whole world, there had already been lynchings in some places for less than the loss of a pig. He scratched his nose thoughtfully, and Summers relaxed, biting off a fresh chew of tobacco.

"Seen an angel last night," he announced importantly, to change the subject. "Big blonde woman on a white horse, singing loud enough to raise the dead, about a hundred feet up in the air, going hell-bent east. Four of us out hunting all seen her—just like the ones all the soldiers been reporting over there. Long about sundown, if there'd been a sun... Of course, we heard about the one in Twin Forks, but..."

Leif let him ramble on, not surprised by it, but trying to pretend interest. Every war has its mass hallucinations, and the stalemate that had begun in Europe was loaded with the hysteria of the weather and the fear of famine to come, as well as tension over the atomic bombs that had somehow not yet been used. It was small wonder that reports kept trickling back of angels riding the sky on horseback. And, like the flying saucers of a few years before, it had spread until everyone was beginning to see them. It had probably been only a trick cloud, catching a stray ray of sunshine, but there was no use in robbing Summers of his importance by suggesting that.

HE WELCOMED the sound of the phone from the house when his ears caught it during a lull in the wind. He started out at a run, throwing words over his shoulder at Summers. No knowing how long it had been ringing.

It was still ringing as he grabbed it up, though, and the voice of his twin brother came from the receiver. "About time, Leif. How soon can you pick me up?"

"What happened?"

"Skidded into a telephone pole. Not much left of the machine, but I jumped in time. Few scrapes and bruises. You should see the nurse I've got bandaging them. Mm-mm…" The phone carried only his chuckle as he said something away from it.

"I told you not to take that damned motorcycle out on these roads…" Leif began, but Lee cut him off, still chuckling.

"So you did, son, so you did. Look, I'm at the Faulkner place—know where it is? Good. Then come and collect your erring brother."

The phone went dead, and Leif grinned wryly, with a mental picture of how the bandaging would be done. Lee was like that. The crazy fool had managed to get into the Second War at fifteen, and had followed that by a trick in China, down into some South American fracas, and over half the unknown world; his letters had come back now and then, filled with exploits, casual heroism, new citations, girls, and money that Leif had used to develop their farm.

Now he was back to recover from a chest wound he'd picked up as a mercenary in the new French Interior Legion, and already bored with the farm and quiet. It was like him to go careening off on his motorcycle before his chest was half healed, and to consider the almost certain accident only a joke and a chance for another conquest.

Summers was gone when Leif came out. He glanced at the shed, saw that Lobo was still chained securely, and headed for the garage. It took time to put on skid-chains and check the car against any trouble from the roads. Lee wouldn't have bothered, Leif realized as he started the motor. But the habits of caution were ingrained. He'd stayed on to run the farm and build up the orchard, to plan and go slowly. Maybe the full cellars and the bank account justified it. But there were times when the letters from Lee came, or on the rare visits, when he wondered. The most excitement he'd known was from vicarious adventure on the television or in books. And as for romance…

Then his thoughts veered back to normal. Now he wouldn't be able to attend the meeting and beat sense into the heads of the would-be-vigilantes who were set to kill Lobo. Lee *would* pick a time like this!

The wind was increasing in strength, and the dull gray sky was hidden by heavier snow. It was still crystalline and sharp, though, bouncing on the frozen mud of the road and whipping against the windshield. Leif hunched over the wheel, staring ahead. He put the heater up to maximum, but the wind whipped out the warmth before he could feel it. Driving back would be rugged.

To make it worse, there were still quite a few cars on the road—probably city people out trying to buy food in the country, and now scared back by the storm. He came to a rough stretch of road, barely wide enough for one-lane traffic, and pulled off at the side, skidding as he slowed to a stop. He waited impatiently as a Cadillac crept by.

THEN HIS foot reached for the gas, just as a rap sounded from the right front window. Leif swung about sharply. There had been no one near, he was sure. But now he stared into a red-bearded face and a pair of dark eyes, set too narrow and too deep. It was a handsome face, from what the heavy beard revealed, but something in it jerked Leif back, before he caught himself and opened the door.

"They call me Laufeyson," the stranger announced coolly, but there was a hint of a chuckle in his voice, and his lips parted in a fleeting smile that held a queerly sardonic twist. "I'll ride with you, Leif Svensen, since you're going my way. I'm happier not to walk, with the Fimbulwinter already upon us."

The word struck a familiar chord, and Leif groped for it, forgetting to puzzle over Laufeyson's knowing his name, or his sudden appearance. Then the word came back from stories he'd heard as a child. "Fimbulwinter—the dreadful winter. Wasn't that supposed to precede the Twilight of the Gods, or some such? The big war between gods and giants?"

"The Ragnarok. And the old blood runs strong in you, Leif, if you know that." The shadowed eyes were still studying Leif, with the wrinkles around them deepening in some sly amusement. "But I knew that. Eh, it darkens early. You're lucky for the lights on this—car."

Leif nodded. The name fitted the weather; it was winter, September or not. He cut on the radio to the local FM station, out of habit, listening to the weather reports. Beside him, the other jumped at the sound of the voice from the speaker, his red beard seeming to bristle suddenly. Then he chuckled, and sat back to listen.

Leif went on with his worrying over the road, listening with only half his mind. Food riots in the east, crime everywhere, fanatic groups in California, another war beginning in South America, and utter chaos in China and India. In nearby Brookville, the Larson brothers had quarreled over carrying in the wood, and killed each other with kitchen knives. And there were three more accounts of the angel riders in the sky, with some inconsistency about their avoidance of holy places, such as the air over churches. Then the announcer let his voice take on forced, almost falsetto optimism as he began on the weather.

Laufeyson broke in on that. "Your Norn in the box makes no sense," he said. "Talk of wind direction, when every fool knows the winds blow from all quarters at Fimbuljahr. Unless I smell it wrong, there'll be three days of blizzard, or more."

Leif nodded and cut off the radio; the forecasts were

usually wrong now. He slowed as he came to a side road.

"Far as I go in this direction."

"I'll go with you, Leif, until you find your brother. I'm seeking a wolf, though not as the One-Eyed thought, and Faulkner's land is as near as any for me."

Leif stole a glance at him, but something about the eyes of the hitchhiker held back his curiosity. He shrugged off a shiver that ran up his spine, and concentrated on his driving over the pitted little road. Lee's motorcycle came into view, crumpled completely, and already being covered by snow. How the rider had escaped injury was a miracle.

He drove up the lane and parked on the shattered side of the house. "Coming in?"

"I'll wait here, now that the wind no longer blows through this. And when I'm warmer, I'll be on my way."

Leif let it go at that, and went up the crackling, snow-covered steps. He rang, waited, and rang again, not surprised at the delay, even though his own efforts to date Gail Faulkner two years ago had been futile. He was grinning as she opened the door, and she dropped her eyes, blushing slightly. Behind her, Lee seemed pleased about everything, though the knees were ripped from both legs of his pants, and one hand was bandaged.

"Come on in and shut the door, son," he advised. "Hot coffee coming up. You run along and fix it, honey, Leif probably wants to bawl me out."

LEIF GRINNED in spite of his intentions. Nobody had ever succeeded in staying mad at Lee, and he was still a sucker for his twin. The expression on their faces was the only dissimilarity in their looks, but it was enough. He let the unconscious resentment of Lee's too-ready success with girls fade, and dropped into a chair before the radiator, soaking up the heat gratefully.

"Go out and tell Laufeyson in the car to come in for some of the coffee, Lee, and we'll forget it. Though you did raise hell with my plans."

But Lee had already gone out, not bothering to put on his jacket. Then he was back. "Nobody there. But why didn't you bring Lobo inside? With the scare on, he shouldn't be running loose."

Leif jerked up, suspecting a joke, but Lee's face was serious. He looked again, then went out after his brother. He didn't need Lee's words to spot the footprints. Laufeyson was gone, and there was no mark of his going in the snow. Instead, beginning at the car, the prints of a large dog or wolf cut off around the buildings; there were no marks to show how the animal had reached the car.

"Laufeyson must have had his tracks covered by a gust of snow," he decided aloud. "But those prints can't be Lobo's—he'd have come to the house after me, even if he could get loose and follow the car."

"This Laufeyson must have been a werewolf then. Come on, let's get that coffee."

Leif dismissed the uncomfortable puzzle, remembering the effect Laufeyson had worked on him. Hell, in another month, he'd be seeing angels riding in the sky. What he needed was coffee and some of the slaphappy conversation that was sure to surround Lee and a girl.

But he was still puzzling over it more than listening to them when a car drove up, an hour later. Gail made some remark about her father and went back to the kitchen, while Lee reached for his jacket. There was a mutter in the rear, and then Faulkner's voice reached them.

"...new guy, never seen him before. Got there just when the meeting was breaking up in a draw. Sure put some gumption into those weak-kneed guys, though. Dead right, too. If Svensen won't get rid of that killer, by God, we'll do it ourselves—going around…"

His words cut off as he reached the living room and spotted Leif and Lee, and sullen embarrassment covered his grizzled face. Gail went scarlet and miserable behind him. Then his stooped shoulders squared belligerently.

"Get out! Get out of my house, both of you, before I throw you out. Sneaking around…"

Lee finished buttoning his jacket leisurely, still grinning, but there was a coldness to the grin that cut off the whipped-up rage of Faulkner and sent the man stumbling backward. "We're going, Faulkner. But if you really feel like losing that temper of yours, drop over any time. Haven't had a workout for weeks. Come on, Leif. Gail honey, I'll be seeing you later. And thanks for the coffee."

The girl stared at her father for a moment, then came forward to open the door for them, disregarding Faulkner's bellow. She came out on the porch, starting to apologize. Lee cut her words off, pulling her face up to his. She tiptoed to meet him quickly—and jerked back with a sudden scream.

They turned to follow her pointing finger.

The sky was black already, the thickening snow visible only where the lights of the house hit it. But something white was coming through it, squarely in the path of the light. A lusty female voice hit their ears, and a big blonde woman with the build of an Amazon appeared, mounted on the biggest white horse Leif had ever seen. She seemed to be riding down the light, staring straight ahead at the Svensens, with the hooves of the horse some four feet off the ground. Then her voice lifted in pitch, and the horse reared, leaping upward over the porch, while the song drifted out into silence. When they reached the rear of the house, she was gone.

CHAPTER TWO

LEIF CLIMBED into his car, waiting while Lee calmed the girl and made his good-byes. He didn't know what was in his mind. The hair on the back of his neck had risen in ancestral instinct, but there had been nothing terrifying about the rider, and he felt no fear. Even the horse had been normal, with no outgrowth of wings. He didn't question the sight. It had been too plain for hallucination. Somehow there were horses that could fly without wings—or there were scientific developments that permitted the projection of such a vision. Einstein's work with gravity was either paying off, or someone had found the secret of television in three dimensions—and color—without a receiver.

But the purpose of either eluded him.

"Valkyries," Lee said, sliding into the car. "Or that's what our ancestors would have called them."

Leif glanced at him sharply. "You don't seem surprised."

"Why should I be? I've seen them before." He grinned, too easily, but his fingers trembled a bit as he reached for the cigarette lighter. "I knew better than to tell you, before. But when I got this stuff in my chest, two of them came swooping down, yelling out that song of theirs. If that bomb hadn't carried me about six feet into the ruined church…well, they'd have got me. Had a former priest tell me the decay of religion was loosing the old demons. He figured they were genuine valkyries."

"What do you think?"

"I think it's a good idea not to think of them. Either they're what they seem—or they're a good trick by someone or another. But I've seen enough not to make up my mind. I…just don't like having them follow me here and stare that way."

Leif nodded, and reached for the starter. Before he

touched it, the back door opened, and Laufeyson's voice reached him.

"It's still easier not to walk in the Fimbulwinter, Leif. With your leave, I'll return with you. Greetings, Lee Svensen."

Lee had swung around at the voice, and now his words were surprised. "De Nal! I thought they'd got you. Leif, de Nal was one of my company in the Legion, the last week I was up. How'd you get here?"

Laufeyson—or de Nal—chuckled. "I was sick of their type of war, Lee. When the bombs dropped and covered me in the mud, I played dead. Now I'm a deserter."

"What about your friend—the big, black-bearded guy? He must have been right where the big one landed."

"Jordsson escaped with me—the same manner."

Leif let them talk of the Legion, forcing his mind off this further puzzle. Their talk soon petered out to nothing, since it was obvious that they had little in common beyond the same service, and the car was silent, except for the beating of the snow and the howling of the wind.

The blizzard was close at hand, obviously, and the snow was already inches deep and beginning to pile up. Driving was something that required Leif's full attention, and he was grateful for it. Even with the headlights, visibility was bad, and he was forced to a crawl. Lee motioned questioningly, but Leif never felt happy when his brother was driving, even under ideal conditions. He went on, judging as much by the feel of the ruts under the wheels as by what he could see.

At that, he almost overshot his own entrance, until he heard the deep barking of Lobo. Then he swung in, hunting for the road, and started up it, just as the dog leaped toward them in the glare of the lights.

"Damn! I thought you said Lobo was chained."

Leif nodded, scowling again. "He was. Here, boy!"

HE REACHED over to open the back door, but the dog growled uncertainly, the hair rising on his back, and sidled away. Laufeyson grunted, and the dog lifted his muzzle and gave vent to a long, uncanny bay.

"Your Lobo doesn't appreciate me," Laufeyson said. "There are times when the dogs don't, and the smell is still fresh on me. Let me forward, and you come back, Lee, before we all freeze."

With the switch made, the dog crawled reluctantly in with Lee, and Leif drove up the long driveway. "You might look at his collar," he told Lee.

"That's what I'm looking at. The chain has been smashed, as if someone took a sledgehammer to it. No, darn it…the links are half mashed, half fused. You'd think a bolt of lightning hit it. Here."

Laufeyson took it from Lee and held it where Leif could just make it out. The description was proper. It did look odd. With the neighborhood worried silly about Lobo already, it would mean trouble if someone had seen him, and there was no way of knowing how long the dog had been free. He wondered who had done it, but there was no way of telling.

The automatic door on the garage had frozen shut, and Lee had to work it by hand. Then they were out and into the warmth and brightness of the house, Leif leading Lobo in with Laufeyson following behind them. The man glanced about curiously, and the wrinkles around his eyes deepened.

"Better than being tied over three rocks," he commented, dropping into a comfortable chair. For a moment, he reminded Leif of a great cat resting in self-satisfied comfort.

Lee had brought down the whiskey and was pouring a shot apiece. Laufeyson seemed to brace himself, but he downed it and his grimace was contented. When Leif came back with coffee, he gave it a disgusted look and refilled his glass with the whiskey.

Unconsciously, Leif pulled the nervous dog closer to him, rubbing the great, wolf-like head. "At least, if the storm keeps up, the fools will have time to cool down. Wish I'd been at that meeting."

"It will let up for an hour or so, shortly," Laufeyson stated.

Five minutes later, the wind died down, and the outer air turned crisper and colder, but the snow stopped falling. Leif cast another doubting glance at the red-bearded man, but he was holding his thoughts in careful abeyance. Too much in one day needed time for digestion.

It was half an hour when the phone rang, startling Laufeyson out of his relaxation. The man caught himself and settled back, even as Leif answered it.

There was an attempt at disguising the voice at the other end, but it obviously belonged to Summers. "Svensen? Just a friendly warning. The men are getting together…"

"You mean they're out to get Lobo, Summers?"

The disguise dropped. "Yeah, that's right, Leif. Now I didn't want anything to happen to you. There's been another killing, over at Engel's. And I figure maybe if you take care of things first…"

Leif hung up, swearing. But before he could get back to his seat, the phone rang again. He growled into it, then turned to Lee. "It's Gail—she wants you."

"Yeah, honey," Lee answered, holding the receiver away from his ear, calming her down. "Yeah…umm-hmm…okay, we'll take care of it. Don't you worry. Nah, nothing to it… Sweet kid. Thanks. See you."

But he was frowning as he faced Leif. "Any weapons, Leif? Gail says the vigilantes are out for blood—Lobo's or ours, and they seem to want both. Dang it anyway, Lobo couldn't have gotten to Engel's place and back, but we can't prove it. Damn these crazy fools—a little fear of hunger, and they go nuts."

LEIF HAD a rifle, but the last shell had been used on a hunting trip a month before, and he'd gotten no replacements. Lee grinned wryly, and was gone for a few moments. He came back with an automatic and several clips. He threw them at Leif.

"You take this. I'll get an axe. How about you, de Nal? You with us?" There was no question between Lee and Leif as to what must be done. Lobo had been in the family since Lee had brought him back from Alaska as a pup; he belonged.

Laufeyson came to his feet gracefully, suddenly looking larger than he had before. "I'm not unfamiliar with an axe, if you have the double-bitted ones. Do you have one?

A minute later, he was swinging it about, testing the balance in the shed. Overhead, there was a dull thunder of hooves, and a sound of singing. The red-beard looked up, grinned at Lee, and made another practice swing. "They gather for the feasting. And one is yet to come."

One did come, almost on his words. The door flew open suddenly, bouncing on its hinges, and a huge bear of a man was through it before the rebound had closed it. His face was humorless, broad, and stronger than any face Leif had seen. The eyes were dark, and seemed to flash in the light of the overhead bulb, while his black beard jutted from his chin like a flag. There was a feeling of sheer power about him that seemed almost a solid aura.

"Jordsson," Laufeyson told Leif. "And a handy man in a fight, though he may bore you at times with the telling of his deeds."

A huge, short-handled maul in the newcomer's hand

flashed up, but the man apparently was used to Laufeyson's humor, even though he obviously could not share it. "The nidderlings come, and Nikarr has the shield maids out. He grows impatient."

"And you grow wordy, as I feared. More, and all will be shown."

Leif stared at Lee, and saw the same doubt in his brother's look. Something stirred in the back of his mind, trying to make sense out of the words. But it was interrupted as the sound of cars coming up the driveway struck their ears. Without a word, Jordsson, Laufeyson and Lee all moved out toward the lane. Lee turned back to switch on the bright porch lights.

"Shows them up, and helps blind them when they try to see us," he told Leif. "How do you feel, son?"

Leif managed to grin, but his heart wasn't in it. These three professional heroes might think this a small business, but he didn't like the idea of an attempted lynching by his neighbors. A week ago he'd have laughed at the idea, but now he was almost sure it amounted to that. He could feel the sweat gathering under his armpits, and his legs seemed to melt under him. He glanced at his hands, and noticed that they were trembling.

Lee tapped him on the shoulder. "Forget it. You're not going through anything I didn't feel. These things take experience, son. You hang back until you get the drift. Hell, a mad crowd can't shoot, anyhow."

"Sure, I should hang back when you belong inside, getting over your wounds, and when two strangers are fighting for me. I'm the man the crowd wants to get."

It sounded good, but he couldn't feel the words. It was all incomprehensible, so muddled that he wasn't sure whether he was a coward or not. Well, he'd envied Lee his casual adventuresomeness. Now he'd find out whether he liked it.

But already, he knew he didn't.

THE FRONT car stopped just halfway up the driveway, and men began piling out, moving purposefully up the road toward them. Someone yelled, in a voice that sounded like Faulkner. But all wore kerchiefs over their faces, or pillowslips with holes chopped out. Inside the house, Lobo started barking hoarsely, and the sound touched off the men, who came boiling forward.

As the only man with a gun, Lee jumped ahead. He started to yell, caught his voice, and finally got it out. "All right, stop where you are!"

"You gonna give us the dog."

"Come and take him!" It was Lee's voice then. "There are thirty of you. We'll save ten for your wives."

"Ho!" The roar from Jordsson was an approving one, and he and Laufeyson moved up to flank Lee, putting Leif behind them again.

A sudden shout greeted the appearance of the red-bearded man. "Hey! It's him—the dirty traitor! Telling us we should take action and then ratting on us. Get him!"

Leif tossed a glance at Laufeyson, but the amused smile was still on the man's face. He stepped forward and began calling out names—including that of Summers—apparently without error. Even as Leif realized nothing could infuriate them more than piercing their disguise, they began pressing forward.

"Ho!" Jordsson's voice rang out again, like a clap of thunder, and the maul left his hand in a savage sweep. Something splattered out on the snow, and the maul seemed to be grabbed by someone and tossed back; it landed squarely in Jordsson's hand. Leif noticed it abstractly, even while his eyes stayed riveted on the headless thing on the ground. The automatic fell from his hands. His stomach heaved, but his throat was too constricted to cooperate.

The crowd flinched, and a few in the front leaped back, but the pressure of those behind was too great. With a strange, animal sound of sheer fury, they charged forward. The three beside Leif were moving to meet them, in spite of the guns that were appearing in all hands.

Leif bent to recover the automatic, and something whistled by his ear. Realization finally penetrated that it was a bullet. He stood there, stupidly drying the automatic and shoving it into his pocket aimlessly for another second. Then instinct seemed to take over, and he leaped frantically after the other three, who were already up to the crowd, too close for the use of guns. In front of Leif, a man was clubbing at Laufeyson's head with a rifle. Lee's axe swept around, leaving a gory trail, and Leif grabbed the rifle before it could drop from the falling man's hand.

There were axes and knives in the crowd, too. Even as the barrel of the gun fitted into Leif's hand, he dropped it, to grab desperately at the handle of an axe swinging down toward him. It grazed his arm, shredding off leather from his coat, and he was down with the swinger, being trampled.

Two legs reared over him, and an axe chopped expertly down. The hand at Leif's throat went limp, and the axe came free in his grip, just as Laufeyson stooped and yanked him upright.

A PART of his mind was still wondering about his cowardice or lack of it, and another detached fragment was fighting at the sickness he could feel all through him. But the hysteria of the crowd and the ferocity of these former neighbors had entered into him. He swung out underhand, feeling the axe cut through the leg of someone before him, and moved up beside Laufeyson, who was now separated from the other two.

He still couldn't kill deliberately, but maiming and crippling seemed almost as effective. Things became a red haze in front of him for a few moments. When it cleared, he could see most of the attackers retreating wildly. They had bargained on a lynching with little danger, but had been swept into something far more vicious and were now losing the frenzy in the face of real menace to their lives. He glanced about quickly, spotting Laufeyson and Jordsson.

Then he saw his brother on the ground, with his blood running out over the snow from a great gash through his abdomen.

Leif jerked forward, just as Lee lifted himself to an elbow and let out a sudden warning yell. But it was too late.

From behind him, something struck sharply against Leif's back, sending him twisting and reeling. He tried to come around and bring up his axe, but the man now facing him had already raised the big corn knife for another stroke. It glistened in the light like a dripping sword, and began chopping down.

Leif jerked sidewise, trying to throw himself back and away. But there was no time. The blade came down, inexorably. It whistled by his ear, bit into his jacket, and went on through. Pain hit him as the muscles parted and the collarbone splintered. He was falling now, the knife dragging out of him. He started to shout, but his voice was a burble, and there was the salt of blood in his mouth.

Laufeyson's arm was suddenly under him, just as a shout went up from somewhere near.

Wild singing was coming from the air above, and with it sounded the thunder of hooves. An object flashed down as the pain in Leif began to sharpen and become unbearable. It separated into a big woman on an immense horse, dropping out of nowhere. Everything was turning into a gray mist, but consciousness had not left entirely. He felt her hand clutch his hair, felt himself lifted with a single heave of her arm, and dropped across the shoulders of the horse.

Then the wind was whistling past him, and he could sense the Earth falling away. Behind him, the song suddenly rose to a strange shrieking set of tones, and they seemed to twist crazily. Rainbow spots merged into great bands and seemed to quiver through Leif's whole body, blotting out the pain.

The horse was laboring now. Its breath came in short, hard gulps, and the huge hooves seemed to slip and slide. Again, the rider urged her mount onward, while the rainbow bands quivered, tightened, and relaxed. Leif felt the sweat from the horse begin to soak into him, stinging sharply as it worked into his wound, lifting the pain to new heights.

Again the horse strained, and something seemed to give with sticky reluctance. The pattern of the rainbow ran together, beating almost audibly. The horse seemed to breast some sort of a rise, and his hooves settled again into a steady pounding, while the woman's shout turned back to the song he had first heard.

There was a violent wrenching that threatened to tear Leif apart, atom by atom, and the rainbow colors poured out in a wild final burst.

Then all grew quiet. Blackness closed over Leif mercifully.

CHAPTER THREE

THE SOUND of distant metallic clashing and the shouts of men reached his ears next, with no apparent passage of time. Leif stirred, before remembering his wounds. But the pain was gone, and time must have passed. He was obviously on some sort of bed, though the usual hospital smell was lacking. He opened his eyes and blinked them. The darkness remained complete and total.

There was a sudden stirring beside him, and footsteps. He

lay quietly, afraid to move and find how serious his wounds were, wondering why the lights were out.

"The trance still lasts," a woman's soft voice said. A hand ran over his forehead caressingly, and Leif could feel the hair being brushed from his face. The fingers remained another moment, cool and with an odd tingle to their touch. "He's slim for a hero, as Baldar was—and comely, too. He looks—gentle, perhaps, kind…"

The lusty answering laugh was amused. "Careful, Fulla. Such words are odd in a virgin of the Asynjur. Remember Freyja's mortal husband."

"Nonsense, Reginleif." But there was confusion in Fulla's tone. "Though it has been a long time since a mortal joined us. And the Aesir… Nonsense!"

The other laughed again, but dropped it. "He was trouble enough. Carrying him through Bifrost was almost too much for even the loan of Gna's Hoof-Tosser. The horse will be useless for a week. Let's hope he's a real berserker with the knowledge Asa-Odin wants. Surtr's hot breath is almost on us."

There was the sound of footsteps leaving, and her voice died with distance. Leif made little of it, and wanted to make less. Baldar, Aesir, Odin—they were dead myths and nonsense. He must still be delirious—but there *had* been the valkyr!

"Bifrost has burned your sight, Leif Svensen." He hadn't heard the man approach, but the sudden voice was that of Laufeyson, and without his usual sardonic humor. "Here, take my hand and make your eyes follow the feel of its motions. You'll need all your senses at the Thing. I've some small skill at sleight, as has been told. Now—by Ironwood's mother, this matter make right; speed minutes, and man, still mortal, gain sight!"

The words were a chant, and the motions a curious hocus

pocus, but it worked. The room sprang into sudden light. Leif blinked, looking at the aged beams of the ceiling. The room was huge, with hard wooden bunks around it, covered with bearskins; weapons of primitive design decorated the walls, and the light streamed in from windows of oiled vellum. Laufeyson stood over him, wearing a helmet with spike and wings and clad in heavy mail (flexible armor), like a scene from a messy production of a Wagnerian opera.

It was no hospital! Leif's eyes jerked to his shoulder. There were no bandages or open wounds. Only a slight red scar showed.

Laufeyson nodded. "Asgard—the home of your ancestor's gods. And you're whole; going through the dimensional bridge of Bifrost revitalizes the body until it can repair any damage. We're myths, Leif—but myths with sharp teeth. To convince you—what language am I speaking?"

LEIF COULD remember the English words for "myth" and "dimensional" in the speech, but the rest—he couldn't place the sounds, though they might have been Teutonic in origin.

"We can't read minds here, but any vocalized words carry their meanings to all—such is the nature of Asgard. Will you believe?"

Leif shook his head, still uncertain. Something was wrong, but he couldn't accept the other's explanation so quickly. Laufeyson frowned.

"No matter—you'll have to believe. Already Fulla returns. Listen! Play dead, but remember Odin is stubborn and sometimes a fool. We were sent for Lee, and only I chose you, instead. To them, you must be the berserker, the hero who could hold back a score in blood-rage to save a friend, as was seen from Odin's throne. Play the part and be surprised at nothing. Odin's rage is not pleasant!"

Steps sounded from outside then, and Laufeyson was suddenly gone. In his place, a leaf drifted on a sudden wind, to blow through the doorway. Leif stared at it. Delirium or not, he was suddenly sure that this was the time to follow orders. He dropped back quickly, closing his eyes and blanking out all expression.

"Still in a trance," Reginleif's rough voice said.

"It should have been gone by now." Fulla's hand again rested softly on his forehead. "But nothing goes right since the awakening. Even the apples... Perhaps appointing me in Idunn's place was a mistake; the tree responds to nothing I do. Well, he *must* be revived, Reginleif."

Reginleif tittered hoarsely. "I've revived enough heroes, Fulla; and Hoof-Tosser needs a rub-down. You do it—since you want to, anyhow."

Leif opened his eyes a crack, just enough to see the buxom woman leaving. Fulla was moving across the room toward him hesitantly, slim and supple, her hair long and golden, bound in the back by a curious metal crown of the same color. Her face had the beauty of a type sometimes called sweet, or wholesome, but with none of that lack of vividness; and the blush that was covering it now added to the effect. Then she was too close, and Leif closed his eyes quickly.

There was hesitation in her movements as she touched him this time. Her arm moved under his head, while her other hand rested on his chest. And suddenly her lips were on his, full and warm.

Leif might have had too little experience, but he hadn't been a total loss as a man. His arm moved automatically around her, pulling her down. For a moment, she permitted it, her hand moving to his shoulder and her lips responding. Then her breath caught, and she sprang back, blushing furiously.

She looked better to him with his eyes fully open.

"It was only customary—to awaken a hero entranced…" She stammered slightly over the words. Then her lips became determined. "But you were revived before. You tricked me!"

The delirium was definitely taking a turn for the better, Leif decided, and the unreality of the situation cut off the last of his inhibitions. "The neatest trick of the week," he admitted cheerfully, and caught her hand.

She struggled, half-heartedly. Halfway to him, she gave up and came to meet him eagerly. His grin vanished, and he was briefly shocked at his own response. Something in him gathered itself into a ball and burst. He was only conscious of Fulla and the need to be near her, to gather her more tightly to him—

"Odin summons!" A hoarse croak announced it, followed by the caw of a crow. Fulla sprang back from Leif, the red of her face rushing up and disappearing into whiteness. Leif followed her eyes, to see a black bird sitting on the shoulder of a shaggy gray wolf.

The bird regarded him steadily. "Odin summons the Son of Sven to the Thing. Let Fulla bring him."

It cawed again, beat its wings, and was off, with the wolf loping after it.

Fulla avoided Leif's eyes and began pulling a helmet and corselet of mail from the wall. "Put them on quickly. The Alfadur is impatient these days. And…we'll forget this folly."

HE WAS scrambling into the odd get-up, finding no time to answer. He had no intention of forgetting, nor, he thought, did she. But he followed her out quietly. The building sprawled over acres of ground, low and massive, with door after door in the front. Other buildings lay around it, some higher, but none over four stories. Most had been gilded once, but now only faint flecks caught the sunlight.

Asgard needed repairs badly.

The land itself was more impressive. Deep blue skies went on with no clear horizon. A high wall cut off one side and a forest lay in front. In all other directions, the greensward of rolling plains continued on and on, soft and springy underfoot. It might have been a well-kept lawn.

They headed for the forest. Then, as they moved away from the buildings, he saw the source of the clashing sounds. The field had been worn down to bare dirt for square miles, and it was covered thickly with men in mail. Some held double-bitted axes, others spears, and most were equipped with broadswords and shields.

As he watched, a warrior not fifty feet away swung at two others, lopping off their heads with a single stroke. He wiped his forehead complacently and went looking for more trouble.

But Leif was beginning to remember his myths. These would be the einherjar, the heroes the valkyries brought back to Valhalla to fight in practice until needed at the Ragnarok. Odin made them whole each evening, so a little head cutting didn't really matter.

"They look dull and sluggish," he commented, following Fulla.

She nodded. "Most are. We caught the vital force at the moment of death, but the white elves' false flesh doesn't hold it well. And to bring back force and body together is…well, you should know how difficult."

Leif looked at his body. Apparently, it was his body, and not some ectoplasmic stuff. It didn't feel ethereal as he watched her moving ahead of him. They crossed a stream on rocks and entered the woods through a well-worn path. Then he caught her again, drawing her to him. She responded briefly, before drawing away. "We'll be late," she half-whispered. "The Aesir are assembled at Yggdrasil even as we talk now."

They were, as Leif saw a few minutes later. The tree was a huge ash, spreading out like a canopy over them, its top tangled with others around it. Odin sat in a hard chair, recognizable by the wolves at his side, the ravens at his shoulders, and the one eye that stared glumly out at the assembly. For a moment, Leif felt pity at the sight of the bowed shoulders and the doom and frustration on the god's countenance.

From somewhere, Laufeyson appeared. "I'm to sponsor you."

Fulla drew back hastily, making a sign with her fingers. "Then are the Aesir mad, Loki. Son of Sven, the air here seems no longer sweet, and I'm wanted. Guard yourself against the Evil Companion."

She was gone, but Loki was chuckling in amusement.

"Who else?" he asked. "Surely you're not surprised to find who I am. Umm, I see you recognize Odin. Vidarr and Vali, his sons, are beside him; they're to live after Ragnarok, and I suspect they welcome it. Then Heimdallr, who'll oppose anything I wish…"

He went on, but Leif was paying only meager attention. He was remembering tales of Loki's treachery; Fulla's warning wasn't unfounded, they indicated. But he had no choice now. He followed Loki, the son of Laufey, or Nal.

Odin glanced down at him, while the cold face of Odin's wife, Frigg, refused to see him. Odin motioned, but it was for Fulla. She came up with a chest, and Odin pulled out a small, green apple. He nibbled at it, swallowed, and passed it on; the bitterness in his voice might have been from ulcers.

"Phaaa! Are we to gain our youth and strength on such as that?" He belched unhappily. "And not even enough of those. Loki, where is my son Thor?"

"Oku-Thor has not returned. Perhaps he seeks more

heroes." Loki's voice was humble and apologetic, but changed to relief as he spoke sidewise to Leif. "We're in luck there. Thor would probably know you and have us both cast into Niflheim."

"And the hero?" Odin asked.

LEIF FOLLOWED him through the mob, noticing the stares directed at the trousers under his mail. Loki's voice suavely began the tale of how they'd tried to get their man in battle, to be defeated by the church. He told of following, of the tricks to arouse the neighbors, and of the battle there. Leif noticed a skillful blend of his own part with Lee's. He also put it down as a count against Loki that the wolf had been Loki's disguise. Apparently men could only be pulled over Bifrost when they were dead or dying—and by tradition, they were supposed to get their wounds in combat.

Odin listened impatiently until it was finished. "Little enough, but I suppose it must do. It's an ill age when men turn to women. Still, if he has the skills they've used to replace their waning courage, we can use him. Loki, you sponsor this Son of Sven against the Ragnarok?"

Loki lifted his hand. Beside Odin, the thin-faced Vali and the fat Vidarr turned quickly and began muttering. Odin cut them off, his shoulders sagging further.

"What more can we do?" he asked almost querulously. "The times are mad, and we grow mad with them. If this hero of Loki's fails us, we can be no worse off, and you may have the two of them for your sport. Son of Sven, step forward!"

"We're in luck," Loki began. But a sudden roar stopped him.

"Hold!" The roaring bellow came from the rear, and Loki swore hotly. The huge figure of Jordsson—obviously Thor—came jostling among them. At his heels ran a tired, panting dog that Leif recognized as Lobo. In the god's arms, Thor was carrying the body of Lee!

"Hold!" Thor roared again. He dropped Lee with surprising gentleness onto the turf and swept his eyes back over the group, searching. Loki had pulled Leif back quickly, losing them in a thicker group. Thor scowled and faced Odin again.

"Father Odin," he announced, "this is the hero, the real Son of Sven. I denounce the other as an impostor, a coward and as great a knave as Loki. I demand justice!"

His eyes swung toward Heimdallr, who stopped polishing his fingernails against his thighs long enough to point to Loki and Leif. Then Thor turned toward them, reaching for the hammer at his side.

CHAPTER FOUR

ODIN'S VOICE took on a sudden note of command as he cut through the confusion. "Enough, Thor! This is a judging place, and these matters need thought. How comes this man without a valkyr to guide him?"

Thor's impatient hand dropped slowly, and Loki breathed a sigh of relief as he began dragging Leif cautiously forward. Thor's anger was obviously still hot, but he was trying to control it.

"There were no valkyries after Loki befuddled them into taking that one." He jerked his thumb contemptuously toward Leif. "Reginleif and the others went off, leaving me with the hero dying at my feet. I carried him through Bifrost on my back. How else would it have been possible?"

"And the dog? Since when is Asgard for beasts?"

"Two of the nidderlings were killing the animal when my hammer Mjollnir found them. But he's a stouthearted beast—dying, he still crawled after us. Over half the way he came on his own. Should I have refused to help him when Loki's dupe rode here on Hoof-Tosser?"

There was a clamor at that, and even Loki's face showed admiration. "Impossible for even our best horse," he muttered to Leif. "But when Thor's angry, he'd carry twenty through Bifrost. It will sway the Aesir to his side, though."

Leif had almost stopped thinking in the chaos of events, but he caught at Loki's shoulder now. "I'm calling it off, Loki. I won't fight against my brother—"

Loki grinned. "Noble, eh? Don't worry. Thor wouldn't carry him here and then desert him. He may not be bright, but he's just in his own way. Lee'll do well enough, whatever happens. But unless we win this, we won't. You *can* be killed, even here, since you're wearing your own flesh instead of elf-shapings. Or Odin can do worse."

Now they were near the front of the throne and Loki raised his hands ceremoniously for attention. Thor scowled at him, but Odin nodded slowly.

"A mighty feat, Thor," Loki began, keeping his voice just low enough that the others had to strain to hear. The trick quieted them. "Bragi will make a new poem of it. But a pity, too—since I'd already sent the real hero on. Alfadur Odin, in the confusion of the fracas, it was easy to confuse two who seemed alike. Only by holding back and letting Thor do most of the infighting was I able to keep them straight."

"What!" Thor's bellow was a fresh shock every time Leif heard it. "You claim I don't know a hero, Loki? Now, by Ymir..."

Loki shrugged. "Not an unconscious one, Oku-Thor. When dying, men are all alike. No, I claim only that you were too intent on the battle to see all, as I did in my humbler role. Fulla, you were present when he arrived. Say whether my candidate seemed a coward."

Leif looked at her quickly. But the warmth had gone from

her face, and her voice was cold and impersonal. "How should I know, Father of Evil? He was grievously wounded, from the scars that had still not gone."

"And did he cower when he learned where he was, Fulla?" Loki asked, the grin back on his lips. "Or did he perhaps seem eager to join Asgard's company? Surely you would know of that."

She flushed under Loki's gaze, and her eyes swung to Leif. Then she turned away coldly, her chin raised a trifle too high. "He was bold enough to be your twin!"

She came by Leif then, not a foot away. He reached out, but she swiveled and passed without looking. "Oku-Thor, your hero needs reviving, and since no valkyr has volunteered, perhaps my help would be welcome."

SHE DROPPED to her knees on the turf, lifting Lee's head in her arms. Leif swore—she needn't have put that much enthusiasm into the kiss. Then he hated himself for thinking it while Lee was in need of help—and swore again as Lee opened his eyes and grabbed for her. Frigg's cold, disapproving cough finally broke it up, though, and Fulla stood erect, staring at Leif with a thin, chill smile on her lips.

Lee shook his head and came to his feet, looking at the group around him. He frowned, shook his head, and suddenly laughed.

"I'll be damned—Asgard! Thor, Odin—and Loki de Nal." He shook his head again, staring into the crowd. Then his face cleared. "And Leif! Damn it, son, I'm selfish enough to be glad they got you, too."

Lobo had spotted Leif at the same time and was leaping up and down, trying to lick his face. Fulla carefully moved to the other side of Lee as Leif came up. Thor muttered unhappily as the brothers came together, showing their complete similarity. His eyes were doubtful as Loki joined them with a grin on his lips.

The puzzled mutter of the group around reached Leif's ears dimly, but his thoughts were churning busily over the fact that Lee could take everything in at one quick glance and seemingly enjoy what he found. Apparently, he could also sweep Fulla to him in less time. But Leif's throat was oddly constricted as he grabbed Lee's hand briefly. "You look a lot better than the last view I had of you, Lee."

"Two heroes, both alike, both wounded," Loki commented loudly, while Thor regarded him with a mixture of distrust and a strange, begrudging respect. "Yet names have power, too. Should the old blood not be stronger in one named Leif?"

Thor's grunt told Leif that it was a telling stroke; the gods were apparently better at tradition than logic. He was trying to fill Lee in on the essential facts, but he stopped to stare at the crowd.

Heimdallr frowned and stopped polishing the metal on his corselet. The god's fatuously self-satisfied look sharpened as he stared at Leif. "Two heroes, Loki? But my eyes, which can see the grass grow at a thousand miles, tell me your hero has one wound on his back. And I think it was the first wound."

Loki's grin slipped for a second, and Leif felt his palms begin to sweat. The seriousness of this was slowly dawning on him. He rubbed his hands against his trousers, bringing them up against something hard in his pocket. The automatic still rested there. He reached for it, even as Loki caught himself.

"Heimdallr's eyes see more than rumors this time, then. Of course it was first at his back that the nidderling thrust— because none dared to face him."

But the hesitation had been too long, and the face of Odin was sharpening into determination. Surprisingly, Thor looked uncertain now, still muttering. But the doubts in the others were going.

Leif caught himself. Then the automatic was out and pointing toward the smirking face of Heimdallr.

"If…" Leif swallowed, caught his voice, and somehow managed to stiffen himself against a picture of Lee in the same situation. "If you're to blow the horn that gives Asgard notice of Ragnarok, Heimdallr, you'll do it better without a hole in your head! Or haven't you seen what one of these can do?"

He pulled the trigger as he spoke, and the report jerked every god up, like puppets on strings. The bullet plowed into a knot in the tree, showering splinters and dust down at Heimdallr, and cutting the smugness off sharply. Leif was grateful for the target practice he'd had with Lee whenever his brother was home. "The next goes through you!"

"No!" Thor's hand leaped forward, closing around the gun and lifting it from Leif's hand. "A good play, Leif Svensen, but Heimdallr's Gjallar-Horn is needed."

LEIF TURNED, expecting the big hammer to come up at him, but the god stood calmly, regarding him. Heimdallr let out a sudden shout, but quieted at a word from Odin, and turned to confer quickly with Vali and Vidarr.

Then Loki was speaking again. "You wanted proof—and you have it. As was shown from Odin's throne, the heroes now have new weapons—which we need. Who but a hero would have such—or can Thor's hero produce such a weapon?"

"You know damned well I can't," Lee said quietly. "But…"

His arm chopped down abruptly on Thor's wrist, and his other hand came out to catch the automatic. Thor blinked, scowled, and gave a sudden booming chuckle of approval that snapped off as Lee tossed the gun to Leif. With another abrupt twist, Lee had a two-bitted axe from a bystander and was moving to cover Leif's back.

"A hero, as all can see," Thor shouted toward Odin.

Loki snorted. "A hero—when Thor drops the weapon into his hands! It proves nothing. Can your hero make weapons, Oku-Thor? We've heroes enough in Valhalla—we need skills."

"What're we supposed to do?" Lee asked in a whisper. "Make guns and ammo for them?"

Leif was careful to hide his lips from Heimdallr. The god might be a popinjay in some ways, but his eyesight was obviously a lot better than average. "Seems so. I suppose we could take some kind of a stab at it. I remember some of my college chemistry, and any farmer has to know how to handle tools. We might make flintlock carbines for ball shot."

Thor was standing uncertainly while Odin looked at him expectantly. Finally the black-bearded god turned to Lee. "Can you, Lee Svensen?"

"About as well as you can," Lee answered. "Using guns and making them are two different things where we come from. Besides, it takes material. You might ask my brother."

Odin turned questioningly to Leif, who shrugged. Maybe he could make weapons, but he had no idea of how long it would take here, nor whether he could even get the materials needed. Besides, he still couldn't trust Loki too far; maybe Thor would take care of Lee, and maybe not.

But Loki had moved in front of him, one hand casually behind his back. He moved it quickly, while addressing Odin. "A difficult task. As Lee says, it takes material. Fortunately, I brought such material for one gun only with me—and at great effort, too. Leif will now make such a gun for all to see."

The hand behind his back moved suggestively, and Leif

glanced down to see an automatic lying in the god's palm. He seized it as Loki moved aside. "It might be best to conceal your motions," Loki observed softly. "At least, pretend you're having some difficulty."

Leif handed the original gun to his brother and bent down, hiding his hands under his helmet. He had no idea where Loki had picked up the gun, but it seemed that the sly god was prepared for most emergencies. Finally he straightened, the second automatic in his hand. Loki's lips were close to Lee's ear, but no sound reached Leif. Lee was grinning broadly, but his face sobered as Leif came to his feet.

Another clamor came from the crowd, and Odin sagged back into his seat, nodding, but still not sure. At the side, Heimdallr was whispering to Vali and Vidarr.

Then Vali's voice cut through the noise. "Father Odin, it would seem that Loki spoke truth for once, and that Leif shall be the man to win the Ragnarok."

Vidarr was nodding, speaking quickly to Odin, while the crowd set up a fresh shout. Heimdallr was on his feet, yelling at Vali, but the crowd noise covered his words. Finally, Vali caught him, making frantic motions until he sat back again, scowling. Then, as quiet slowly came, Odin turned to Leif.

"We have decided, then, Leif, Son of Sven. We distrust much, but we have no other choice. Prepare the weapons against Ragnarok and you shall have anyone request within our not inconsiderable power to grant. Betray us or give us further cause to doubt, and Niflheim shall claim you. By Ymir, we swear it. As for the other—"

"As for the other," Thor's voice broke in heavily, "I have brought Lee Svensen to Asgard under my safe conduct. Does any question the honor of Thor?"

Obviously, nobody did. "Then Lee shall lead the einherjar with me," Thor finished. He started off, motioning for Lee to follow.

"Be seeing you, son," Lee told Leif. He went off after Thor, whistling snatches from the *Ride of the Valkyries,* winking at Fulla as he passed her. She turned to follow.

BUT LOKI'S voice reached out, all sweetness and honey now. "Good Fulla, as you can see, I may be busy in conference. Why don't you show our hero to the workshop of the dwarves, since it's there he'll work? And you might tell them they're to do whatever he says."

Fulla's protest was stopped by a nod from Odin. She came up to Leif then, jerking her head for him to follow. They went back over the same lane through the woods. She quickened her steps, marching along, head high, not looking back to him.

Leif caught up with her, and spun her around. "What's going on? Just because Lee's around, you don't have to treat me like dirt—"

He tried to pull her to him, but her hand came out, smacking sharply against his face. Lee would have grinned and gone ahead, and for a second Leif considered it. But the look in her eyes was too much for him. He stepped back.

"Dirt I could endure," she told him coldly. "But a tool of the Evil Companion—a trickster, a false hero—even one who looks like Baldar and…"

He grinned wryly. "Go on and say it. You haven't forgotten being kissed, any more than I have."

"No. I remember that—to hate you for it. But don't feel that you've won everything yet, Leif Svensen. Heimdallr saw through your trick."

She was pointing at his hand, and he looked down now, conscious that he was still carrying the automatic Loki had given him. Then he swore. There was no gun, but only a short stick of wood, shaped something like one. Loki had tricked them, and Heimdallr hadn't been fooled, but only silenced somehow by Vali. Something came to his mind—Loki's doubts of Vali and Vidarr, who would survive Ragnarok, and might like a false hero to speed it. He swore, and threw the stick aside.

Damn Loki! Leif scowled, wondering just what he'd gotten into. Loki was supposed to be on the side of the giants originally; maybe he was only pretending to go along with the gods. And if that were so, Leif was nicely stuck in the middle, while, the millstones were grinding out trouble. To make things worse, he was sap enough to fall for the only girl who'd ever really appealed to him! And she had to be a goddess, as well as hating anything that Loki touched.

They came out of the forest by another trail into rough ground near the great wall, almost at the entrance of a sooty, huge building that ran back into a hill and disappeared. Fulla pointed to it. "The dwarves are in there, where you'll find them. Modsognir!"

A short, ugly creature came out, his face covered with warts, and his whole body filthy—more dirty than the rags that covered him. He was perhaps four feet high, but most of that was torso and his chest expansion must have been better than sixty inches. He nodded ponderously.

"This," Fulla told him, "is your master. The Alfadur commands that you obey his orders."

She turned quickly to leave, jerking her head aside as she swept past Leif. The little grin on her face indicated that she knew she had him going, and enjoyed that part of it thoroughly.

It was too much. He caught her by the shoulders this time, and forced her around, pulling her to him before she could draw back her arms. She was kicking and scratching as she came, but he was pleasantly stronger than she was. She tried burying her face in her shoulder, but one of his hands in her hair forced her head around. Her lips were thin and hard.

Then slowly they relaxed and parted. He pulled her closer still, letting his hand fall from her hair.

She bit him!

His hands dropped completely in surprise, and she was gone, almost stumbling in a mixture of fury and embarrassment. The snickering laughter of the dwarf behind her didn't seem to help. Leif wiped the blood off his lip, but he wasn't sorry. At least she'd remember him now!

"You're growing," Loki's voice said behind him. He spun to see the god lounging beside the dwarf, grinning. "Fulla needs a bit of taming—as who wouldn't, after being a virgin for fifty thousand years or more?"

"I'm growing sick of it all," Leif answered. "Why should I try to do anything for this cockeyed heaven of yours? I don't even know what's true and what's fakery."

LOKI SMILED with his lips, but there was no amusement now on the rest of his face. "Maybe we have been a little hard on you. I had to be—I couldn't reason with the Aesir. But don't think you can walk out on us now. Niflheim isn't any fake."

"What is this Niflheim?" Leif wanted to know. He had a vague idea of a cold hell, and no more. Idly, he noticed that Loki's speech sounded less stodgy now, particularly since leaving the meeting. Or maybe his ears were just getting used to the language, and he was hearing it as he would English. Probably Odin didn't approve of the normal, casual speech.

Loki reached into a bag at his side and pulled out a small mirror set in a frame with a handle. "I borrowed this from Odin's possessions, you might say. It's a small version of the big one on his throne. A—umm, you'd call it a window through the dimensions, perhaps. Here's Niflheim."

Leif took the mirror, looking into it curiously. Then he tried to drop it, but his hands refused to move. Something strained at his eyes, and the sight began clearing—showing people—people with…with…

The next second, he was vomiting while Loki supported him. The god had pulled the mirror out of his hand, but nothing could ease the sickness that ran through Leif. Finally he quit gagging and sat down shakily.

"That's Niflheim," Loki said, and his own voice held a tinge of what Leif had felt. "It's a place where everything is wrong—and where men can't go crazy, even, since it has two times, and one is fixed, immovable. The longer you look, the more you see—and that's true even though you stay there a million years. Some of the ones… But keep the mirror. You may need it to see the processes as they are done on your world, since you and I know you're no master of the skills we need. I wanted a few experts, but Odin would have heroes or nothing. So I did the best I could. And if I made a mess of your plans—"

"If!" Leif grunted weakly. "I couldn't go back there if you'd let me. They'll have me down for sixteen types of crimes, not to mention what will happen to the farm."

"Umm. Well, Thor protects Lee, and I'll try as much for you. When the time is right, perhaps I can visit Earth and set matters in order for you. This is the workshop."

Leif looked from the crude forge to the way one of the dwarves held a piece of heated metal in his hands on a stone anvil, while another swung at it with a crude hammer. But most of the dwarves had only their bare hands and mouths as tools. Beside him, one held a crude spear and was biting off flakes of metal with his teeth to smooth it into shape.

Loki spread his hands. "They have talents—of a sort. But—"

Leif dropped onto a rock, holding his head. This made everything just lovely. And if he failed with such equipment—Niflheim!

"Suppose I win your war with the giants?" he asked.

Loki shrugged. "Godhood and the wench, maybe. And the Aesir will take over your world and run it their way again."

Leif had a vision of that. Lord knew, men had made enough of a mess of things, but with the Aesir ruling, hell would really pop. He came to his feet suddenly, but Loki had already stepped out of the doorway.

CHAPTER FIVE

THE WORKSHOP had changed, later. The armorers had been moved out to a separate building, and the addition of a real forge, a flat anvil, some tools, and a crude grindstone had freed most of them for other work. The arms and armor were better for the new equipment.

Inside the caverns of the dwarves, the rear was filled with equipment of the same kind, but in the front sections there were simply big iron cauldrons and hoppers, joined by queerly twisting lead pipes. Leif stood beside Sudri, his foreman, watching two of the dwarves busily shoveling crude ore into a hopper. As far as he could tell, there were simply two pipes under it, with nothing further to do the work. Yet the iron sulfide ore went in, ran through the pipes, and came out as sulfur on one side and iron on the other.

Sudri clucked sharply and reached forward to taste the sulfur. He ground a lump between his teeth, swallowed, and scowled. He twisted a loop of the pipe half a degree, tasted again, and burped happily. "Pure now."

Sudri had been picked by Leif as the easiest to remember, since he was the ugliest one of them all. He looked like a maimed frog with severe glandular trouble. His nose was buried in the growths on his face, and the face was little more than a huge mouth, carried on a squat body that hopped about with grotesque joints stuck on haphazardly. The elevation above his fellows seemed to have done him good, though, and there was no question of his loyalty.

Well, they'd have gunpowder in plenty, at least. Leif had used the dimensional mirror to find and copy an up-to-date periodic table of the elements, after his first surprise at finding the dwarves had a very clear idea of atomic arrangements. They seemed to make their tests by tasting, but it worked. Now he could get any element or simple compound he wanted from them by telling Sudri what it was.

Leif grinned, remembering their slightly unorthodox method of producing nitric acid. Learning to control the kidneys really meant something here, it seemed.

Then he sobered, and turned back to his private room, lined with lead on the assumption that what would stop X-rays might stop Heimdallr's vision. He picked up the dimensional mirror glumly, and began staring through it. Using it was simple—think about some place on Earth, and there it was. But it had its limits. He could locate a library, even scan the backs of the books; but until someone opened the book at the right place, he couldn't read it.

Sudri came in expectantly. "What next, boss Leif?"

"About half a ton of U-235," Leif told him sarcastically. "Either that or some detonators."

"What are detonators?"

Leif explained as best he could. They'd been mixing small batches of the gunpowder, and they had casings for grenades, since those were crude enough for the dwarves to produce. But getting some way of setting off the grenades that would be foolproof and simple enough for the dopey heroes was another matter. He'd figured out ways, but none that the dwarves could follow in production.

Sudri scowled thoughtfully, and Leif shrugged. "Okay, I didn't really expect you to get them. Suppose you send in my milk, instead. About time Reginleif brought chow over."

Sudri's face cleared, and he was gone. Leif had found that the legendary Heidrun—the goat that gave mead—was just a plain herd of goats, giving honest milk before the gods let it ferment and mixed it with honey for the sickeningly cloying drink they used. And the boar that was supposed to be killed and eaten every night, to be restored by Odin's magic, had proved to be nothing but a horde of half-wild pigs running in the woods behind Yggdrasil.

Boiled pork and mead three times a day! No wonder Odin had ulcers. Leif hadn't found vegetables yet, but he had been able to milk the goats on the sly. The stream in back of the dwarf caves made a good place to cool it.

THERE WAS a *"hallooo"* from outside, and Lee came clanking in. He put a platter and bucket on the bench and tossed the big shield on the floor. "Met Reginleif coming with the chow. Ooof, I'm tired. Son, if we're to win this war, it looks like it's up to you. Dumb einherjar couldn't lick sugar without someone melting it for them first. How's it going?"

Leif told him in detail. He had more respect for the Ragnarok now, having gotten a good look through the mirror at the giants—frost and fire gangs both—who were massing against them. They were beasts in everything bad about the word, but they were strong, and numerous enough. Odin had good reason to fear them—and if they won and got through to Earth…

He tossed something over to Lee that resembled a gun. "Barrel inside that looks as if a dyspeptic caterpillar had crawled through butter. Two weeks work for a dozen dwarves. I'm still trying to build a lathe, but just try cutting threads on anything with no guide and no decent tools."

Lee threw the useless gun aside. "And even if we get the grenades, I'm not too sure how well they'll work against the giants, from what I hear. Thor's son Ullr—no, his stepson—anyhow, he's a nice enough guy, and quite a bowman—he wants to meet you, by the way…"

Leif grinned, in spite of himself. "Here, stop eyeing the milk and help yourself. Maybe you'll remember what you were saying then."

"Ullr says Odin's getting impatient. He didn't like your not coming to mess with the rest, and now you've been holed up here for months with no results."

They were interrupted by Sudri, bringing with him a bent, grizzled old dwarf whose skin indicated he was one of the stone dwarves. "Andvari," Sudri announced happily. "Andvari, make some detonators for the boss."

Andvari tucked a chunk of flint into his mouth, followed it with iron dust, and chewed busily. He spat suddenly, dropping a few hundred tiny crystals into his open hand. Sudri picked one from them, put it into a powder-filled grenade casing, and squeezed the hole closed with his fist.

Lee gulped, but Leif was used to it. Some day he'd have to find what these original inhabitants of Asgard were made of; it certainly wasn't protoplasm. But now he gestured for the grenade. "How's it work?"

"You throw it. When you want it to go off, it goes off when it hits."

Lee grabbed it up and was out the entrance. A moment later, the explosion sounded, and he was back. "It works. I tried it without and with thought control. Only works when you mean it to… Look, son, I'm late now. Make up some of these and send them over to Thor's place. It ought to keep them happy for a while."

Sudri looked for Leif's nod, and dragged the old dwarf out after him. Lee downed the rest of the milk and grunted wearily. "Lord, I'm tired! Tossing one of those axes around all day is work."

"You might try sleeping nights, then," Leif suggested. Lee laughed contentedly and stretched, before reaching for his big shield. Then he blinked at the three dwarves, loaded down with grenades, who came to the door to wait for him. He shrugged, winked at Leif, and headed for the entrance, the dwarves following dutifully.

Leif let the forced grin on his face die, and got up impatiently. If Lee was seeing Fulla, he didn't want to know about it. He'd seen her twice since the day of arrival, but each time she'd turned hastily and gone off elsewhere, without a word. It was a cinch that Lee wouldn't have been here all this time without feminine companionship, and most of the goddesses and valkyries were worth more by the pound than the looks.

Outside, the dwarves were busy making grenades under the direction of Sudri, while Andvari sat spitting out detonators. Leif pulled down his armor, stuck the automatic Lee had returned to him into a pocket, and went to the door. The brightness in the sky that substituted for a sun here was dimming, and the air was cool and pleasant after the closeness of the caves.

Off to the side, barely within vision, he could make out the valkyries and more energetic einherjar pairing off. Beyond that lay Thor's sprawling Bilskirnir, the most pretentious building next to Odin's. Leif grunted as he saw someone walking toward it, a figure that might be Fulla.

There was a sudden barking, coming toward him, and he saw Lobo galloping along, just as the dog seemed to see him. The next second, he was being pounced on, while a wet tongue ran over his face. Leif staggered backwards, grabbing for the dog. Then he stopped.

"All right, Loki, come off it."

THE DOG disappeared, leaving the sly god in his place,

carrying a bundle in his arms. "Either you're getting used to illusions, Leif, or I'm losing such skill at the art as I have."

"Lobo makes a whining sound in his throat when he does that. What's happened to him, anyway? I haven't seen him in three weeks."

"Nor me in two. He's been in a fight with Odin's pet wolves, and Thor's patching him up." Loki chuckled. "Thor's getting a soft spot for the dog. First he carries him over Bifrost, then buys him from Lee, and now he plays nursemaid. Smoke?"

Leif stared at the cigarette package and did a double take. His mouth watered at the sight, but he shook his head. "Not here, or we'd all blow up. Yon know we're making grenades, I suppose? Umm. How'd you get these?"

"I went back to Earth to fix things for you, as I agreed. Did you know time is different there—that five of your days go by while one passes in Asgard?"

"I guessed it from the way my watch acted, and what I saw through the mirror," Leif admitted. He was outside, lighting up eagerly as Loki joined him.

"Umm. Some of your neighbors remembered me, and it was a bit difficult for a time, though they've already passed a law making all previous crimes of the winter outlawed. But I'm not bad at convincing men of things. And after the past months, food means more than hate, and your money is still good. I've hired Faulkner to guard your place and care for it. You're in China, by the way. Ha! A pretty girl, Gail Faulkner... I brought back twenty cartons of cigarettes. A hard habit to break, once it's started."

"Loki, why can't we bring up tools from Earth? Cigarettes are fine, but—"

"Metal," Loki cut him off. "It resists the twists of Bifrost. Hoof-Tosser could carry you easily, but it took the help of two other horses to bring you, because of the metal in the automatic you carried."

"The valkyries come through wearing metal armor."

"That's elf-stuff, not regular metal. When Odin led us through Bifrost long ago, it was easier. Then Asgard seemed down hill from your Earth, but now it is otherwise. There were nine worlds connected through Bifrost then. Now only Jotunheim, Muspellheim, and Niflheim are easy to reach. Your world is closing; Vanaheim, Alfheim and the other two are closed."

Leif let it go. Loki's sense of logic was stronger than his traditions, and if he said it couldn't be done, then there was no use trying the idea on others here. He puzzled again over the contrast between what mythology he remembered and the facts. There seemed to be a logical solution behind all the magic, and that might be useful, if he could find it. But it was like the shoes of the valkyries' horses. The elves had made them, and somehow they could harden the air into a firm roadway back on Earth, but nobody knew how; even the few surviving elves from lost Alfheim no longer knew why they worked.

He'd learned a lot from Loki, but there seemed to be too much that even Loki didn't know. "How come Fulla takes care of the tree? I thought…"

"It was Idunn's task," Loki finished. "It was, until the valkyries picked up a certain hero who was also a fanatic priest of some odd new religion I note you still have. He raged first, then quieted down and turned into quite a poet, as well as hero. Bragi—he's the verse-cryer—took him in, and Idunn was all too willing to be kind to her husband's guest. Umm. Most kind. The priest got the chest with all the apples, and was across in Niflheim, next we knew."

Leif stared at Loki, shaking his head. He shivered as he remembered his vision of that place. Loki nodded.

"I said he was a fanatic. Tyr—the one-armed god—tried

to follow, but it was too much, even for him. So—well, that's why we slept a thousand of your years. The scent awakened us when the tree bloomed again, as it does each such thousand years. Odin remembered another time, with a giant named Thjazi-Idunn blamed that on me, if your myths tell of it—when the apples were lost from Idunn's carelessness, so he sent her after the priest."

So Christianity hadn't killed off the Aesir, but only put them to sleep. Apparently a taste of the apples periodically was vital to life here, though Leif wasn't sure whether it was an actual need or only a habit-forming drug.

"Heimdallr says there's an eagle around," Loki commented idly, lighting a second cigarette. "A huge one. The little illusions I cast may not be real, but some of the giant folk can actually change form, in time. This eagle may be a spy."

LEIF SUDDENLY remembered something. He pulled a little telescope from his pocket. "A gift for Heimdallr." Even though Sudri had shaped the lenses in his bare hands over the fire, according to Leif's sketches, it showed a quite clear image. "Tell him it'll triple his sight, and maybe he'll gloat about it enough to stop hanging around spying on me."

Loki looked it over and tried it out. "A good trick. It may make him as much your friend as he can be. But if you're trying to get rid of me, I can take the hint—when I'm ready to! I found and read a rather interesting book on the care of fruit trees in your collection of books."

Leif kept a careful poker face, though it hit him. "So?"

"So I think Fulla is due for a surprise. Strange. We never could get the seed to produce a tree with the same fruit, and now I find that's only normal. But we didn't know about grafting, though it's too late for that this blooming. Still, it seems there are many things that can be done to better the yield. Well, I'm back to Earth, for a little while. Good luck with the tree."

The god chuckled, and again the form of Lobo went off through the dark.

Leif picked up a sack of chemicals, a crude spade, and a saw. Then he headed out through the gathering dusk toward the tree. He'd been examining it for some time, and the samples of dirt from around it had confirmed his suspicions of the trouble. Loki had guessed right, though he hoped none of the others got the idea. They were suspicious enough to kill first and examine motives afterwards.

But it was as nearly dark as Asgard ever became as he reached the tree. Against the glow of the sky, he could see the worn old limbs, and the dirt in his fingers smelled wrong to his nose. It was a shame to neglect a fruit tree, and the farmer in him hurt. Besides, if the gods were to win the Ragnarok, they'd need more strength than from green, stunted apples.

He spaded in the fertilizer, which the dwarves had made to his specifications, getting the feel of the earth again. It was pleasant, after the crazy life he'd been leading. He finished that, finally, and began carrying water in the leather sack, washing the fertilizer in. Sometimes lately he even began to believe that the gods should win the war for Earth's good. Afterwards—well he had one wish. Maybe something could be done with it. And he no longer was sure the gods could take Earth; they were a lot less powerful than he'd first thought. And they were lousy horticulturists!

He climbed into the tree and began sawing off the dead wood, pruning it back. It was a smallish tree, completely unimpressive, and the work was less troublesome than he'd expected. At least the armor protected him from sharp twigs, as he'd thought. He painted tar over the cuts, hauled the brushwood away, and stood back, examining the tree again from the ground. It looked lean and plucked now, but the dead wood wouldn't sap all its energy, and the ground would nourish it.

Finally, he wrapped the spade and saw in the sack and headed down the trail. Luck was with him, it seemed. None of the gods had spotted him, and Heimdallr was probably busy with other things, not looking this close to the center of Asgard.

He turned around a bend in the path and collided sharply with the figure of a woman! Then, as he bent to help her up, he saw it was Fulla!

CHAPTER SIX

SHE WAS moaning slightly as he lifted her, and she winced as he started to release her. Then she stood upright, and he took his hands away.

She started to step toward him, and moaned again, stumbling. He paused, irresolute, but only for a moment. The next second, he had scooped her up into his arms and was carrying her off the trail, to a spot where he'd seen a smooth, mossy section a few days before. As he moved with her, she glanced up, and he realized his face must show against the sky. She jerked a little, before sinking back against his armor.

"What's wrong?" he asked, as he dropped her gently onto the moss.

"It's my ankle. I twisted it. It's nothing—it'll be all right in a few minutes." She winced again as his fumbling fingers found the ankle. "No, don't stop. It hurt at first; now it feels nice, Lee."

Lee? Of course, they looked and sounded alike, except that their attitudes colored their expressions. He puzzled over her choice, until the clinking of his armor penetrated his senses. Naturally—he'd left it off since the first day, while Lee had apparently grown into his. She'd guessed by that.

"Better?" he asked.

"Mmm. Sit here, Lee. I thought you were with Gefjun tonight. She'll be jealous if she finds you're out alone— worse, if she finds you with me."

Leif grinned, remembering Gefjun, another of the virgin goddesses. So Lee had been doing all right, even if he hadn't been seeing Fulla. He tried to call up some of Lee's mannerisms. "Let her be jealous then. Who kissed me first, you or Gefjun?"

"True." She slid downwards and closer to him. After the unwashed naturalness of most of the females of Asgard, he was surprised to notice that her hair was faintly and pleasantly fragrant. "I began to think you'd forgotten that kiss, Lee Svensen."

"Had you forgotten, honey?" It wasn't good, being mistaken for another man, but it was better than nothing. The armor was suddenly hot around him, and he was sweating. He reached for the buckles.

She bent to help him with it, and her hands we're caressing. At last it was off, and she was closer. Her voice was a whisper. "I haven't forgotten, Lee. But even a goddess can't remember forever—one kiss."

He tried to laugh as Lee would have laughed. It sounded hollow to him, and the blood was pounding in his ears, but it seemed that she accepted it as Lee's laugh. "There should be a moon now," he tried to say lightly, as he bent forward. "With that, maybe this Asgard of yours could be heaven."

The moon had nothing to do with it, though, as he discovered. It was heaven—a strange, bitter heaven. He tried to forget that she thought she was with his brother, and failed; but even that bitterness couldn't steal all the pleasure from him.

She sighed softly as he withdrew reluctantly, letting his lips break slowly from hers. Then her arms tightened again, and she was pulling him down, her mouth demanding. Her breasts strained tautly against him as his hand tightened on her back, and her body turned slowly, bringing the flat of her hips against him.

"Oh, Leif! Leif!"

FOR A SECOND, there was only the caress of her voice, small and hoarse in the darkness. Then the words penetrated. He jerked suddenly away, freeing her. "You knew me?"

She shuddered, pulling herself slowly up. Leif fumbled for a cigarette, and he could see her face white and tense in the light of the match. Her eyes widened as he drew in the smoke, but it was unimportant to her now. Her lashes were dropping as the match went out, her fingers twisting into odd shapes. Her voice was tiny and lost in the space around them.

"I knew, Leif. I saw you going this way—and I started to follow, to watch you and—hate you. Then I didn't want to see you. I went back—but I came, after all. I thought I'd never find you! And I didn't hurt my ankle."

"But what about the Lee act, then?"

"I had a plan—I thought. If I met you and you thought I took you for Lee...then it really wouldn't count." Her voice was even lower, and she hesitated. "I knew how you felt, or I thought I did. And I wanted you to suffer. I couldn't mix with Loki's treason, but if you thought it was Lee that I liked...somehow it would be all right for me then. And you'd be even more miserable afterwards. Oh, Leif, I—" She let out a deep breath and then said, "And then—then I couldn't pretend. You could hate me, Leif."

He tossed the smoke aside and turned toward her. "I could—but I don't."

She sighed, slowly relaxing back onto the moss. "Fifty thousand years is a long time to wait." She pushed the hair back from his head, her long fingers lingering and trembling faintly. "I'm glad I waited, beloved."

DAWN WAS creeping up as Leif tossed the last cigarette in the package aside and climbed to his feet, reaching for his armor. Fulla stirred, watching him, before putting out her hand for him to lift her. "We'd better be getting back," he told her. "I should have taken you home hours ago."

She nodded, but pulled his arms around her again, snuggling against his shoulder. Her cheek rubbed against his arm, and he lifted one hand to the back of her neck, drawing his fingers around and past the lobe of her ear. Suddenly he felt her body stiffen. She began drawing back, her hand slowly going to her breast, as she slid out of his arms.

"My tree!"

He'd forgotten the blasted tree, but he looked now. Seen in the full light of day, it was a bleak sight, with most of its branches missing, and the thinness of its foliage showing fully. Every scar he'd put on it stood out clearly. Then another gasp came from Fulla, and he looked down to see her staring at the sack dropped on the trail, with the saw sticking out from it.

There was disbelief in her voice. "You! You ruined the tree—the life of Asgard! My charge...and I—I—"

He caught her shoulders, pulling her around to face him. "Of course I did, Fulla. It was dying from the deadwood, and from lack of food in its soil. I did it because I couldn't see you failing your job. Damn it, I did it because I was in love with you."

"My tree!" She sagged in his hands, slipping out of them, and falling flat on the moss. Her eyes remained fixed of the tree, and there were tears in them, while sobs slowly began to wrack her body. "And I trusted you—loved you. Oh, don't worry, Loki's companion! You succeeded in your plan. I won't tell the Aesir on you. You made sure of that! But I hate you, hate you, hate…"

"Fulla!" He bent toward her, but she screamed.

"Don't you dare touch me!"

"Fulla! You said you loved me. Now you jump to the first wrong conclusion against me. Will you listen, let me show you what I did and why? Or are you going to go on believing the worst—on circumstantial evidence?"

He bent again, and this time she didn't scream. Instead, she turned viciously, swinging her right hand—with a rock in it.

Leif stood back coldly, spitting out a tooth and blood without feeling the blow. He was numb and empty. "All right, Fulla. Tell your damned gods, if you like. And when you find what a fool you've been, remember I tried to tell you the truth—and that I did love you. I thought you were someone I could hold to. I thought a lot of fool things. I should have known you were just a goddess, like Frigg—no good without your pedestal. Well, if you ever want me, whistle. It'll give you something to do while you wait fifty thousand more years!"

He picked up the sack and slapped it over his shoulder without looking at her. Her painful sobbing went on as he turned down the trail, and something in him hated the sound and ached to go back and still it. The larger part of him was frozen with hurt and anger. Love without respect and trust might do for the gods, but he wanted more than that out of life.

Heimdallr and Loki were doing the impossible by standing amicably together at the foot of the path as he came out of the woods, but he barely noticed that the self-styled son of nine mothers was busily polishing the little telescope and beaming. He nodded toward them and went on grimly, heading for the workshop. Sudri would look beautiful after this past night.

"Leif." Loki was running to catch up with him. "Arroo! I'd better get our lady Fir to bandage that lip. It looks as if Thor had hit you."

"Grin just once, Loki," Leif told him, "and you'll wish Thor'd hit *you!*"

LOKI BLINKED and stepped back, his eyes shrewdly appraising, and a touch of malicious amusement showed on his lips. "Oho! So. And our farmer is suddenly turned into a berserk hero. Well...Odin *will* be happy..."

His grin slipped off as Leif moved toward him. There was a haze in the air and a rattlesnake drew back fangs and threatened, where Loki had been. Leif reached for the automatic, judging where Loki must actually be, and the snake turned back into the god, this time with no amusement. "Enough, Leif. Sometimes my mouth is a fool. Consider it unsaid."

The anger suddenly evaporated from Leif, taking most of the numbness with it. Only the pain was left. He could feel the starch running out of his system, and made no effort to stiffen again. Loki's eyes were sympathetic now, as he slapped Leif gently on the back.

"There was a girl once—about so high—" he said casually, indicating the point of his chin, but there was a curious edge to his voice. "Only she didn't stay that high. Giants mature at no greater height than ours, but like the snakes of old, they keep growing. Sigyn was seventeen feet when I saw her last; she called me a ridiculous runt and threw me out. Funny how I still remember the girl she was. Well..."

Something like the boom of thunder crossed with the crack of a board breaking rolled over them then, in sound waves that were physical enough to stir the leaves of the trees. Leif snapped out of his trance.

Above the entrance to the dwarf cave, a plume of smoke was rising, with a billowing cloud under it that still contained bits of timbers. The powder there had obviously exploded, all at once.

A picture of Sudri's misassorted body coming down in pieces jumped to Leif's mind, and his legs began moving. Loki looked startled, and then went along, matching his leaps. They came over the rise of ground, and were among the hillocks, darting along the path, while the acridly sweet smell of powder hit their noses.

Leif gave a quick look to the leaning timbers, and then was inside. A yelling voice reached him, and he turned toward it. Sudri was bent over the broken form of Andvari, shouting in the glottal stops and Bantu clicks of the stone dwarf dialect, but the mouth of the old dwarf barely moved.

Surprisingly, the damage hadn't been as great as Leif feared. The solid stone wall separating the front section from the rear still stood, and the explosion had reached only the front wooden entrance. There were no other bodies.

Sudri saw him then, and faced him. "Someone came in and threw a grenade. I yelled. Andvari held back the detonator. It was still partly his to control. We all went to the back, but he had to stay. He was too old to hold it long, and it went off. Not too bad. Most of the powder was in the grenades, already stored in the rear. But you see how it is."

Leif nodded and turned to the old dwarf, whose pain-filled eyes were raised to his. "Who?"

Sudri shrugged, but the old one motioned, and Leif bent over. There was a gasp as the stone dwarf fought with the unfamiliar soft sounds so foreign to his speech. But he formed them and Leif heard.

"Vali Odinsson."

Then he dropped back, dead before his head touched the floor.

Sudri touched Leif reassuringly. "Don't worry about the detonators, boss Leif. Andvari told me the trick in his speech. I don't understand all, but any stone dwarf will. We have lots of detonators, already."

The foreman turned, shouting back, while the cowering dwarves began to come out, staring at the wreckage. "You, Bifurr, Nori, Onarr, Mjodvitnir, Vindalfr, Fundinn, Throinn—you fix things. We'll be in production in three hours, boss Leif."

"Yeah," Leif said absently, still staring at the old dwarf. He'd only seen the grim old figure a few minutes, but...he wondered what he would have done with a bomb he could delay but not stop. Damn Vali!

HE HEARD the sound of others behind him, and swiveled on his heel to face the crowd that was collecting. "Lee, you can stay if you like—Thor, too. The rest of you get the hell out of here before I set Sudri's crew on you with grenades. Gods, heroes, whatever you are, beat it! And from now on, anyone who comes too near this place—even Odin himself—without my okay, gets a grenade in his guts."

Thor came up, stern questions in his eyes. "Why, Leif Svensen?"

Loki spoke quick words into the ear of the black-bearded god, and Thor nodded. "So? Then good. I have little use for a leader who will not safeguard his men, even if they're but dwarves. Back, all of you, before I try my fist on you."

Leif could see Fulla racing up as the crowd turned, her eyes darting toward the entrance and striking his. He tightened his lips and swung back to the cleaning up that was going on; a moment later, he saw her running off again, toward the path to a tree, while the crowd grudgingly left.

Vali! It would do no good to confront him, since he was one of Odin's sons, and Leif had nothing more than the word of a dying dwarf, heard by himself and apparently by Loki. Or had it been only Vali? He'd warned Loki about the danger from a spark here, and Loki had known what a grenade could do from Leif's words. Leif no longer wanted to distrust the sly god, but...

"Look!" Loki caught his arm and pointed. High above, gliding like a vulture, a dim speck showed in the sky. From it came a harsh, mocking cry. "The eagle—much too big for that height, too. It must be a spying giant."

"Fine," Leif commented. "So he knows we have boom stuff. He didn't set this off, though. All right, Sudri, carry Andvari's body back gently. We'll bury him in whatever rite his people use. Lee, sometimes I'd like to be one of those blooming berserkers. But there's nothing you can do here, if you've got other business."

"I'm supposed to demonstrate the grenades," Lee said. His face was serious, and he tipped his helmet as he passed the body of Andvari. "Let me know if you need help."

Leif moved back through the caverns, examining the packed grenades that hadn't gone off; production had been fine. He kicked a small sack on the floor and swore at its weight. He stopped to toss it aside, just as Sudri spotted him.

"No!" The dwarf was suddenly under him, waving excited hands. "Bad stuff, boss Leif. It's okay for dwarves, not for men. That's the U-235 you wanted. Half a ton. It keeps better in small pieces."

Leif gulped, and nodded. "It does, son—it certainly does."

He should have known better than to try sarcasm on a dwarf; he'd mentioned it, it was an existent isotope—so here it was. Half a ton of it, in little bags of less than critical mass. How did the dwarves know that, and what did the gods need of humans to show them how to beat Ragnarok? Then he realized that some dwarf had probably gotten too much together in assembling it, but that it wouldn't explode when brought together slowly—that had to be done instantly, before its own heat boiled it away. Apparently the dwarves were radioactive-immune.

He watched them storing it away carefully, and went back to superintend the reconstruction, noticing his tooth was already growing back. Idly, he heard the detonation of grenades, and wondered how the gods were impressed by Lee's display. There were explosions again, followed by a long, sustained yell.

The walls were almost whole once more when Reginleif came up, stopping well beyond the entrance and hallooing.

Leif shrugged and moved out, with Loki behind him. Now what? They'd probably heard about the tree—unless it was something worse.

"If I don't come back, Sudri," he called, "look me up in Niflheim."

But it wasn't a very humorous crack. It had too much possible truth in it.

CHAPTER SEVEN

LEIF'S eyes skimmed over the crowd as he reached the Yggdrasil judgment place, trying to estimate where he stood. It didn't look good. Loki whistled faintly in surprise behind him.

Frigg was speaking to Odin, and her righteousness was all too evident. Beside Odin, Vali and Vidarr were nodding vigorously at what she said. Odin's shoulders were slumped more than usual, but they straightened as he saw Leif coming, and a gesture cut off the words. Heimdallr was intently polishing the lens of his new toy, and his face was inscrutable.

Fulla sat at the foot of Frigg's dais, her face lowered. She glanced up at the stir around her, and her eyes met Leif's for a moment. Something that might have been the beginning of a wan smile touched her lips, but vanished as he stared at her.

Lee started toward his brother, and Thor lifted himself from his seat holding Lobo's collar in one hand, the big hammer in the other. A lithe young husky Leif recognized as Thor's stepson, Ullr, scratched his head, and moved with them. They lined up beside Leif.

"Tell 'em to go to hell," Lee whispered.

But Odin's voice cut off any chance to ask for information.

"Leif Svensen, a time has come for judging. There is treason in Asgard, I have promised to my son Thor that your words shall be heard. But as a pupil of your patron Loki, who shall believe those words? Speak, though, and defend yourself."

"Nice unbiased justice, Valfather," Leif commented disgustedly. "Well, I've had a sample of Asgard's judging before this, today. I should have expected it. What in hell am I supposed to have done? If you mean the explosion in the workshop, there was treason, but none of my doing. You might try cleaning out your own household, on that."

He saw Fulla's face whiten at his reference to the morning, but his eyes snapped back quickly to Odin, whose one eye seemed to be shining from a thundercloud. Vali came to his feet, his ferret-face tautening. Leif stared at him, spat on the ground, and rubbed it out with his foot. But the son of Odin only grinned nastily.

"You are accused of trying to destroy the einherjar," his bland voice announced. "The grenades which you gave were to be safe when not thrown with intent to destroy. And, to be sure, they behaved well when your brother handled them. But Vidarr and I have been given cause to suspect all is not well, and we demanded the right to test them. Behold!"

Leif's eyes followed his pointing finger to a gory mess on the ground near Odin's throne.

"Fifty or more loyal einherjar, Leif Svensen!" Odin took up the tale as Vali sank back to his seat. "From but two of those creations of yours, thrown by my sons. Nor can all my skill call them back to life again, scattered as they are. Shall we gather at Vigridr for the Ragnarok to find our weapons shall remove our heroes, leaving us defenseless before the Sons of the Wolf? Nor does it seem that your treason stops there. But speak!"

Leif turned his eyes to Loki, but the sly god was staring intently back down the trail toward the shops. Niflheim pressed close, and Leif could feel the sickness of that vision stealing back over him. He turned to Lee, to see his brother holding a single grenade in one hand, doubtfully figuring the chances. It wouldn't work, Leif knew; there'd be some left, at least—enough to send them both to Niflheim if Lee threw the grenade. But—if he could get his hands on it and move back from his small group of friends, it could put him in no condition to be revived for Niflheim. Compared to that place, death would be a vacation.

HE MOVED slowly toward Lee, facing Odin again. "Okay, I suppose you expect me to scream protests you wouldn't believe anyway. What good would it do? All right, so the mishandled grenades wiped out some of your einherjar. And so I did mess around with the sacred tree of yours…"

Fulla was suddenly erect, screaming something, but the clamor of the others drowned the words. Leif slipped the few remaining feet to his brother and grabbed the grenade. Now if he had time to get into clear space…

"More grenades, boss Leif?" Sudri's voice asked roughly

beside him.

He jerked his head down to see the dwarves mixed with the little group around him. Loki was grinning, rubbing his hand over a grenade, and the dwarves all held weapons of their own. But before Leif could adjust his mind to the new facts, Loki's voice cut through the din.

"It would seem that the question is now whether Leif Svensen can be sent to Niflheim safely, Odin," he announced. "There are those present who feel that justice has not yet been rendered, and among them is Oku-Thor and myself. You have seen what two of these can do. We have scores of them, and the skill to use them, which it would seem Vali and Vidarr lacked. Am I right, Thor?"

Thor nodded. "The grenades worked when I tried them, as well as Mjollnir itself. Until the facts are clear, this man has my protection, Father Odin. I demand justice."

Surprisingly, Heimdallr was coming toward them, pulling a huge sword from its scabbard. There was nothing foppish about him now; the softness seemed to have vanished, and the sword was a living thing in his hand. He took his place as far from Loki as he could, but clearly lining himself up on Leif's side.

Fulla had also left the front and was moving to them, but she hesitated as Leif faced her, pausing irresolutely.

"But the tree?" Odin was unused to having his court divided, and uncertain of the menace confronting him. Most of the other gods were shifting unhappily, not knowing what to do. "Thor, you heard him admit to defiling the tree."

"Then I say send one to the tree to examine the damage first, and judge later!"

Heimdallr waved the big sword casually. "No need. I've been watching the tree through this bit of magic which our young warlock rightly thought useful to one of my skill." He pulled it out and stared through the telescope, preening himself a bit as the attention of all focused on him. Leif still couldn't see how his sight could penetrate through the obstacles between him and the tree, or how the telescope could help there; perhaps it was extra-sensory sight, and the telescope helped only psychologically. But Heimdallr seemed satisfied.

"The apples are ripe, and new shoots come forth," he announced. "It would seem Leif Svensen has certain abilities with such things."

Another yell went up from the gods, and the ravens suddenly left Odin's shoulders, darting out toward the tree. Fulla's face abruptly came to beaming life, and she sprang forward toward Leif.

He grinned crookedly. He'd expected that. Now that the weather was clearing, she wanted to be out in the sun. He jerked his thumb back at her, and swung on his heel to face the more forthright figure of Thor.

He wasn't too surprised when the ravens came back, each with a yellow apple in its beak. Time here could do funny tricks, it seemed, such as compressing weeks into hours for the fruit to respond to his treatment. Odin took one of the apples, smelled it, and bit into it. He bit again, and ten years seemed to fall from his shoulders. Others were reaching for the apple, but he shook them off.

"Leif Svensen, you have permission to stand beside us."

Leif scowled, but Loki's hand shoved him forward, and he moved up to the seat, mounting the little dais. Odin's hand reached out with the apple, and there was only benevolence on the god's face.

REACTION was hitting at Leif, making his legs tremble as he stood there, and the bravado that had somehow lasted through all the danger was gone. But as he managed to control his teeth and bite down on the apple, a sudden raw current of power rushed through him. He swallowed automatically, while a warmth and strength diffused over him. Whatever was in the apples, it was powerful stuff.

"For this, Leif Svensen," Odin told him, "I would gladly forgive many things. And because this was no traitor's act, I am moved to accept Loki's explanation that it was but lack of skill in the hands of my sons that caused the grenade to wreak such evil. Or perhaps the influence of the spying eagle Heimdallr has seen. The matter of turning some of the Aesir away from me is otherwise, but there was some justice on their side. You may go back to your work, and we shall consider the events of this day to have struck a balance. I declare judgment, and the Thing adjourned."

Leif stepped down, considering. But this was no time to try to take care of Vali. He slipped back, letting his eyes flicker across Fulla's face quickly, and rejoined Loki. The god was turning the dwarves back hastily toward the shop, and Leif realized that it might go ill with them if they stayed around to remind the Aesir that they had come out to rescue him. He began leading them off quickly, while the gods clustered around Odin, waiting their turn for the apples.

But Loki was back with him before he reached the workshop, and Ullr had followed him.

"The youngster has brought something forth which is unexpected in the Aesir," Loki told Leif, grinning. "He's had an idea! And by now you know how rare that is, and why I spend so much time with you. Well, out with it, Ullr."

"I was thinking that those grenades are good things. But even better would be arrows—made hollow and with the same stuff inside—to explode when they hit. Can that be done?"

Leif took one of the arrows that the god held out and examined it. It was thicker than most he'd seen, and he estimated the matter quickly. The dwarves could produce crude sheet metal, and they could weld it in some mysterious way. The inner side wouldn't have to be perfect for this, provided it was ground straight and in balance on the outside. He passed it to Sudri, and the dwarf nodded his big head, while his mouth opened in a grin that went three quarters of the way around his neck.

Later Leif watched Ullr go off with Loki to try out the new arrows. Since they wouldn't explode until wanted, the same ones could be used for target practice. He turned back to his private room, rebuilt and relined. On impulse, he stripped the wristwatch from his arm and handed it to Sudri.

"Nice work coming up with those grenades. Thanks."

The dwarf gobbled incoherently, strapping it onto his thick wrist and listening to it tick. He'd been fascinated by it since he'd first learned its purpose. Leif grinned and shut the door after him. Sudri could use it for an interval timer, even if it didn't keep Asgard time.

HE PICKED up the mirror and scowled at it, jerking it quickly past his eyes. But even the brief glimpse of Niflheim was too much. Shuddering, he put the mirror away. Well, he'd passed the first crisis, and he knew who his friends were.

Loki apparently could be trusted in a pinch; the trouble was that he was the most intelligent of the gods, and the only one to prefer wit to muscle. Maybe it had led him into some of the tricks of which the legends accused him, but it also put him firmly on the side of anyone who could meet his intelligence. Thor was a god of absolutes, but he could be trusted so long as someone didn't pull the wool over his eyes. Ullr was so hopped up over having become an inventor that he'd go to any lengths, practically, for the man who could make the arrows. And Heimdallr was more or less on Leif's side—though his foreknowledge of the condition of the tree made his position a little doubtful.

But the rest of them would be just that much more against him because of the split that had occurred. They wouldn't like the idea of a mere man challenging them and getting away with it. Odin might be happy now with his apples, but the best that could be said for the day was that it had produced another truce. And there was the combination of Vali, Vidarr and Frigg lined up against him.

The next time, there wouldn't be any convenient apples to sway their decision.

He got up as a halloo sounded from outside and went out for his supper. Then he stopped in the doorway, staring. Reginleif had been replaced by Fulla. Well, why not? Wasn't he the boy who'd saved her precious tree and hence assured her of her new job?

He cursed the weakness in him that made his hands tremble as he took the bucket and platter from her.

"I found some vegetables," she said tonelessly. "Loki told me you wanted them, and how to make what he called a stew. Perhaps Loki is not all evil. There is fresh milk, not mead. I—I've never eaten stew."

He stared at it slowly, noticing that there was something that looked like cabbage and carrots mixed with the rest, as well as grain to thicken it. "Okay, wait a minute."

He went inside, and came back again a minute later. "I've taken half of it—that's plenty. You might as well have what's here; better for your complexion, anyhow, than straight meat."

She'd seized the bucket as if to dump its contents, but now she let it fall to her side. Without a word, she turned slowly and headed back toward the main buildings.

Drat women, goddesses or otherwise! He clumped back in and started to eat the stew. It wasn't too bad, but each mouthful was harder to swallow than the one before. Finally he pushed it aside and picked up the mirror.

He found what he was seeking at last, and carefully watched operations that were supposed to be so secret that not a hundred men knew them fully. Obviously, the making of atomic bombs had been simplified considerably since he'd first read the descriptions of them. In a pinch, the dwarves could turn them out. The means for bringing the two masses of U-235 together violently weren't too difficult, and the same trick detonator would set off the charge that would start the operation.

Just what could be done with them when they were made was another matter, though it seemed a shame to have all that power lying around without using it.

He tasted the stew again, muttered to himself, and began putting on his armor. The trouble was, he needed some company. And the solution to that was to go up where Lee and Lobo were, at Thor's place. He clumped out, automatically started along the trail that led to the tree, and then swore again as he struck out firmly for Bilskirnir.

REGINLEIF brought his next meals to him, but the vegetables and milk continued. If Fulla was preparing the food, she at least showed signs of being a fair natural cook, since the food improved, and began developing a certain amount of variety. Leif avoided Loki's eyes when the god was around at the arrival of the meals.

But the work in the shop was going well enough. They had grenades and to spare, as well as a good supply of the explosive arrows. Leif delayed the final decision on the U-235 bombs, but finally called the dwarves in and outlined it. He was right—the things were within their powers, though he had no way to test the finished ones, and could see no way to use them. Still, it kept the shop busy, and would furnish a good talking point for any trouble that might arise.

The group at Thor's proved as dull as his own company,

since Lee was chiefly worried about some means of getting a measure of efficiency out of the heroes, and Thor's lack of humor grew ponderous in time. Leif even tried spying on the news back on Earth, either from the few newspapers that were beginning again, or by watching the events as they happened, but the difference in the time that had passed there and what he felt had passed made it all seem unreal. Things had been unbelievable during the winter, but the worst was now past, and the prophecy had been wrong about there being three such years with no summer. The lethargic hopelessness of near starvation—and real starvation—was giving place to a surprising cooperation in getting back to normal life, but he could work up no real interest in merely watching it. If he could get back to his farm…

Finally, when Reginleif brought a rather good meat loaf with vegetables on the side, Leif gave up. He told himself he was sick of being reminded of the fool he'd been, and that something was going to have to be done about it. He'd see Fulla for once and for all, and take care of things properly.

He felt better as he buckled on his armor and went out the doorway.

Then he paused. Coming toward him in the gathering twilight, with a happy smile on her lips, was Fulla. Beside her, Vidarr strode along, motioning down toward the shop. They were still a couple hundred yards away, but obviously coming toward him. Leif started to duck back, just as Vidarr caught her arm. Leif was puzzling over the two of them together when a sudden cry from above jerked his head up.

Huge against the little light of the sky, the giant eagle was plummeting down, headed straight for the two. Leif fumbled for his automatic, yelling. But Fulla had seen it already, and was trying to run. The wings of the bird suddenly shot out, stopping its fall, and it drove toward her, blotting her from Leif's sight. Then it was lifting. Fulla was clutched firmly in its talons.

And still strapped at her side was the chest that held all of the apples.

Leif fired at the eagle, knowing the distance was too great, and took a shot at the running figure of Vidarr—futilely. He could see the eagle rising rapidly now, heading out toward the wall. Another cry came from its beak, and it began to struggle heavily. There was a corruscating flash of rainbow fire and the eagle and Fulla seemed to dwindle into nothing.

It had crossed Bifrost into Jotunheim, taking Fulla and the apples with it to an unknown fate!

CHAPTER EIGHT

FOR A FROZEN second, Leif stood there cursing himself. It was obvious that Vidarr had told Fulla Leif wanted her, and she had been coming to a tryst that would have been pointless if he hadn't been such a pig-headed fool. Now, without the apples, the gods would be sleeping pushovers for the giants, leaving Bifrost wide open for them to get on to Earth. He'd seen enough of the giants through the mirror to know what that would mean.

Maybe he couldn't win Ragnarok, but he'd done a nice job of losing, it—in the worst possible way.

Then he swiveled and dashed back into the shop, tossing savage words at Sudri, and grabbing for the mirror. He took one quick look, spotted Fulla and the eagle in it, and tucked it into his pocket. Sudri was pelting away toward Bilskirnir as Leif came out and struck across the field at a full run, cursing the weight of his armor, but having no time to remove it.

He could smell the stables as he came near them, and he turned in hastily. Reginleif was busy currying one of the horses, while the goddess Gna was watching. Leif grabbed Gna's shoulder and swung her around. "Which is Hoof-

Tosser?"

She started to protest, but her eyes had tipped him off. He dropped her and headed for the horse. Gna came after him, trying to hold him away, but he had no time for fooling. He planted his fist under her chin, watched her crumple, and faced Reginleif. The valkyr blinked, squirmed as the automatic came out, and then plunged in to pull the horse out.

"Saddle him!"

She obeyed, and Leif came up. Hoof-Tosser was skittish, but Leif knew horses. He gentled the animal, forcing his excitement away, speaking into the stallion's ears. Then he swung into the saddle, lifted Hoof-Tosser onto his rear legs, and pivoted about and out of the stable.

He headed straight for the wall, wondering how to steer upwards. He wasn't even certain that the animal could lift into the air, except on Earth, as it was mythically supposed to. But it seemed to understand when he drew back on both reins, made a convulsive leap, and was airborne. Leif had no idea of how to cross Bifrost or whether the armor he wore would cause trouble, but it was too late to wonder.

"Jotunheim, Hoof-Tosser," he ordered.

The horse whickered, then drew back its head and screamed. Leif tried to imitate it, and realized it wasn't unlike the cry Reginleif had given in going from Earth. Already, the air was taking on the rainbow ripples he remembered. His armor was growing warm, and there was a queer twisting resistance, but the steps of the horse didn't falter this time; Loki had been right in saying entrance was easier to the other worlds than to Earth.

Under him, Asgard turned to nothing but color ripples, that disappeared in turn; Leif looked down to see a cold gray landscape under him, scraggy with huge boulders, and looking like something left over from a period of glaciation.

He glanced at the mirror now, turning it until he could find the giant. But it refused to work—naturally, since it worked only *through* the dimensions!

Far ahead, there was a victorious scream, such as a bird might make, and Leif headed the horse toward it. But though Hoof-Tosser went on eating up the distance, he could see nothing of his object. He shook his head, to swing suddenly at a call from beside him.

For a second, he thought it was the eagle, only to realize that this was a great hawk. Hoof-Tosser nickered, and the hawk drew up. "You're headed right, Leif," Loki's voice called.

THE HAWK somehow landed on the horse's back, and began to struggle. A fine membrane seemed to peel off, and Loki emerged from it, stuffing a small bundle into a pouch he wore. "Freyja's hawk garment—elf work at its best. Do you know what you're getting into?"

Leif shook his head.

"I can't help you," Loki told him. "At least, not inside one of their forts. They'd smell Asgard on me. You may be able to pass. Look, Sudri only barely told me that you were off after Fulla and the apples. Who's responsible?"

Leif told him, and the god nodded. He began to fill Leif in as best he could on the general habits of the frost giants, wasting no time on anything but practical details. Most of his knowledge was unencouraging. Then he pointed down, and Leif could see a rugged castle below, apparently hewn out of one of the great boulders. He made out a lighted courtyard of some kind.

Loki had the reins of Hoof-Tosser and was urging him down. "We'd best land yonder, and you walk the rest of the way. I'll try to conceal Hoof-Tosser and work my way close. If you get free, whistle three times and the horse will come.

Don't worry about me—I can find my way back. Just get Fulla to Asgard; those apples are our first worry."

Leif slipped from the horse's back, shaking his head as Loki held out a sword to him. He'd do better with the automatic. And if he was lucky, maybe he wouldn't need even that. These were the giants near Bifrost, picked to resemble and spy on the gods—and through their own careful breeding, he wouldn't be too unlike some of them; according to Loki, the barely mature giants were no bigger than a man. He might be able to pass as one.

Getting into the castle proved easy enough. There was a spillway for rainwater at the side, and he hoisted himself up and through the wall. Light shone out from an opened door, and there was no one in the courtyard. Inside sounded an excited babble. Leif gritted his teeth, and stepped in as if he had business there. But no one was looking toward him.

All he could see was a pair of twisted, hairy legs blocking the door and supporting a massive body. Then they moved, and through them Leif could see bits of giants and chairs, and something at the far end that looker like a glass case with a big sword in it. The top of it was suddenly opened by a huge hand, and Fulla's chest of apples dropped beside the sword. There was a hoarse bellow of laughter, and Fulla's voice shrieked.

Leif twisted through the legs of the giant, and moved into the room, an immense place, well packed with giants of all sizes and types, some with tusks, others with long fangs, and a few that looked almost human in a bestial way. All were intently watching a thirty-foot giant at the head of the table, who was casually holding Fulla in one hand. The other hand came out, swishing the thick hairs on the knuckles across her face. She flinched, twisted her head, and spotted Leif.

She covered the expression almost at once, but it had betrayed him. The giant over Leif looked down and yelped.

"Baldar!" Leif felt a taloned hand suddenly grab his middle, and he was sailing fifty feet through the air. "Hey, Skirnir!"

The giant who'd held Fulla reached out a hand and caught Leif. The breath whistled from his body, and his ribs creaked, but the hand had cushioned the shock. The giant turned him over, staring out of narrowed eyes. "Hmm. No, not Baldar, though he looks something like that one. New one, and he doesn't smell like a hero, either—real flesh. Thought I'd learned everything. As when I was a kid spying on them as Freyr's messenger."

From the back, a croaking bellow came, and Leif saw something that was neither eagle nor giant, but turning slowly from one to the other. The thing croaked again, and its head became all giant. "It's the warlock—Leif they call him. Hai, Vali said he'd come."

"Of course I came," Leif yelled. The quiver that was running through him wouldn't show so much if he bellowed back at them. "As a warlock—Witolf's kin—do you think I'd work willingly for the Aesir? When all the confusion came up, I lit out over Bifrost for your group on the double."

SKIRNIR laughed heartily, slapping his thigh. He wasn't bad looking, in spite of his size, and he was unlike all the others in wearing a smile. But under it, there was something Leif had seen only in the eyes of a man who had tried to beat a dog to death. That man had been smiling, too, until Lee had knocked him unconscious.

"It won't work, warlock. We heard of you from Vali and Vidarr. Here, since you love the wench, join her. We won't separate you. We'll roast you together, and after you tell us of Asgard, I personally will eat both of you. How's that for real uniting?"

He chuckled at his humor. Fulla moved toward Leif, her legs tottering under her. Leif's were in a little better condition. He was reasonably sure the giants didn't eat people, but a lot surer of the sadism behind the taunt. Fulla's eyes were hell-wracked as she slumped against a big mug beside him.

"I got you into this. Oh, Leif, I'm such a..."

Then she screamed, and Leif saw Skirnir picking up a huge ember in tongs, to begin moving it toward them. He reached for his automatic, yanked it frantically out and squeezed the trigger. Nothing happened! He'd forgotten to reload. Skirnir had started to duck, dropping the ember, but now the giant grinned again. He flicked the gun from Leif's hands and pulled the pouch of clips away in a snapping motion.

He tossed the ammunition into the case with the sword and apples, and tried to examine the gun. It was too small for him, but he seemed satisfied. With a malicious smile, he threw it back to Leif and reached for another ember.

A bellow came from the rear, cutting off his enjoyment of the scene. One of the smaller giants rushed up, tossing Loki's helmet onto the table. "Aesir!" he exclaimed loudly.

Skirnir frowned. "Damn! Vidarr swore he'd send them to Muspelheim after Surtr's tribe. No matter, they can't be in full strength, or they'd have struck. Here, Hrymr, throw these two into the cage and get our horses. We'll have to look into this."

Hrymr grabbed Leif and Fulla in hands that resembled steam shovels and began dragging them off. All three of his mouths were drooling as he tightened his grip. But a bellow from Skirnir ended whatever ideas he had. He clumped behind the case, into a series of corridors, down some stone steps, and back to a cave covered by a huge oak door. There he tossed Leif in quickly and sent Fulla after him, landing with a thud that threatened Leif's already aching ribs.

The big door swung shut firmly with a positive click of the lock, leaving the cell completely dark, while the giant's footsteps pounded off toward the others.

Leif groaned, and Fulla began to roll off him, taking more time than seemed necessary in the process. She left one arm over his chest, and her lips were beside his ear. "Leif, I'm scared!"

He chuckled wryly, forcing himself up on his elbow. "Then that makes two of us. I'm afraid I wasn't cut out for this sort of thing."

Leif got to his feet and lifted her up, testing himself and finding no bones broken. He was surprised to notice that the weakness wasn't bothering his legs now; apparently he was getting used to being afraid. But he still couldn't laugh at danger, as Lee did. Then suddenly he realized he had laughed—and wondered whether the heroes might not be laughing at their own knowledge of fear.

BESIDE HIM, Fulla caught her breath, snuggling against him. The warmly personal scent of her hair penetrated, even over the musty odor of the cell. He pulled her closer, his lips tautening in a twisted smile. If the giants were coming back soon, he'd probably be screaming in agony too intense for thoughts of her within the hour, but he didn't have to die now in anticipation. The future couldn't take away any pleasure from the present, at least, and only a fool would do less living than he could while life still stirred in him. He caught her chin, and found her lips in the darkness.

For a minute, it seemed to work; then a vision of Skirnir smiling and moving the ember forward captured his mind. He drew back, grimacing. This was a hell of a time to be billing and cooing—particularly when he had no way of knowing what sort of a jam Loki might be in.

"We've got to get out of here," he stated. "As soon as I can get a light to see what the set-up is..."

But Fulla sighed softly, reaching out a hand from which all

the trembling had vanished. She took the matches he'd been striking futilely and thrust them back into one of his pockets. "There's no air for the flame sticks to burn on Jotunheim, Leif. We only seem to hear with our ears and to breathe because Bifrost adjusts us in passing over. And the fire the giants have is magic. But I don't mind the darkness or what the giants will do, as long as you're not angry with me anymore. You do like me now, don't you, beloved?"

"I do, kid," he told her. In spite of the fifty thousand years she may have lived, she was still only the twenty-year-old girl she seemed, at heart.

She made a purring sound in her throat. "Even if you had ruined the tree and killed the Aesir, I'd still be yours. It wasn't my heart that hated you and hit you, Leif—it was all the traditions that die so hard. But after you went away with a frozen face, I knew the tradition didn't matter. Only then you were so cold and distant. Leif, why did you come to rescue me? I'd caused you so much trouble already."

Shhh." He'd never had much use for story heroes who dropped their important work to rescue some clinging vine from the villain, but it seemed natural enough now. It was probably a tradition as deep in his race as the traditions of the gods and giants—traditions that could hold back Ragnarok for the right signs, even when the giants could have found Asgard asleep and undefended. Or maybe it was because he was responsible, and he'd had to develop a sense of stubborn responsibility in the long years of running the farm for Lee and himself.

"Shhh," he repeated. "I'm not sorry."

It was the right answer, and she leaned against him, content. Or as nearly so as a woman can be. "I must look a mess, beloved. If we only had a light and a mirror..."

His sudden yell cut off the words, and he was fumbling in his pocket, cursing himself. Of all the darned fools, forgetting the dimensional mirror! Somewhere in a big city on Earth, there'd be a searchlight he could locate. His mind directed the focusing, letting it draw gradually closer, while a growing beam of light began to lance from the mirror surface, strengthening as his focus came closer to the light. The massive walls of the cell sprang into view.

He swung the light over them, finding no trace of weakness anywhere. And the door was solid, locked on the other side with no hole to pick that lock. His heart sank for a moment, and then he grunted. It was supported on four bronze hinges, each fastened with three brass screws instead of the pegged construction he'd expected. The giants had more technology than he had thought.

"Hold the light on the door," he told Fulla, giving her the mirror. He drew out the automatic. There were things about the gun's army design that the giants hadn't suspected, such as the fact that it was specifically made to be its own toolkit. He began disassembling it rapidly.

FINALLY the rod that served as a screwdriver lay in his hand. It was apparently pitifully weak and slim, but the metal in it was sound, and brass screws turned easier than iron ones. He found bits of rock to prop up the door and take the weight off the hinges, then began working on the first screw. It was rough going, and his hands ached with the effort of forcing the screws, but they turned. In minutes, the last screw dropped into his hands, and Fulla cooed admiringly, reaching for the door.

He shook his head, massaging his fingers until he could reassemble the automatic. They'd have to reach the case to get the apples, and once there, a new clip would make the gun his best chance of getting free.

The door moved reluctantly as he heaved at a crosspiece, and began to swing in. He took its weight on his shoulders, somehow easing it down to the floor. Maybe there was no air, and hence no sound—but if he'd thought he heard Hrymr's footsteps, then the giants might think they had heard any loud noise from a falling door.

Leif wiped the sweat from his forehead, and peered out into the corridor, but it seemed free, and he reached his hand back for Fulla. They crept forward cautiously, but the place seemed deserted. He began dashing down a long passage, just as a figure stepped out of one of the side corridors.

Leif brought the automatic up without thinking, but a quick whisper reached him. "Hold it, Leif!"

"Loki!" Fulla moved forward to the god, making a few quick gestures, and nodded. "It is you, and not a deception. We thought you were caught."

"Too bad I wasn't, eh, Fulla?" Loki asked, grinning at her. Then he made a whistling gesture. "Well, what's this? You seem almost glad to see me. Leif, you'll have the wench tamed yet. No, they didn't catch me; I used the helmet to distract them when they had you, and slipped in here under illusion to save you. I can't hold the trick long here, though, so you found me in my own form. Come on."

He'd been moving forward as he whispered to them. Leif gripped his shoulder silently, and the god grinned again, accepting the gesture properly as thanks. He led them around a complicated course, quite different from the way Hrymr had come, but a few minutes later they were cautiously edging out behind the case holding the apples, sword and ammunition.

"Luck," Loki commented. "No giants. Open it."

Leif lifted the lid—and a sudden clangor began from a big hammer beating on a brass gong imbedded in the floor. The giants had a warning system, and already he could hear a yell from outside. The big creatures would be there in seconds—long before they could reach the door!

CHAPTER NINE

LOKI HAD already snatched out the things from the case. He tossed the chest of apples to Fulla, handed her the sword with a low whistle, and gave Leif the clips. Leif began shoving one in at a run toward the door, while Fulla swung the great sword experimentally. It seemed to be light and almost paper thin, but amazingly tough, passing through one leg of the case without apparent resistance.

There was a louder clamor outside, and the giants began boiling in, answering the gong. They came shoving through the door, ranging from ten to thirty feet in height, forming a solid wall of swords and spears as they charged at a full run toward the three in the middle of the room. Leif brought up the automatic, but he knew it was a futile gesture against that amount of brawn.

Hrymr clapped two of his mouths together in surprise as the bullet hit his chest, but the spear in his hands rose to throwing position without a tremor, and started for Leif.

Something whipped past Leif's head from behind, just as Loki's hand caught him, dragging him down beside Fulla, flat on the floor. Then the room shook to an explosion, and Loki was bouncing to his feet again. Where Hrymr had stood, there was only a gory mess, and the giants were backing away, except for a few who were making no further plans due to sudden death.

"I've still got two grenades," Loki said grimly. "With enough luck, we may be able to get outside in the dark. After that... Come on, we've got to find cover before they strike again."

He led them at a run across the floor, dragging the corpses of four of the giants into a crude barricade. Fulla blanched at the prospect of dropping into that mess, but she was down with them when the giants started forward again. They'd learned this time. Skirnir was sending them in well-scattered, to minimize the effect of the grenades. Spears came up, and the floor behind the three trembled as the heavy weapons landed. But the bodies had given them protection enough, until some bright giant decided on a forty-five degree cast.

Leif was shooting, taking his time and aiming for their throats. The big torsos seemed unharmed by a .45 slug, and the head would be too well protected by bone. He reloaded, counting three more clips. Loki waited until several in advance came almost together, and threw the second grenade.

Skirnir yelled, but it caught several of them. This time, though, they made a forward rush as soon as the explosion ended, and Loki was barely able to get the final grenade thrown in time to halt the leaders.

They hesitated, and Loki nodded, "Next, they'll loose the rest of the spears, and then charge. Here, this one had a sword you can manage. Keep low—in a brawl, sometimes, being shorter is an advantage. Strike to cut their tendons, and then into their throats when they fall. Fulla, I'm calling Hoof-Tosser. If he can get through to us, grab him, and get to Asgard."

She gripped the amazingly versatile sword and shook her head. "I can kill giants with this."

"You scram!" Leif ordered harshly. He heard Loki let out a piercing whistle, keeping his eyes on the giants, who were already drawing back their spears.

Hoof-Tosser suddenly crashed through the door, high and coming fast, with his feet beating down at the giants' heads. For seconds, it disconcerted them, and the horse dropped. Leif made a sweep as his arms came around and threw Fulla into the saddle. The horse rose at a yell from Loki.

Then the spears fell, one grazing against Leif and catching in the cloth of his trousers. He yanked free, as the giants came boring in, and was over the barricade with Loki.

THEY WERE lucky enough to dart into the thick of the charge before the giants realized they were coming. Leif began struggling to stay with Loki and avoid the giant legs at the same time. The god was right, since the giants had difficulty in separating enough to get a clean sweep at the pair. Leif chopped out with the sword, ducked as a giant started to fall, and managed to drag the point across the huge flabby abdomen, disemboweling the creature as it fell. Beside him, there was a snick of metal against bone as Loki's sword found a throat on another fallen giant.

But that gave the opening the giants needed. Leif felt a huge hand dart forward, leaped to avoid it, and found himself in another hand, with Loki also encircled. Their chance was finished before it really began.

Then the hand suddenly opened, and the giant began falling, his head jumping from his shoulders toward the floor. Leif's eyes darted up to see Fulla coming down again on Hoof-Tosser, the sword drawn back for another swing.

And a roar from the doorway seemed to shake the whole room and drag every giant around.

"Thor!" Loki yelled. "Get behind that barricade and lie close, before we get trampled."

Leif snatched a glimpse of Hoof-Tosser carrying Fulla toward the doorway, before he dropped beside Loki. Thor's fighting bellow came again, and there was a deep, hollow sound that could only be his hammer finding a giant skull. Almost on its heel, the sound of a grenade came, followed by another. There was a sudden thump of giant feet, and the first giant leaped over the bodies shielding Leif and Loki.

Leif's sword leaped up and the giant landed with a stumble, to fall on his face, and start crawling away on hands and knees, the tendon in his heel sliced through.

"Good man," Loki said approvingly, and his own sword licked out.

Then the flight ended, and Thor was over the bodies, dragging Leif and Loki to their feet and shoving a bag of grenades at them. The first of the giants had just reached the exit when Leif's toss crumpled him. A minute later, there were only parts of giants lying around.

Lee came running up. "Okay? God, son, you had us worried when we couldn't see you among those giants. Hey, Fulla, come on down and let's see one of those apples."

She was dropping already, and Leif accepted the fruit gladly. He could barely stand and hold the sword now, though it had seemed a part of him during the fight. But the first bite of the apple sent its usual heady strength through him, and he managed a fair grin.

He was surprised to see even Thor wiping sweat from his forehead, and accepting the next bite of the apple. "Without those grenades, things might have been different. They were more than ten times what we expect in a fort, by usual rules. Ho, you'll do, Leif Svensen. There's a place for you on my right side when the Sons of the Wolf come down at Ragnarok, if you want it."

Leif realized that Thor was handing out the highest honor he could, and apologizing for his comments that first time at the tree. Somehow, he felt like a peasant who had just been knighted by a king. This queer tradition of theirs began to get in the blood in time. But Thor cut off his thanks by lifting Fulla from Hoof-Tosser and into Leif's arms, then picking them both up and carrying them toward a tank of liquid at the side.

"And maid worthy of a berserker," the big god rumbled, in his closest approach to humor. "But my goats won't like the stink of giants on you."

He doused them into the tank and out again, rumbling

what was probably meant for a laugh, then seized Loki and treated him the same. They came out surprisingly clean, and almost instantly dry.

"How'd you reach us?" Leif asked.

Lee grinned. "We were already following Sudri's story when Vidarr came up with a big story about giants from Muspelheim. Everybody else went off there, but I persuaded Thor that there was a lot better reason to trust the dwarf."

"THEY WENT out into the courtyard then, where Thor's two goats were waiting, each slightly larger than a Percheron stallion. Thor climbed to the front of the vehicle, looked back to see all were accounted for, and yelled. They were off at full speed, with Hoof-Tosser trotting along at their side. Loki and Lee stood beside Thor, looking forward, and Leif and Fulla were alone at the rear. But he was too tired to do more than hold her close quietly, and she seemed content to fit his mood. It was over an hour later when Thor's bellow rang out, and they began crossing through Bifrost, to pelt on over the sward toward the judgment tree.

Thor's yell sounded again, and the gods scattered to let Thor through. Leif grabbed the reins of Hoof-Tosser and vaulted into the saddle, unfinished business bringing new strength to his body. He stared through the crowd, noticing that Odin and several others were missing, but his eyes searched for Vali and Vidarr.

Then he spotted them, off at the side, between Odin's seat and a small pile of grenades Odin was keeping for his personal testing. Their faces were incredulous, but hardening into sudden action as they turned toward the grenades. Leif reached for the gun, to find it had twisted in his pocket.

Thor shouted, and the hammer cut the air with a scream, lifting Vidarr from his feet and splashing him against the tree. But Vali had reached the grenades and scooped one up before Leif's gun was fully out or Thor's hammer could return.

Vali was confident now, his rat-face smirking. "Safe conduct, Thor, or the lovely Fulla *and* the apples will be supping with Baldar! You've won now, but…"

The gun in Leif's hand spoke sharply, and Vali's face blanched as the grenade fell from his pierced wrist. Thor's hammer came up, but Leif was remembering Andvari as well as the threat to Fulla, "Mine, Thor!"

Thor nodded. "Yours, Leif Svensen."

Hoof-Tosser was already in the air, overtaking the running Vali. Leif brought the horse down, kicked as carefully as he could at the treacherous god's head, and was off, gathering the thin figure up and lifting it in front of him on the saddle. Fortunately, the blow had only stunned Vali, briefly. His eyes were opening as Hoof-Tosser began lifting up and into Bifrost at Leif's shout.

Then all hell was tearing at Leif's mind, and even the horse was whickering unhappily. Vali screamed, and began to struggle, to cease in a paralysis of fright and horror as the ripples of color began to die down, Leif closed his eyes, but the hell still poured over him. He held back his vocal cords, savagely fighting to keep from ordering Hoof-Tosser back, and summoned the last desperate effort of his will. There was apparently little gravity there as he lifted Vali over his head and tossed the god forward. Then he found he couldn't order Hoof-Tosser back; but the horse had had enough, and suddenly reversed of his own will.

Niflheim's cold fingers released reluctantly, but Leif's eyes were frozen shut, and his mind teetered and gibbered at him, even when the voices of the gods were around him again. He felt hands reaching for him, and then passed out.

Fulla was cradling him, and there was the taste of apple in his mouth when his mind began creeping back. His brain had mercifully refused to remember anything clearly; somewhere, there would always be a section of scarred memory from the few minutes, but its very horror had burned all connections to his consciousness. He grinned feebly at Fulla and looked up to see Odin on the seat, finishing some remark to Frigg. The eyes of Odin's wife were frozen lightning as they stayed fixed on Leif.

The Alfadur looked older and more beaten than usual, but he was holding the hell of the treachery of two sons to himself, and Leif was surprised to see no anger in the god's eye. Odin watched Leif rise, and nodded wearily. "I have removed the burn of Niflheim, Son of Sven, in small gratitude for saving me the need of dealing such justice on one I had thought my son. Henceforth, by virtue of all that has happened on this day, be known as Leif Odinsson!"

There were incredulous sounds from the other gods, and Frigg screamed, her hands contracting to claws as she turned on Odin. Leif shook his head and looked to Loki for information.

LOKI'S expression was both puzzled and more sardonic than usual. "Yeah, that makes you an official god, Leif, adopted by Odin himself. But don't get any ideas—Odin probably did it to spite Frigg as best he could for siding with Vidarr and Vali. And there are catches to it—it doesn't mean you are any freer; you're bound now to win Ragnarok more than ever—or you'll join Vali as a traitor. And it takes several thousand years before you begin to develop any powers you don't already have, so you're still a god in name only!"

Put that way, it was easier to believe. Leif liked Thor's accolade better than this empty honor. But Odin had quieted Frigg and was speaking again.

"And lest Loki make you think this a mockery, though it is the only honor we have to give, all former oaths apply.

Should we win Ragnarok, the boon of which I swore here is still yours to ask."

He shook his head slowly, stepping down from his seat and approaching Leif. The arm the god laid on Leif's shoulder was a tired one, and Leif felt a stirring of sympathy that deepened as Odin went on in a low voice. "But to the son who replaces two unnatural ones, I admit victory seems most unlikely. The giants now know of our newer powers, and the Gaping Wolf already seems to course beside the dog, Garm, while my eyes saw the hordes of Surtr assembling in Muspelheim. We have won back a weapon worth ten thousand einherjar, since the sword you found in the case is the great weapon of Freyr. But without Vidarr, who shall kill the Wolf when I have been swallowed? Thor! Leif! I grow weary. Lend me your strength as I go to Mimir's well to read what shall come of the future now."

Leif shook his head slowly, conscious of the never-ending surprises of this paradoxical world. He looked at the icy, venomous face of Frigg, and back to the god who'd given an eye to learn only that he must rule with the certainty of eventual defeat—and to whom being swallowed was a lesser evil of the dire things to come. Suddenly, Leif had enough of it.

"Father Odin," he asked, "as Leif Odinsson, do I have a voice in council?"

Odin nodded gravely. "Even as Thor."

Leif's eyes swept over the crowd. Heimdallr was busy polishing a part of his golden armor; Freyr was fingering his newly restored sword with open delight; Fulla's face was beaming, and Lee had his hands clasped together over his head in a vote of triumph; even Thor was looking on with a brotherly acceptance. Then Leif turned to Frigg again, and all the life went out of the company, leaving the hopelessness of all of them open and obvious.

"Then I demand to be heard," Leif stated.

Odin shrugged and stepped back to his seat. "Speak, Leif."

LEIF FELT like a fool at the attention focussed on him; well, he'd never enjoyed making speeches, though he'd made enough at farmer's meetings. Loki could have made a better one, but he could at least tell them what he thought.

"My ancestors had a lousy religion once," he began abruptly. "It was the gloomiest, most futile one created. For every major god, they had something evil to kill him; and the better the god, the worse his fate. To make it neater, they had those gods knowing what was to happen. But that was all right—those ancestors were only rude barbarians. They could have a serpent to kill Thor, Surtr to kill Freyr, Garm to kill Tyr, the Wolf to kill Odin, and a general burning of the universe by Surtr after evil had won.

"But then I get brought here to find that they got those notions from you—after you'd had thousands of years to learn better! You're still swallowing the hogwash today— even when you've already seen half of the predictions turn out to be a pack of has-been lies. You still think the Norns— who couldn't even predict the sleep—are infallible. They were right about so-and-so, weren't they? The idea that you made it come true by believing every word they put out never entered your heads.

"Or take Frigg. Once, in trying to show off how well she could protect her mama's-boy, Baldar, she got him killed. So now she sits there crying over it, hating everyone, and doing everything she can to ruin you. But she gets away with it because she told you she knows all the future—though she can't tell it to you. That's the line little kids tell when they haven't studied their lessons: 'I know but I won't tell!' She couldn't even tell you how Thor will avoid death from the

Serpent's venom!"

Odin was staring at his wife with a speculative look in his eyes, and there was iron firmness in his voice. "Speak, Frigg!"

She snarled at Leif. "No one can tell that, since Thor dies by the venom. Tradition and my foreknowledge say it!"

"And both are liars," Leif told her flatly. "The dwarves have made me plastic sheets that even hydrofluoric acid can't touch. In an inner suit of that, Thor can swim in the venom, and laugh at you—as he will live through it. And what of all that bunk about Vali and Vidarr living beyond the Ragnarok to found a new world? Am I greater than your whole world, that I can upset your fixed future?

"When I was brought here, I may have been a coward, as I was accused. But I wouldn't have sat around a witches' cauldron with a bunch of old women being scared sick by fairy tales. I'm one of you now, and it's my future, by your own choice. So—do you really want to win this war? Because you can."

Odin had been saying something to Frigg, and the god waited until she stepped down with blanched face and unbelieving eyes and began moving off woodenly. Then he turned back to Leif. "How, Leif?"

"Forget your traditions, stop waiting for the giants to bring the war to you. Use the courage all of you have, individually, and take up the weapons I have against the giants, before they can organize. Wipe out their leaders while *their* traditions keep them helpless!"

Thor's bellow seconded it, with Loki and Freyr joining. Odin nodded slowly. "I say good, Leif, but this is something on which all the Aesir must decide. Those who would join in that, stand to the left of my throne. Those who would await the Gjallar-Horn, choose the right."

Leif stared incredulously. Beside him, to the right of the

throne stepped Loki, Thor, Freyr, Fulla, Odin, and Ullr. Even Heimdallr stuck to tradition and moved to the right.

They were to wait like sitting ducks for the giants' timing.

CHAPTER TEN

LEIF SHRUGGED, letting the spirit that had prompted his appeal die out, and went up to Odin's seat. "All right, then, I suppose Thor and I might as well help you to Mimir's well. It's as good as anything."

Odin smiled faintly, and shook his head, motioning Leif back. "Leif, my son, traditions are things beyond reason. For the logic you have used and the thoughts it has given me, I like you—as I've liked Loki in spite of all the traditions against him. Well, the others have won, but let Mimir's well be. I have enough for thought already. The giants are warned now, and will strike too soon. Fulla needs you more than I—go to her and the work that is needed."

He turned and moved away, leaving Leif blinking, while Loki chuckled in the background. Fulla was moving slowly toward the buildings, her eyes on the ground, as Leif caught up with her, and she refused to meet his eyes.

"Well?" he asked at last.

"The Alfadur had no business... Perhaps I said things while you were burned from Niflheim, but...maybe I even said I needed you."

She shook him off as he caught at her. "But Leif, I know your heart isn't with Asgard. I know you mean to use Odin's boon to return to your Earth. And since you have eaten of the apples for only a short time, you can return, though it may be hard at first. I thought there was still a little time until then, and that we... I should have known your words were only to soothe me while the giants had us."

He caught her to him then. "The words were what I felt

in my heart, you precious little fool," he told her gravely. "And if I can go back to Earth, I'll want you to go with me— if you can give up all this to be just a farmer's wife. You'd have to pretend to be just a woman—no goddess."

"It wouldn't be pretense—I'd be no more there than any woman. Only Odin, his true sons, or Loki can retain any of their powers on Earth."

"Oh." His hands began to drop from her shoulders.

She pressed them back. "Do you think that matters to me? I'd go with you if I turned to a giantess! But it would never do. I've eaten the apples too long, and without them, I'd grow old on Earth and die as a hideous hag—when you were still in your prime."

"We could take a few apples and put them in the deep-freezer…"

"A few apples last all Asgard a thousand of your years, Leif—because there are only a few, ever. But on Earth, all of them would be less than enough for one of us for a single decade! *If* we could have even one…"

She threw off the mood and drew his head down to her. "But we still have a few weeks before Ragnarok, Leif—if you want."

He looked down at her, comparing her to the girls he'd known, and even the dreams he'd had when he was very young and naive. He could see the smirks from Gefjun and other goddesses, and knew he should refuse, for her good. Then he smiled at her. "A few weeks can be a long time, honey."

But long after night had fallen, he lay staring into the blackness of his room. They were short weeks, before the giants struck, and the gods were hopelessly outnumbered, the einherjar almost useless. The giants would have all the advantage of choosing the time, and the Aesir would be defeated by their sense of inevitable defeat.

If the miracle of victory for the gods occurred, Leif had practically an eternity of life in a tradition hounded world where there was nothing to do but turn Earth into a vassal peasant state, subject to the whims of the gods. If they lost, Leif wouldn't know it, but the giants would wrack and raze Earth with fire and destruction.

It was just a question of time before one of the two alternatives was thrown at him. He wondered idly how much time, and dismissed it, to sleep and dream of Fulla growing old and wrinkled, cackling at him out of toothless gums.

But a month later, Fulla's face was still the same and her teeth seemed highly capable as she sat chewing a mouthful of pancakes and bacon. And Leif was still wondering when the giants would strike.

SOMETHING that sounded like all the klaxons invented answered his question, wailing and keening through the air. Fulla paled, horror running into her eyes. "Heimdallr blows the Gjallar-Horn! The giants are at Vigridr!"

Leif poked the last of his breakfast into his mouth, considering the fact that Ragnarok had begun. Now, as Leif Svensen, he could go to the shops and await the returns. But as Leif Odinsson, his place was to the fore. He got up and began buckling on his armor, with Fulla's help. Finished, he blinked as she came out with a suit of mail, motioning him to help her.

She met his eyes firmly. "I'm fighting. Do you think I care what happens if you don't come back to me, Leif?"

He knew he should protest, but he felt no desire to. If she wanted to be in the battle, that was right for her. He helped her quietly, and went out through the workshop entrance, where the worried dwarves tried to yell encouragement after them. The work there was done, as best it could be. Leif moved toward the stables, seeing no other god near them, trying to realize that this was it. But the fear he expected refused to come. He was only conscious of a vague relief that the waiting was over.

Lee caught up to him, swung him around to stare at him, and grinned. "You got it, son. I always knew you'd make a better hero than I, and by Ymir, I was right. You'll be around after this is over—you can't kill a man with that stuff in him."

"I'm not scared, if that's what you mean, Lee. But I'm not looking forward to it for the thrill, or laughing about it."

"No—no, of course not." Lee frowned in thought. "You don't have to. You can go in cold and dead serious, like Thor and Tyr. Look, my godly twin, d'you know what would happen if Loki or I quit pretending it was all just a joke or a thrill? We'd funk out. We don't dare take it seriously. Damn it, if I don't get off the soapbox, I will funk it! See you at the wake tomorrow!"

He chucked Fulla under the chin and was gone at a run toward Thor's group on einherjar, his voice taking on parade drill tones before he reached them.

Leif found the valkyries busy saddling, and cut through their chatter. "I'm guessing that nobody gave you orders. What are your plans?"

Reginleif looked doubtful, still not used to his godhood. "To the battle, as always—to rescue the…"

She fumbled, and Leif grinned wryly.

"Tradition, isn't it? To rescue the new heroes! Not this time, not by a damn sight. All right, get on the horses and go over to the shop of the dwarves. Sudri has his boys ready, and they'll load you up with grenades and tell you where to haul and dump them. You don't like taking orders from dwarves—but you'll do it, or I'll give your horses to the dwarves. Fulla, you get along well with Hoof-Tosser, and Gna doesn't know enough about the whole business. Take him and a few of these girls. They can lug the small U-235 bombs up to Bifrost, where you can carry them over to the trails in Muspelheim and Jotunheim. You know what to do?"

She repeated the plans she had heard. Under the stupid tradition, he hadn't been able to take precautions in advance, but he could cut off most of the reinforcements from getting out of the giant worlds by dropping the atom bombs on them where they were massed outside the entrances to Vigridr. The stone dwarves had modified the time element on the detonators to give the bomb carrier enough time to escape.

Leif nodded approval as she covered it. "Good. Hoof-Tosser is the only horse that can get off the ground, except over Earth, and probably the only one strong enough to carry a bomb across even those easy borders. Take care of yourself, kid, and don't get too low."

She matched his mood by avoiding all emotion. He left as she began to give the valkyries orders. He located Loki and Thor and drew up to them, noticing that the black-bearded god was wearing his plastic underarmor properly. "How bad is it?"

LOKI GESTURED toward Leif's mirror, and they all moved toward the wall, where they could watch Asgard and examine Vigridr through the mirror. Sometimes Leif almost forgot that the little battle-world lay across Bifrost, in another dimensional twist, since it lay so close, and passage through Bifrost to it was so easy that the pigs had to be chased back regularly from it.

Odin and Freyr had already assembled their troops at the end of the battlefield nearest Asgard, and Tyr was coming through with his. Vigridr field was better than two hundred miles on a side, taking up most of the largest landmass on the world. Lee came moving through then with the left wing of Thor's band—the strongest and smartest of the heroes, on the whole. As Leif watched, he saw the valkyries begin to move down, dragging wooden sleds of grenades behind them, in addition to those belted to the heroes.

But there was a mist over the field, and at first Leif could make out nothing of the giants. Then it began to clear, and he groaned at what he could see. The forces of the Aesir seemed lost in a tiny corner of the field, compared to the seemingly endless expanse of giant forces. And only the picked monsters were there—none less than thirty feet in height and one whole company running to nearly twice that. They were armed with everything from swords through pikes to maces—and the last looked the most dangerous. But he could see no sign of bows and arrows, or of the cement-tamper gadget he'd dreamed up as the best answer to killing off the Aesir forces, if he'd been on their side. It had seemed so obvious that he'd half expected it, though he knew that what was obvious was actually so only against a millennium of a particular cultural development.

"It isn't quite that bad," Loki said. "Vigridr has a gravity only about a quarter normal, and we're more agile. But as you may have noticed, Jotunheim has even less, and the frost giants feel too heavy for comfort, while the fire giants are used to nearly three times our gravity. They feel themselves so light that they have to remember not to use their full strength, and it slows them up."

They'd need the advantage, and then some, Leif decided. "How'd so many get there anyhow?"

Heimdallr came up and caught the question, buckling on the plainest, dirtiest, dullest and heaviest armor Leif had yet seen, and swinging a sword that seemed designed for two men. There was a curious drive to his voice, totally unlike his usual affected drawl. "My fault, brother. While I watched the main trails for the march to begin, these were coming in on small trails, a few at a time, hiding in the grasses, and waiting for this day. You were right—we should have struck them first. Well, good luck among them."

Leif felt the three clips left in his pouch, made sure all his grenades were in place, and loosened the buckle of his new sword. He had Sudri alloy and forge it from the toughest formula he could find on Earth. It was thin and light, but its cutting edge could sheer through normal steel as if it were paper. He'd imitated Freyr's sword as best he could, and tried to sell the idea to the others. But they preferred the familiar, just as they distrusted the thin, tough solid armor he'd had forged. They were used to chain mail, and he couldn't convince them that this spread the shock better. But a lot of them were carrying the little polished shields that could be carried horizontally, to signal reflections of any sudden movement above the wearer, giving almost full-circle vision against the giants.

He started to climb into Thor's chariot, to stop at an exclamation from Loki. "Naglfar!"

Something was coming through from Jotunheim that looked like an immense ship, but which must be a huge mobile fort—complete with ballistas, which he'd never expected. It rolled on immense wheels, powered by the barely visible feet of some incredibly large monster. Then Bifrost seemed to buckle and develop diffraction patterns, while a blinding light ran along Naglfar, seeming to crumple the fort like a paper toy.

"Hrymr was supposed to steer it," Loki said. That probably caused the delay while they trained a new driver. But what ruined it?"

"U-235," Leif answered, and waved up as Fulla went overhead on Hoof-Tosser. The bomb had come in handy; that thing had seemed ugly enough to wipe out the gods by itself.

THEN THOR made ready, and Leif waved at Loki, who

would be the messenger, since his skill at sleight could serve as enough disguise to make him pass unnoticed during the rage of battle. Thor yelled at the goats and they went slipping through the faint ripple of Bifrost, while the einherjar followed. Leif looked at them and grimaced. They were going into something that was beyond their imagining, but most of them didn't have enough of the life force to realize this was more than a routine day. And the ones that were almost without life force in their elf-shaped flesh had been left behind for reserves.

"I've had no training at this, Thor," Leif commented. "I won't be much help to you."

"Training—it takes something else! I'm glad to have you with me, Leif, and if the Serpent gets me, it will be good to know you're there to lead my band. Ho! They're moving."

Odin's band had started, and the distant figure of Odin could be seen in his gold helmet, holding what seemed to be his spear. Leif grinned, glad of the last-minute inspiration that had made him change the spear to a bazooka and furnish Odin with a load of trick shells for it. It had taxed the abilities of the dwarves, but they had succeeded.

Out of the giant group, a band moved forward, headed by something out of a nightmare. "Fenris Wolf, the Gaping Wolf," Thor said, but Leif had already guessed it. It looked something like a wolf, though it rose to a height of forty feet at the shoulders, and had teeth five feet long, dripping a raw, green fire of radioactivity. Leif shuddered, looking for the other monsters. He saw a great creature, looped into coils, projecting a head larger than a twenty-foot boat, but it wasn't a true serpent, since it sprouted hundreds of short, stubby legs and bore a dozen arms, all loaded with weapons. The third was harder to see—something that seemed to flame and blaze, in outlines that the eyes refused to admit. That must be the dog Garm.

He shuddered again. Somewhere in his mind, a dim memory of things like that in Niflheim tried to clarify itself. Thor nodded. "The fire giants, being more terrible than the frost giants, dragged three creatures from Niflheim long and long ago—so long that they believe Fenris Wolf is the father of them all. They are dreadful opponents."

They were more than that, and Leif's admiration for Tyr increased as he watched the god drive his forces against the thing called Garm. Then Thor yelled, and his own band was moving toward the Serpent. Thor handed the reins to Leif, checked his hammer, gloves and belt, and dropped over the side, running forward. The band behind the Serpent came forward with a rush.

Leif's eyes dropped to the long blades projecting from the axles of the chariot, and he hoped the accounts he'd read of the Egyptian use of them were true. It had been another last-minute idea. He whooped at the goats and let them go all out, fairly sure that their armor, built like his own, could take the first encounter.

At the last moment, he swerved, dug deeper into the protective front of the chariot, and shaved down the side of the giant ranks. There was a series of grinding jolts to the chariot motion now, and a howling above that threatened to break his eardrums. He came to the end of the rank of giants, stealing a quick look back. It seemed impossible that so many giants could have been robbed of their legs in that one brief passage. The blades at the sides really worked, and the old Egyptians had been smart boys.

The giants were swinging toward him now, though, and he cut around their rear, barely shaving through as they tried to close up. This time, while they were swinging to face him, he cut up the other flank, catching their legs from the rear before they could face him. He came erect and began tossing grenades into their ranks. He shook his head at himself, wondering how he could take it with the same attitude as butchering time on the farm.

The giants lacked discipline—but it was nothing compared to the einherjar. Some of those were standing off at the side, happily swinging away at each other, as if they were back practicing in Asgard! Leif let out a yelp and was in among them, trying to bring some order out of their behavior. He indicated the grenades, and they began picking them up and throwing them toward the giants. Half didn't explode, for want of will, but those that worked helped considerably. Leif swung back.

And a grenade from his own einherjar hit the back of the chariot, knocking one wheel to splinters!

CHAPTER ELEVEN

LEIF HAD begun jumping at the sound of the explosion, and he landed with a jolt that tested his body and found it unharmed. He dived to the goats, swearing again at the dumb heroes, and began unhitching the animals. At a swat from the side of his hand, they went loping off toward Asgard and the stables.

Fulla yelled from high overhead, and Leif waved up to show he was doing all right. She dropped a rain of grenades into the ranks of the giants nearest him, and went wheeling back for more. At that rate, she'd be their best warrior, and safe enough in the bargain. Leif struck off at a lope that covered some twenty miles an hour at the reduced gravity, refilling his belt with grenades that had not exploded, and avoiding the thickest clumping of the giants. But it was necessary to stick somewhere near the einherjar, and try to keep them from straying, and he found himself bottled suddenly, with one of the heroes. Leif's grenades ran out, and there was still no opening in the giant ranks. He motioned the hero and went leaping in, ducking in where their grouped legs kept them from getting a good swing at him, and where even poking with a spear was hard. Beside him, the hero was happily taking care of those that Leif managed to drop, with a cooperation unusual for one of the einherjar. Then Leif came onto an unexpected group of grenades, and began throwing them as the giants broke away. One giant threw a grenade at Leif, but the detonators were not attuned to giant minds. He caught it and fired it back—to remove the last of the near giants.

The hero grunted amicably. "We fight now, huh?"

Leif strangled over the words, but managed to keep his voice calm as he sent the hero after some giants in the distance. Still, if they were all like that one, it wouldn't be too bad. He counted over a score of dead giants and loped down the field, wondering if there was anything in Lee's theory that a man who was both cold and unafraid couldn't be killed in battle. It should make a good combination for survival. He leaped ten feet into the air over giant dead, and started back toward his einherjar.

"Ho, Leif!" It was Thor, apparently wading through giants, his hammer a steady tattoo that left a string of broken giant heads, while he was swinging a big battle-ax with his other hand. Leif saw the giants closing around him like cornered rats making a last desperate bid, and went in from the outside, scattering them again, to give Thor room for his hammer work. Actually, it wasn't too much different—except in reverse—from his experience in digging rats from a granary foundation. Try as he would, he hadn't been able to hit one of them, though Lobo had been killing them right and left. They had been much too small for Leif, just as he was for the giants.

"Garm got Tyr," Thor announced sadly, swinging the axe over Leif's head to chop off part of a giant, and reaching out for the returning hammer. As he did so he spotted one leg temptingly near, and swiveled on his hip, locking a leg into the giant's, and tripping the grotesque monster where Leif could take care of him. "Though Garm died after, from the damage Tyr's one arm had done. And you've proved better than Frigg or the Norns, since I've killed the Midgard Serpent and Odin has a tooth of Fenris Wolf as a trophy. Where is Lee?"

LEIF SHOOK his head, and backed against Thor as three of the giants came charging at them. He barely caught the spear on the slant of the shield, deflecting it without trying to stop it. Even then, it sent a surge of pain up his arm. He had noticed that it was getting harder to dodge and save himself, as the giants grew accustomed to Virgridr and the style of the gods. And he was having to watch himself, to make sure that his success didn't make him careless. Thor did it by pure conditioned reflex, but he couldn't risk that.

From the edge of the field, there was a piercing hail, and a group of the valkyries and goddesses came swarming out, armed heavily with grenades, and intent on finding giants for targets. For a time, they turned the tide back to a condition of giant killing, rather than war, and the giants began to retreat. Some of the better einherjar worked more smoothly with the women, and there were knots that operated at almost full efficiency. The normal einherjar remained more of a menace than a help, however; the fighters were always in danger of getting a bomb in the back from one of their own supposed allies.

Thor found a lull in the action and began pulling out hunks of the plastic underarmor, shaking sweat from his body with it. Leif tried to help him, so they could get back into the fight sooner, and most of it came out through openings in the armor. They were pulling the last away when Loki seemed to materialize out of nothing before them, trying to keep up with their questions; there was no good way of estimating the battle from the field.

"Lee's collected five heroes who seem to have some gumption, and he's got Gefjun and a couple other Asynjur freighting grenades. He's doing more damage to the giants than any group. And we're doing miracles, thanks to the grenades and the bombs that killed off the giant reserves. But we're losing, badly. They hold most of the field, except around the entrance to Asgard, and they're closing in there. Even if every hero kills twenty of them, they can still beat us. The dwarves are hauling in the grenades, now. And Sudri and a bunch of volunteers are right in the fight."

He pointed to a section where a few dwarves were busy hurling grenades. A giant suddenly caught one dwarf. Leif saw it was Sudri, and groaned, but a second later, the dwarf dropped back, spitting, while the giant's hand dropped beside him. He darted forward and grabbed a leg of the giant, his mouth working, before an eddy of battle cut off the sight.

Leif stared after the dwarf, and then jerked back as a flicker on his shield caught the corner of his eye. He leaped, fifteen feet sideways, just as a great mace thwacked down into the dirt, the sharp spike clanging off his armor and opening six inches of skin along his leg. Half a dozen giants had sneaked up while they were conferring with Loki.

Leif went into action that was now automatic, while Thor's hammer and axe began a thudding dirge. A grenade from a hero went off in the midsection of one giant. Leif groaned and swore, picking himself up from the ground, but he was only bruised, and in a few moments Loki was cutting the ugly throat of the last giant.

But the battle was obviously being lost; the giants had been cautious of the heroes at first, but now were largely disregarding them and working on their real enemies. "How much longer can we hold out?" Leif asked Loki.

"Maybe two hours, but certainly no more."

"Thanks. Good fighting."

He finally found Sudri, slipping back for more grenades, and the dwarf paused in delight at finding Leif whole. But Leif had no time to waste. "Can you build rails out over Vigridr—higher the better—from Asgard through Bifrost— and store a score of bombs over the field?"

"Sure, boss Leif. Stuff won't weigh much here, and that part of Bifrost is thin. Brace the platforms from Asgard. You want it done?"

"On the double, Sudri," Leif ordered, and headed for the section where Odin was supposed to be, avoiding giants as best he could. It was still odd to be able to run a mile in less than two minutes, but handy. He found Odin in a little time, mixed into the thick of things, with a couple of the valkyries, a hero, and a dwarf helping—the screwiest mixture Leif had seen, but a surprisingly effective one. The giants were well thinned out by the time Leif reached the group and began helping to clean up the tag ends.

ODIN LOOKED good now, more vigorous and youthful than Leif had seen him before, but the worry in his eyes showed that Loki had been in touch with him. Leif wasted no time on preliminaries. "Can you order a complete retreat, and have it work?"

He accepted the god's doubtful nod, and braced himself for what he hated about the plan. The reserve einherjar were certainly no use to even themselves—actually less alive than mythical zombies. But because the elf-shapings had once housed the complex life pattern of real men—whether it was a soul, or as synthetic as the bodies he couldn't know—it bothered him to demand their cold-blooded sacrifice. And Odin was somehow fond of all his heroes.

The idea of sending those reserves in to their sure death didn't sit well with the Valfather's conscience. But he nodded at last recognizing the harsh laws of military necessity. "As you say, Leif, there are many who are less than beasts, knowing neither pleasure nor pain. If those will suffice, you have my permission. And here, we shall try to organize for the quick retreat you need. Now go back where you're needed. I can do what is needful here."

Leif headed for Bifrost, still trying to avoid further fighting now. He ducked around a huge corpse, leaped over a pile of squashed einherjar, where a giant foot had trapped them, and dived rapidly under the falling sword of a smaller giant. Then he was clear and searching frantically for Fulla. She caught his wave, and Hoof-Tosser plummeted down, to touch the earth lightly, and dart up again as Leif flopped wearily behind Fulla.

Her hand squeezed hard on his wrist, but she made no comment, and he was too exhausted to waste words. He found a scrap of the bit of apple all had been given and swallowed it, as they flashed through Bifrost. It helped enough to let him jump from the horse and move briskly to the workshops.

The dwarves were almost finished with the crude rails that ran from the shops to the top of the wall and headed out through Bifrost. He followed it out, to a platform at the edge of Vigridr, perhaps two hundred feet high and two hundred square feet in area. The bracing back to the wall on Asgard had already been installed, and the first sled with its load was dragged up the greased rails as Leif watched. He made a few minor suggestions, and moved back to Asgard.

It was amazing how time was slipping away. Loki was waiting for him, with Heimdallr at his side, as Leif stepped from the wall. The vain god was now blood-spattered and filthy, almost unrecognizable, but the horn in his hand still sparkled like a precious jewel. "I'm to sound retreat when you're ready," he announced. "But who's to lead the sacrificed einherjar?"

Leif frowned, shaking the cobwebs from his brain. Of course there would have to be a leader, since the heroes couldn't even remember orders more than a minute or so, unless they could simply ape the acts of a god in front of them. They needed only brains enough to keep the giants from realizing it was retreat, and not replacement, for five minutes, but that was beyond their ability. He'd overlooked that need.

But now he faced it. "All right; it was my idea."

"Don't be a fool," Loki snapped. "It means death."

"It means the same death to anyone," Leif pointed out. "And I can't ask someone else to die for my plans."

Fulla made a low moaning sound in her throat and slumped to the ground. He smiled at her grimly. The month had been longer than they'd expected, and once Ragnarok was over, he could only be a source of trouble to her.

HE MOTIONED Heimdallr to sound retreat, and the horn came up, wailing as if ten thousand banshees were attending the wake of the last idshee in the world. Heimdallr dropped the horn with a scowl, and stretched out his hand. Leif started to meet the gesture, only to feel the god's arm push suddenly against his chest. Something caught behind his knees and he went sailing over the kneeling form of Loki, victim of a trick older than even their traditions.

He was on his feet almost instantly, but Heimdallr was running toward the apathetic ranks of the oldest heroes, waving them forward. They started mechanically into Bifrost, with Heimdallr at the front.

"You never know about him," Loki muttered slowly. "But in a way, he was right. You did your job here—and more. He'd made a mistake in not catching those early giants drifting in. Now he has to undo it."

Fulla was with them as Leif and Loki stepped along the rails into Vigridr again, watching the retreat. Odin had somehow managed to marshal his forces into a thin strip before the entrance, and even to force the giants back temporarily. Now Heimdallr broke through Bifrost, his horn wailing, and went boring in, mingling his ranks with the others. Leif could now see that he was the man for the job. He did it with a flair that somehow made every faded hero a temporary extension of himself, and he got them through undivided and into motion against the giants. Odin waved, and gods, valkyries, dwarves, and heroes with enough intelligence to obey pelted for Bifrost. The giants hesitated, uncertain about the strange maneuvers, and even gave ground a little before Heimdallr's force. Then they began a forward movement again, but still cautiously.

Leif felt something touch his arm, and turned to see Hoof-Tosser delicately stepping along the rails, rubbing his muzzle against Leif. Apparently, he'd gotten tired of being alone. Leif grabbed the horse and pulled him forward onto the platform, noting that there were still a few grenades on the saddle. Then Leif was mounted and urging Hoof-Tosser into the air.

At first, he could see no sign of Heimdallr, until a toppling giant showed the god briefly. Leif urged Hoof-Tosser down, his sword swinging for a giant neck, and continuing on to another. He saw others running up, tossed the grenades, and brought the sword down again. For a second, there was a clear space. Heimdallr was not fool enough to argue; the god leaped up, lifting his arm, and Leif caught it, yelling for Hoof-Tosser to get back to Asgard.

The weight of the god and armor was too much for Leif to heave up to the saddle, but Heimdallr caught a stirrup with his other hand and gradually floundered up behind Leif. Below, the last of the forces of Asgard were retreating through Bifrost, while the giants were pelting across the field, disregarding the hopeless einherjar.

Leif yelled to the dwarves as Hoof-Tosser leaped through Bifrost and drooped down beside Loki and Fulla.

The dwarves were darting back as Leif and Heimdallr dismounted; the god nodded casually, and reached for the mirror. Leif knocked it from his hands, just as a stabbing beam of radiance lanced from it, and Bifrost became visible for miles of its length, arcing and leaping in rainbow fire. But it held back the shock and lethal radiation. Twenty of their strongest U-235 bombs going off together weren't very gentle. Leif reached for the mirror, and they could see no evidence of life on the little world, clothed in decaying radiance. The giants were no longer a danger.

ODIN AND Thor found them some time later, still unsure of this victory that had replaced certain doom. Leif was dead inside with reaction from the flux of emotions he'd never known he was experiencing, and he could sense Odin's mood. The god stood looking down at Asgard without seeing it.

"Five gods, four goddesses, eight of my valkyries, four-fifths of the einherjar, nine dwarves—let Sudri have a seat on the council for his work...but we won. Gna is dead, and Hoof-Tosser is yours, Leif. Frigg has killed herself, since the prophecy failed. Tyr and Ullr. But I have still my three strongest sons—Heimdallr, Thor, Leif. My heart is full. Leif, Lee follows us; he got safely from Vigridr. Now I must reckon accounts at Yggdrasil."

The gods, except Loki, drew away, just as Lee reached Leif, too tired to do more than nod. Heimdallr looked back at the rails for the bombs. "A good trick," he commented.

"A better trick than Leif's others. With it, we can build through to Midgard; we can regain it easily—and hold it!"

Leif sat frozen as the gods moved out of range, realizing slowly that Midgard was Earth! Finally he turned to Lee. "Are you coming back to Earth with me, Lee?"

Fulla gasped, drawing a slow shuddering breath. But Lee nodded, grinning suddenly. "It's going to be pretty fossilized around here with no war, Leif. And Gefjun is getting the darndest ideas."

Fulla stood up slowly, and the smile on her lips seemed almost real. "You have to go, Leif."

He climbed to his own feet again, sighing. "It will be hell without you, but I can't betray a world—even for you."

"Then I'll run ahead and not interfere. You'll have business with Lee and Loki." She raised on tiptoe and kissed him softly, making no attempt to linger or stir his emotions. "It was a perfect month, beloved."

Then she moved down to the path, neither too fast nor too slow, her body set to a masterpiece of music. Leif watched her go, trying to photograph the strength and fineness of her on his mind. At last he turned back to the others.

Lee looked uncomfortable, but the sardonic smile was etched deeper on Loki's mouth, though his voice seemed husky. "How are you going to protect Earth, Leif? Going back won't do it."

"No." He hesitated, then shrugged. "I have a boon from Odin—and I'm claiming it against all Asgard, for today. I want the right to take all the apples back to Earth! Let them sleep a thousand years—it's better than being dead forever—and by then Bifrost may be completely closed from Earth here. But it will stop them."

"Unless they stop you. Well, I'll put it up to them, Leif. Maybe I can get it for you—unless they decide to drop all of us into Niflheim for the idea. Be seeing you."

He started after the others, the grin stronger on his face, and Leif turned to the shops of the dwarves. He still had some instructions for Sudri.

CHAPTER TWELVE

DUSK WAS settling on Asgard when two figures approached the shops. Lee was pacing about, but Leif sat quietly smoking, while Sudri stood watching with mournful face. The figures drew nearer, and turned into Thor and Odin, but Leif made no effort to rise.

Odin came up first, looking down at the man, and his shoulders were tired. Gravely, he dropped a chest to the ground at Leif's feet. "The apples are all there, Leif, my son, Loki has preached from Jotunheim to vanished Vanaheim and back, to no avail. But no man or god may say that the word of Odin is an empty thing. The Aesir pay their debts."

"I'm sorry, father Odin," Leif said slowly, rising at last. Something in the grave old figure had made the acknowledgment of relationship more than a formal salutation. "I had no wish to add another of your sons to the list who are traitors to you…"

"Nor have you." Thor's voice was brusque, and as low as it could ever be. "We heard Heimdallr's words; Loki made them clear enough. When a man or god betrays his roots, he is a traitor; when he protects them, nothing can make a traitor of him. By Ymir, if you didn't chain us, I'd chain you between Asgard and Niflheim. Anyhow, what is another thousand of your years, when we now have a thousand times that to live? Take the apples, Leif Odinsson, and go back to your Earth with a clear conscience."

Leif picked them up slowly. He'd expected everything but that. Asgard would always be a place of surprises, and not the least of the amazing things was the length of Thor's speech.

"Sudri knows how to care for the tree while you sleep," he said, "And he may even be able to develop more trees. It is a possibility."

There seemed nothing else to say. He strapped the apples to his belt, feeling strange without the armor he'd gotten used to. Then he lifted his head and whistled. An answering nicker came at once, and Hoof-Tosser dropped down beside him, nuzzling him gently. Leif gave Lee a hand up onto the bare back, and prepared to mount.

Odin dropped his hands on Leif's shoulders. "Wherever you are, Hoof-Tosser will come at your whistle—to carry you about on Midgard, or to return you to Asgard. We'll be sleeping, but there'll be room beside our dreams for yours. I shall look for you when I awake."

Thor came forward to shake hands gravely with both twins and to lift Leif up onto Hoof-Tosser. Then the two gods turned and moved back down the trail, and only the sobbing wail of Sudri was left. Leif looked over Asgard again, savoring all the good about it for the last time, and hoping to catch a glimpse of Loki or perhaps another. Then he clucked softly, and Hoof-Tosser was breasting the swirls and patterns of Bifrost.

"Make way for the Svensen twins," Lee called out.

But Leif shook his head. "For Lee Svensen and Leif Odinsson," he corrected, before the swirls of Bifrost blotted out further words. It was easier this time since he'd left the automatic with Sudri, and Hoof-Tosser moved forward at a steady rolling gait. Then that cleared to a sudden swoop, and the horse was landing, while bright sunlight poured down on them. They were back on Earth.

LEE WAS off at a bound, staring about, and Leif slid

down slowly. They had landed in a small clearing in the woods, near a trail that led to the house, not two hundred yards away, almost as if the horse had known enough to avoid publicity.

"Home, sunlight, people—and some real whiskey!" Lee cried, stretching and sniffing the air, with his spirits high again. "Me for the whiskey. Coming, son?"

"Be along in a minute," Leif answered. He was vaguely conscious that Asgard had made him older than his brother, so that the old familiar relationship of admiration toward Lee's glamour was now almost a fatherly one on his part. He grinned faintly as he watched Lee hopping over the little obstacles on the trail, and started out.

Hoof-Tosser nickered again, and touched him with a nudge. Leif turned back, and his smile was fuller. "Go on back to Asgard, Hoof-Tosser; this is a lousy world for horses that can run through the air above anti-aircraft guns. But sometime, I'll whistle you down again, and we'll take a ride at night when it's safe. How's that?"

The horse blew its breath sharply through its nostrils, shook its head, arched its neck, and was suddenly lifting and vanishing in a rainbow of color. Leif turned up the trail, coming out on fallow land. He stooped and smelled the dirt, rubbing it in the palm of his hand. It should have been plowed and planted. And the dead wood back there should be trimmed. There'd be work enough for him.

"Hi, Leif!" He looked up to see Faulkner working on a broken fence-post, with Summers talking to him. There had been no real cordiality in the voice, but there was acceptance. "Heard you'd be back soon. Be over to get things straightened out tonight. Okay?"

"Fine," Leif told him. He climbed the back steps, pushed through the screen door, and was in the old, familiar kitchen, with the warm Earth smells of an honest dinner cooking on the stove. It was…

She turned toward him, smiling with a hint of tears in her eyes, and pulling the apron up over her head. Then she stood there, uncertain, waiting for his reaction.

"Fulla! Oh, you fool!"

She was in his arms, half-crying, half-laughing. "Fool yourself, Leif Odinsson! Did you really think I'd leave you alone down here—when I could ride Hoof-Tosser, too, before you needed him? There'll be a week—maybe two—before I change. And I can always go back then!"

Then she cried out as she felt the coffer of apples at his side and was tearing them out, counting them.

Loki's voice drifted in from the doorway, and Leif looked up to see him standing with his arm about Gail Faulkner, grinning at them, with Lee in the background. "Fulla couldn't wait to find you'd have the apples. She barely waited for me to tell her where to go. But while your apples can keep us going—it's all right, Gail, I'll explain later—can keep us for a while, I've got better news. Come here."

The sly god picked up one of the apples and moved into the dining rooms, munching on it in total disregard of the precious time it represented. He pointed out into the orchard.

"I told you I found out about grafting from that book! Do you think I wouldn't remember the years we slept? I had experts working on some cuttings the next day. Ten trees out there, all with Asgard apples!"

Leif looked at them, shaking his head. "They're blooming."

"Umm. Have an apple, Fulla. We'll have enough till they bear…I guessed they might bloom. They're on Earth now, and plants are supposed to bloom every year here. So they bloom—and so can we."

"But…" It was coming too fast, and Leif could no longer

adjust his ideas to fit the facts.

LOKI TOSSED the apple core casually out onto the grass. "Don't worry, I promise to take none back to Asgard, but until I have to, I don't intend to go up there for that type of sleeping, either. Hey, Lee, did you see the newspaper? They're building rocket ships for the planets—somebody found a miracle fuel. Come on, I'll show you the paper. I've got an idea Venus is actually Asgard, Jupiter is Muspelheim, and the moon is probably Jotunheim. Fits, from all the experts know. Come on, Gail."

Leif heard sudden enthusiasm come into Lee's voice, and a sudden babble of immature plans of getting into the crews and losing no time in getting a berth on one of the rockets. He flashed Loki a grateful glance, and led Fulla out into the yard and toward the orchard.

She linked her hand in his, her figure slim and golden in the sunlight as they stood looking at the little trees. Then she dropped down, running her fingers through the soil, watching it as it packed into a loose ball in her hands.

"We'll have to dig up a preacher, Fulla," he told her. "It wouldn't do to have our children think we were fallen gods, just because we didn't go through the right formalities. Think you can stand being a simple farmer's wife?"

"Oh, Leif! But the rockets…"

He shook his head. "You've got me wrong. I'm not a hero, honey. I'm just what I said—a plain, old-fashioned dirt farmer. Do you Mind?"

She showed him she didn't.

Well, in a way, it was good to have been a hero. Every man should have a chance to win his girl, kill a few giants, and be a god for a while—and most men probably could if they could forget their fears long enough to try. It was comforting to know that those fears were gone, and that he wouldn't have to dream about questing for grails or going to other worlds, envying those who did it.

But it was better to get back to the things a man really wanted.

He settled down onto the grass beside her, letting the sun shine on them, relaxed and content. Then he grinned.

"Or maybe I am a hero, of sorts. Giants are easy enough to kill, and they stay dead. But now you take quack grass…"

THE END

If you've enjoyed this book, you will not want to miss these terrific titles…

ARMCHAIR SCI-FI & HORROR DOUBLE NOVELS, $12.95 each

D-11   **PERIL OF THE STARMEN** by Kris Neville
THE STRANGE INVASION by Murray Leinster

D-12   **THE STAR LORD** by Boyd Ellanby
CAPTIVES OF THE FLAME by Samuel R. Delany

D-13   **MEN OF THE MORNING STAR** by Edmund Hamilton
PLANET FOR PLUNDER by Hal Clement and Sam Merwin, Jr.

D-14   **ICE CITY OF THE GORGON** by Chester S. Geier and Richard Shaver
WHEN THE WORLD TOTTERED by Lester Del Rey

D-15   **WORLDS WITHOUT END** by Clifford D. Simak
THE LAVENDER VINE OF DEATH by Don Wilcox

D-16   **SHADOW ON THE MOON** by Joe Gibson
ARMAGEDDON EARTH by Geoff St. Reynard

D-17   **THE GIRL WHO LOVED DEATH** by Paul W. Fairman
SLAVE PLANET by Laurence M. Janifer

D-18   **SECOND CHANCE** by J. F. Bone
MISSION TO A DISTANT STAR by Frank Belknap Long

D-19   **THE SYNDIC** by C. M. Kornbluth
FLIGHT TO FOREVER by Poul Anderson

D-20   **SOMEWHERE I'LL FIND YOU** by Milton Lesser
THE TIME ARMADA by Fox B. Holden

ARMCHAIR SCIENCE FICTION CLASSICS, $12.95 each

C-4   **CORPUS EARTHLING**
by Louis Charbonneau

C-5   **THE TIME DISSOLVER**
by Jerry Sohl

C-6   **WEST OF THE SUN**
by Edgar Pangborn

ARMCHAIR SCIENCE FICTION & HORROR GEMS SERIES, $12.95 each

G-1   **SCIENCE FICTION GEMS, Vol. One**
Isaac Asimov and others

G-2   **HORROR GEMS, Vol. One**
Carl Jacobi and others

.

Made in the USA
Charleston, SC
11 April 2013